THE LITTLE WALLS

She was dark with a streak of hair dyed blonde like a caste-mark, and big ear-rings that clinked. For her type she wasn't bad looking and not as bold as some. She was wearing a purple kimono, stockings that didn't match and tarnished gold slippers.

I said, "Are you Herminia Maas?"

"Sure." Then she looked at me more narrowly. This wasn't quite the usual lead. "You got a cigarette?"

I lit the cigarette for her. As the light flickered over the mascaraed lids and the plucked eyebrows I said, "My name's Philip Turner."

"O.K. That's swell. Now we're . . ." She stopped and lifted her head. "Turner?"

"Yes. It was my brother who was drowned in your canal . . ."

WINSTON GRAHAM

The Little Walls

This be our wall of metal; to be in nowise
conscious of our guilt, and to turn white
at no fault laid to our charge.   HORACE

I ask, is it not madness to die,
lest you should die?   MARTIAL

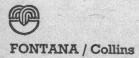

FONTANA / Collins

First published by Hodder & Stoughton Ltd 1955
First issued in Fontana Books 1967
Second Impression March 1969
Third Impression January 1970
Fourth Impression November 1972
Fifth Impression July 1976

Made and printed in Great Britain by
William Collins Sons & Co Ltd Glasgow

The characters in this book are entirely imaginary,
and bear no relation to any living person

FOR JEAN

Chapter One

When my brother committed suicide I was in California so I wasn't at either the inquest or the funeral. It was nearly two weeks before I could get away, and I then flew back and made straight for his home near Dorking, where the telegram had come from. But when I got there the house was closed and a neighbour said Grace was staying with my eldest brother Arnold in Wolverhampton. So I spent a night in London and drove up by car the following day.

I could guess the sort of shock it had been for Grace, so I thought I would see Arnold first. His letter, the only one, had been scrappy and muddled, showing up if anything needed to his own confusion of mind, and it had told me precious little more than the original cable. Nor had the American papers had a lot to say. They avoided committing themselves as to the causes of his death, because apparently no verdict or conclusion had yet been reached by the police. But what had happened, so far as I could make it out, was that Grevil, on his way home from the Far East, had stopped off for a few days in Holland, and had apparently thrown himself into a canal in one of the back streets of Amsterdam. It made as much sense to me as if I'd been told he had hanged himself with his bootlace in his own back kitchen.

I drove the car to the works and round to the side entrance, noticing the new building nearly completed in Green Street, and drew up under the old sign which said: " Humphrey Turner & Sons, Engineers." That hadn't been repainted, and I was glad, because it looked better the way it was. It seemed more than ever a pity now that I'd never really known Humphrey Turner, who was my father.

In the main office there were two or three girls, but no one was typing and I could hear Arnold's heavy voice from behind the frosted door. Dictation stopped when a girl gave my name in, and after a minute I was shown up.

Arnold had always been the fleshy. type, but there had been a robustness about his weight. Now it looked flabby for the first time. I knew what *I* felt for Grevil, but I hadn't known what Arnold felt. Perhaps he hadn't known himself until now. Or perhaps, I thought as he began to tell me of it, he was upset because of the stigma that it left.

". . . A terrible thing. Still a young man, with so much of his achievement still before him. In spite of some slight waywardness of purpose, his whole record . . . It's impossible to imagine how he must have felt, what he must have thought. . . ."

"I only saw the American papers."

"The English didn't leave any doubt. There wasn't really much doubt, you know, from what the Dutch police told me."

"You went over, then?"

"Yes . . . Grace went with me. We—flew him home. The funeral was on the ninth."

"How is she?"

"Better now."

"And Peggy?"

"Back at school. It's been a terrible time for us all." He looked at me a bit resentfully; in the family I had always been the young one who got out of things. "We should have been glad of your help then. Of course there is still a lot to settle up."

"There's a lot to *explain*," I said, on my feet again because I couldn't sit calmly to discuss what had happened as if it were something which could be pigeon-holed already and put behind us.

"There's a lot that will probably never be explained."

6

"Had he been ill?"

"I gather he had a bout of fever. But it was well over, and one expects that."

I said: "What sort of reason is there? A man like Grevil—the last person. I heard from him about two months ago; he wrote from Java. He was coming home from there, I suppose?"

"A man like Grevil," said Arnold, getting up too and sitting on the edge of the desk. He picked up the cigarette-box and held it out to me, but I shook my head. "A man like Grevil. That's just what I thought when I first heard. It's queer the same sentence should occur to us both."

"It's likely to occur to most people who knew him."

After a silence Arnold said cautiously: "Of course one can't evade the fact that a brilliant man, with the gifts that Grevil had. . . . Such people live at a higher pressure than the ordinary man. Father did. They all do."

They all do. An uncomfortable epitaph, and one that I still rejected. One that it seemed to me it was important we should all reject. "Grevil was finely balanced if you like. But he'd much the clearest mind of the three of us."

Arnold blew his nose and then lifted his head and peered over his handkerchief at me. It was the old, unwinking stare. "Events appear to prove you wrong, Philip. He may have been less well than we know. And his assistant was away sick nearly all the time. You know how he drove himself. Something at the end . . ."

I stared back. "Why is accident ruled out? A false step in the dark. . . ."

"It was rather difficult for us over there—though of course interpreters were provided. A woman said she'd seen Grevil jump into the canal. Under questioning she qualified it a little, said he might have stumbled; but one could see what she thought. Then—of course then there was an unfortunate letter found on him. That was what clinched it."

"A suicide letter?"

"No. One from some woman. Telling him she was finished with him."

Arnold put away his handkerchief. I don't know if I looked as unbelieving as I felt. "Does Grace know about this?"

"She had to. But it wasn't mentioned publicly and it did not get into the press. The Dutch authorities couldn't have been kinder, and it was entirely due to them that we received so many facilities. Of course they very much esteemed Grevil—not only for his archæological work but because of the friendship that grew up between him and members of the Dutch Royal Family during the war. He was due to go to dinner with Count Louis Joachim, the evening after he died."

I said slowly: "Well, I just can't swallow this part at all."

"I don't see how we can get away from it, Philip."

"He was happy enough with Grace, surely. I've always thought so. Who is this woman? Did she give evidence?"

"She hasn't been traced yet. It was only a Christian name on the letter. The notepaper was that of the hotel where Grevil was staying."

I thought it out. Is one more tolerant of one's own morals than other people's? Not tolerant. It wasn't tolerance I lacked here, but understanding.

Arnold said: "I think now you're here I'll run you home to lunch. Grace is staying with us, you know. Or you can run me, if that's easier. It's nearly twelve, and I don't think I could settle to work after your visit."

We went downstairs and got into my car.

He said: "How's your work going?"

"All right."

"You still like it?"

"Yes, it's all right."

"Are you in California permanently?"

"For a year or so. I should have flown back as soon as

your first cable came, but things were in a balance and I simply couldn't drop them."

"How long can you stay?"

"About a week. You look prosperous here."

"Fair. Supply and delivery dates are our greatest problem. One loses contracts. Only last week a Belgian firm . . . Of course, the death—the sudden and unexpected death—of one of the family gives one to think rather seriously about the future of the business."

"Well, yes; but you're young enough yourself."

"Even though Grevil was not an active member of the firm—certainly not the head and founder the way Father was—it still has an unsettling effect. It would be nice to see a greater distance ahead."

I knew what he meant and he knew what I meant and so we said no more on the way home. Lunch was difficult. Grace welcomed me, as she always had done, but you could see that my turning up now had only brought things back to her in their first rawness. We carefully said nothing about it at the table, and afterwards Arnold went back to the works and Mary made a lame excuse and left us together. Then we talked about California for a bit until I broke off in the middle of a sentence and said:

"Grace, I wish I'd been on hand—nearer home anyway —when all this happened. You know what I felt for Grevil, and the cable was pretty hard to believe when it came."

Grace's face had that over-clear emotionless look that I think comes sometimes to people when they've lived for a long time with a bad thing and have at last seen the worst of it.

"I knew how you'd feel. Arnold wanted to send you a guarded message, but I thought you would prefer . . .

We began to talk of it then. After a bit it seemed to have a better effect on her. She'd been frozen up too long.

Grevil had left England in November, as I knew, and

had been in Java ever since. By arrangement with the Dutch and Indonesian governments he had gone out to make new diggings at Sangiran, where excavations had been interrupted by the war, and also at Trinil, where the original Java man was found; and at the end of last month he'd flown back to Holland, where most of his archæological finds were to be deposited with the Rijksmuseum. He had been in Amsterdam only two days when he died. Grace had had a cable from Jakarta just before he left, and had been more or less expecting him home any time. Then the English police had called to tell Arnold what had happened.

When she finished I didn't speak but picked up a snap of Grevil in a little silver frame and looked at it. He just looked tall and ascetic, and all the qualities I remembered didn't show at all.

" Arnold told you about the letter?" she said.

" What letter?"

" From the woman."

" Yes, he did say something. . . . I didn't altogether accept it."

" Didn't you?"

" Not as it was told to me. I haven't seen it—I don't know what it said—but some things fit into people's characters as you know them, and some don't. That doesn't fit into Grevil's as I imagine I knew him."

" No," she said.

" So if he did commit suicide I don't think he did it for that reason."

" Why do you say, if he did commit suicide?"

" Well, are you convinced?"

She got up and took the snapshot out of my hand. " What else is there to think?"

" Are you more inclined to believe it because of what happened twenty-three years ago?"

She flushed. " No. Why should I be?"

"Weaknesses run in families. Like talents."

"Not necessarily."

"Not necessarily. That's what I want to think."

"That's what you must think. I was saying so to Arnold."

"Did you ever believe Grevil was the sort of man who would take his own life?"

"No."

"And this woman. Do you know anything about her?"

"Not yet. Grevil's friends and callers at the hotel weren't much noticed, and the police have very little to go on. There was certainly no one in the hotel."

"What was the name she signed?"

"Leonie. L-E-O-N-I-E. I don't know if it's Dutch."

"Arnold said he hadn't been too well in Java."

"He said nothing in his letters except that he'd been confined to his tent for a couple of days. Of course his health was never of much concern to him."

"Does he sound depressed in any of the later letters?"

"No. You can read them if you like."

I said: "But if he'd only been in Amsterdam two days, how could he be in that deep with any woman?"

"He'd known her before—must have from her letter. He'd been over to Holland two or three times recently —making arrangements for this trip, meeting various friends. I don't know how long he's known her——"

"Or I suppose she could have been on the plane."

"No. The passenger list was checked. All the women passengers were traced. There was a friend of his on the plane called Buckingham, a man he met in Indonesia —but no woman."

"And what does Buckingham say?"

"They haven't found him yet either. He'd left Holland before the police began to inquire."

I went to the window and looked out at the garden. One or two of the trees were promising green, and a recent shower had silvered the early tulips.

She said: "I expect you feel I'm being disloyal to him in believing in this woman at all."

"No. But I think you've more reasons for believing it than you've told me."

She looked confused. "I wish I hadn't said that now. You see, I haven't any other reasons at all, this time. Nothing more than the unexplained letter."

It took a second or so for the sting to begin to work. "You mean there have been other times?"

"One other."

"I'm sorry."

"It was years ago, and I've never told anyone else. The last thing I want to do is to say anything that will make you think differently about Grevil."

"This has all made me think differently about Grevil," I said; "but if you're afraid it might make me think less well of him, then it won't. Because if you're fond of a person you don't judge them; and anyway I'm the last one to be able to do that. But was it important, this other occasion?"

"To me? At the time, yes."

"For long?"

"I don't think it was important to him for long. When I knew that, it made the difference. After a while, after it had been over for a time, it didn't mean anything or come between us any more. We were just as happy as we had ever been."

"I see."

"I hope you do see, Philip. Because of there having been one woman—though it was eight years ago—it's easier to believe there was one now. I certainly didn't know it; I hadn't a ghost of a suspicion; and in any case it doesn't make me see the suicide as an understandable thing. I'd rather he'd taken six women. . . . But it *happened*, didn't it. It has happened. We can't make it disappear by refusing to believe it—not any of it. However hard we try, there's no escape."

That night I sat in my bedroom for a long time with a packet of cigarettes. Thinking about it and thinking about it on the way over, I'd kidded myself that when I actually got here and was able to hear all the facts and talk everything out with Arnold and Grace, then the pain and the tension inside me—the first deriving from his death, the second from the manner of his death—would ease up. So far not so.

Perhaps it would happen yet. Early days. All I felt to-night was a higher dissatisfaction at what I'd been told and a mild savagery at the manner of the telling.

My more sensible self told me it wasn't Arnold or Grace's fault that they were apparently sitting back and accepting what I wasn't willing to accept. I hadn't identified the body. I hadn't been there personally and heard the evidence of the woman who said she saw Grevil jump into the canal. I hadn't seen the note from the other woman. Two weeks of build-up, details adding on bit by bit like a miser's interest, had brought them to this way of thinking. In their shoes I should by now probably have felt the same.

But at present I just wasn't willing to go along with them. There'd always been a particular link between Grevil and me. The elder by ten years, he had done far more for me than the average father and done it in a more comradely way. Arnold, four years older still and a bit out of range—and already pretty well preoccupied trying to take his father's place in another way, in a business suddenly short of its founder—had never meant much to me at all. Grevil was the one.

And Grevil was brilliant. Intellectually he stood a head above his plodding persevering elder brother and his rash unreliable younger one. A first-flight scientific brain —switched from its first choice to archæology nine years ago—had gone along with an unusually stable sense of values—unusual in the mid-twentieth century anyway. These days it's unfashionable to be religious—that's unless you happen to be a literary Catholic—but Grevil was never afraid to be unfashionable in an unfashionable way. He had gone about his own life certain in his own beliefs, but never making a show of them; and his worst enemy couldn't have called him a prig.

And now he was gone, soon after his fortieth birthday, drowned indecently in a muddy canal; and the long narrow head set on its rather slanting shoulders, and the sallow face with the alert eyes and sharp amused mouth, were already changing themselves into bacteriological compounds which might be pretty exciting to the chemist but were very unsatisfactory for the people who remembered him.

" I am not resigned to the shutting away of loving hearts in the hard ground." Some American poet had written that. Maybe we all had to come to it. But what I was not resigned to was the wanton useless waste of a fine life barely half spent.

But what did I propose to do about it? I might carry on a perfect vendetta of inquiries and kick up hell with the police, but it wouldn't put one stone back where it had been. All I could hope to do was some sort of justice to his memory, and perhaps in the process recover some of my own peace of mind.

I picked over the newspapers Arnold had given me an hour ago. They didn't help much. " *British Archæologist Found Drowned in Holland.*" " *Woman's Testimony in British Scientist's Suicide.*" And one of the picture papers had of course got hold of his earlier career: " *British Atomic Scientist Meets Mystery Death in Amsterdam.*" The most detailed account was in the *Guardian:* " *Grevil Prior Turner, the English scientist, who was found drowned and on whose death an inquiry is being conducted in Amsterdam. . . . Medical opinion is that the body had been in the water about three hours . . . no evidence of violence . . . shortly before midnight a woman from a house overlooking the canal saw a man fall. . . . Dr. Turner is believed to have brought back valuable archæological material which is at present being studied in the Rijksmuseum. . . . Educated at Winchester and New College . . . distinguished physicist while still in his twenties . . . turned later to ethnology and archæology . . . his book last year on the significance of the dolichocephalic skull. . . ."*

I chucked the papers in a heap and turned to the letters Grace had given me. They were much the usual thing, comments on weather, conditions in the country, progress of his work; they went with the minor domestic interchanges usual between husband and wife. Nothing to set the world on fire. Only one thing was noticeable—that the man Jack Buckingham, whoever he might be, had been in the picture for at least a couple of months and that his name constantly recurred. Grevil mentioned him first as "a lone white man, a surprise to come across in Surabaya, particularly one of his calibre. I don't yet know what he's doing here and he looks a trifle down on his luck; but what a pleasant fellow to talk to! I hope to see more of him."

In the next letter things had moved on. Dr. Pangkal, Grevil's Indonesian assistant, had fallen ill and Buckingham was helping in his place. Buckingham was "a keen amateur archæologist himself and has visited several of the principal European sites." More than this, they were preparing to move camp some thirty miles on Buckingham's suggestion, to a place called Urtini, where they were going to make excavations in a river-bed. All the later letters Grace had given me were dated from Urtini except the last. In one he wrote: "I don't know what I should have done in Pangkal's continued absence without Jack Buckingham. Did I say he had a good brain? Perhaps good isn't the right word. He's very much anti many of the things I care most about. All the same I would take a bet with anybody that—to quote Hopkins—the motion of this man's heart is fine. Anyway, whatever one thinks about him personally, and even if one ignores the emergency of Djandowi, his help and companionship have been quite invaluable."

I searched in the earlier letters for some previous reference to the emergency at Djandowi but found none.

The last letter of all said: "It's a relief to be up in the mountains for a day or two after that snake-house heat. J.B. has come along too. I hold him in increasing affection; and it's queer the sense of affinity there is —knowing each other so short a time and finding so much to share. I have persuaded him to come home with me, and have invited him to stay with us for a few weeks while he gets on his feet and looks around. Hope you don't mind. I'm sure he'll not be much trouble, and I'm certain you'll instantly take to him. Most people seem to."

In the end I gave it up and got into bed. I wondered if Buckingham would in fact be able to help us at all when he was located. I wondered why he had not come to see Grace or made any attempt apparently even to write. Were any efforts being made to trace him or had the police of two countries already put away the file of Dr. Grevil Turner, F.R.S., who had come to a nasty end while the balance of his mind was disturbed? I didn't know. I meant to find out.

Hours later when I finally went to sleep I dreamt that I was standing beside the tree of life, and it looked green and flourishing. But when you looked closer it was rotten, rotten at the heart, and I looked beyond it into the canal and a man's body was stuck in some sluice-gates. At first I thought it was Grevil and then I thought it was my father, and sometimes it seemed to be neither and sometimes both. The water that gushed over the body was the bright mud yellow of corruption.

Chapter Two

My contacts with officialdom weren't worth a commissionaire's salute; but the name of Grevil Turner still meant something, and after two useless interviews I sat down on the Friday morning in the office of a Colonel Powell who worked on the less fashionable side of Whitehall. Powell was a tall grey-visaged man near sixty whose face looked as if it had suffered a good deal of wear and tear keeping the Empire together. He was abrupt and rather stiff, and probably fundamentally shy.

He said: " The case certainly hasn't been dropped, Mr. Turner. We're satisfied that it has been handled—and is being handled—very competently by the Dutch police. We have kept in touch with them throughout, and I can assure you that neither they nor we will consider the case settled until at least two people have been traced. Whether we shall trace them is another matter; but that's our chief concern at the moment."

" Have you any leads on them up to now?"

" No. A Mr. Jack Buckingham certainly arrived on the K.L.M. plane with Dr. Turner and registered at an hotel. But he stayed only two nights and then moved on. No one of that name has since left the country. He may of course be living with friends in Holland and have omitted to register, but he has certainly not come forward in answer to the broadcast appeal. With the woman we have still less to go on. A Christian name—though an unusual one—nothing more."

" Have you a copy of the letter she wrote?"

" We have the letter itself, if you'd like to see that."

A minute later, with a queer feeling of putting my fingers on something unclean, I was staring at the message which had been found in Grevil's pocket. The envelope was plain and untorn, the notepaper bore the heading Hôtel Grotius. Both were wrinkled and faded, but the ink of the letter, which I think had been written with a ball-pointed pen, had run surprisingly little. It was a woman's writing, clear and the letters well formed, but I thought in a hurry—particularly the last part.

"This is just to say that I am leaving to-day. This time everything must be over between us, please believe me, it's really and truly the end. I came along this afternoon meaning to face you, but at the last I've suddenly funked it. What *is* there to say except what has been said before —and except good-bye?

"My dear, it's been rather a bad mess from the beginning—my fault every bit as much as yours. My fault that there ever was a beginning. Oh, I know there have been times—I don't deny them—but they don't make up for what goes with it—at least they don't for me. Everything that's happened these last two days makes the same point over again.

"If you still feel any friendship for me, please don't follow me and please don't write.

"I'm very sorry.

"Leonie."

I handed the thing back. "Her English is good."
"So is that of many Dutch people. But probably she's not Dutch."
"Have you reason to think that?"
"Well, we've a rough description of a woman who called to see your brother on the afternoon before he died, given us by the receptionist of the hotel. Er —here it is: 'Spoke to me in French, then in English. About twenty-four or five, fair hair cut short, grey-green eyes with some brown in them, shoulder-bag, English- or American-style coat. Slight build, about five feet six or seven. Dr. Turner was engaged and she said

18

she would wait. I do not know if she saw him, for I was busy with new arrivals.' It gives us a little to go on but not a great deal. She may not even be the woman."

"And this other woman who says she saw him jump into the canal?"

Colonel Powell rubbed a finger down his leathery cheek. "Hermina Maas? A lady of easy virtue. But there seems to be no particular reason to doubt her testimony."

"Not unless she had something to hide."

"What could she have to hide?"

I went and stared out of the window. You had an excellent view from here of the comings and goings of the London County Council.

Powell said: "Your brother hadn't been robbed, and there were no marks of violence on the body except a cut hand and a bruise on the forehead which could have come about in falling. The Dutch doctor said the bruise was not severe enough to have caused a loss of consciousness."

I said: "Why was the body three hours in the water if this woman saw him go in?"

"Apparently she saw it happen from her window, and by the time she got into the street he had disappeared from view. She told the police and they began a search."

"And this man Grevil met in Java, who travelled back with him; could anyone on the plane describe him?"

"One of the air hostesses gave us some material to go on, but it was all rather un-precise."

"There'll obviously be other sources."

"Not so obviously. Between ourselves, we shouldn't be displeased to trace Buckingham. That's if he's the person we think he is. There's a man called Buckingham been in trouble two or three times in the Near and Far East since the war. He first appeared running Jewish immigrants into Palestine; there was a good deal of notice taken of him there because in the end he fell foul of the immigrants themselves. Then there was trouble in Cairo, and later we heard of him in Bangkok. He probably knows that a number of people would wish to interview him if he showed up, and not solely about Dr. Turner's death; so that will make him a less easy fish to net."

"Is he an Englishman?"

"We don't know. He travels on a British passport. The trouble is that almost all his activities have taken place outside our range of contacts. We have one fairly reliable description of him, but it isn't definite enough to help us when there's all Europe to search."

Someone was stoking the furnaces in St. Thomas's Hospital. I said: "I want to go to Holland on Sunday. Can you give me the name of the man in charge of things over there."

I could tell I was being thoughtfully looked over. "Is there any special point in your going at present, Mr. Turner?"

"There is, I think, to me."

Colonel Powell got up and twisted his pencil round in his fingers. "The investigations in Holland are not yet complete. Our Dutch friends are doing all they can, and we're giving them full co-operation. I think, if you'll permit me to offer an opinion, that it might be a mistake to intervene personally at this point. Later perhaps you could go over and see Tholen. . . ."

"Later will be too late. I've only a short time in Europe. And anyway I'd prefer to know what exactly is being done."

He frowned at his pencil. "I don't think the final conclusions we reach are likely to be very different from what they are now, do you? Everything points to your brother having killed himself as a result of this unfortunate love affair which had gone awry."

I came back from the window. "Everything points to it, except Grevil's character. I think I knew him well. It's possible that I knew him better than anyone else. I mean to find out."

"Of course I never met Dr. Turner. But from what I've been told I gather he was an impulsive man, wasn't he? Given to sudden decisions. Prone to periods of high spirits and depressions. Given to *unusual* decisions sometimes."

"Such as?" I said, getting that dry feeling in my throat.

"Well, it was unusual to say the least for a young physicist rapidly coming to the front rank to abandon his work suddenly in nineteen forty-two and to join the Army and serve in the ranks."

"He could see where his physics were leading—towards the discovery of the atom bomb. He suddenly felt he could have no hand in it."

"A gesture perhaps, but a rather unavailing one. To throw away his whole career——"

"Evidence surely of being the one sane man."

Powell glanced at me. He could see I was angry. "Well, it's a matter of opinion, isn't it. But the quixotic sacrifice remains. It doesn't seem altogether out of bounds that a man who for a principle threw away his life's work might, on another occasion, throw away his life."

A clerk came in with a sheaf of papers. He was a little pimply chap and looked as if he would be no loss to the world at all. When he went out neither of us spoke. It seemed to be rather a deadlock. Eventually I said more equably: "I'm afraid that what you've told me makes me more than ever sure I want to see things for myself."

"What I've told you about Buckingham?"

"Yes."

Powell flipped through the papers. "Very well. Sir Derek asked me to help you in any way I can. You say you want to go to Holland?"

"Yes, if you please, I'd like a letter to the man in charge over there."

"Inspector Tholen. Very well." He pulled a sheet of paper abruptly towards him and began to write on it. After a minute he stopped and stared at the end of his pen.

I thought there was something wrong with it, but there wasn't. He said: "It might just possibly be worth your while meeting Martin Coxon before you left."

"Who is he?"

"The one man we know who has met Buckingham. But it's a very old scent."

"I'd like to."

"He lives in Rye. That's if he's at home. Perhaps we can find out for you." Powell pressed the thing on his desk and spoke into it.

There was another long silence. Powell finished his letter, read it through, blotted it with one of those semicircular pads, put it in an envelope, handed it to me. Then the thing clicked again and a voice said that it wasn't known whether Commander Coxon was at home, and as he wasn't on the telephone there was no quick way of finding out. Should they send a prepaid wire?

"No, thank you," said Powell when I shook my head. He switched off and stared at me thoughtfully. "Coxon's one of those men who couldn't settle to civilian life after the war and went foraging for himself. Quite a few did. We employed him ourselves once or twice, but he hadn't quite the temperament for our work and so we've rather lost touch with him recently. Apparently he met Buckingham near Jaffa in the spring of 'forty-eight. We haven't inquired too closely what Martin Coxon was doing off the coast of Palestine at that time, but I suspect he was turning a faintly illegal penny himself."

The moment of irritation was gone now, and he was talking to smooth off the edges. I knew well enough that I'd been "pressing", as a golfer would say, all through this interview, and he'd been aware of it but not of its causes. I was annoyed with myself for having so obviously risen to the bait. Because if Arnold and Grace had come to accept the coroner's verdict as a true one, what hope was there that a stranger like Powell would do otherwise? Why resent it when he followed the natural line?

Perhaps it was because I hadn't realised before how glib assumptions can seem when they're made on surface evidence and without an inner knowledge at all.

All the same, I had to take myself in hand and try to see this as a detached problem, not as a key to old conflicts and old loyalties.

I nearly didn't go to see Martin Coxon, but there was nothing better to do with the afternoon, so I drove down.

He lived on the coast about a mile east of Rye in a biggish modern bungalow, one of the sort put up in the thirties without benefit of architect. You went along crazy-paving flanked by big white stones, and climbed five steps set in a rockery to a key-shaped front door, and the bell you pulled went *ding-dong*.

The door was opened by a tall dark woman of about sixty. She looked as if she'd seen me coming. I asked if Commander Coxon was in and she said no, but she expected him back any time, and when I mentioned Powell's name she invited me into a living-room full of twentieth-century furniture. It was also littered with books, which made it look a lot better.

"I don't think my son will be long," she said in a genteel voice. "He's only shopping for me in Rye. I expected him before this."

I thanked her but she still hung about the door, neither in the room nor out. She'd been a handsome woman but her looks had grown scrawny and angular. I said I didn't want to disturb her if she was busy, and she coughed behind her hand.

"Forgive me, Mr.—er—Turner, but I do hope you're not going to ask my son to take something else on. He really hasn't been well, and he'll never learn to relax or let up. He drives himself."

23

"No," I said. "I came only to make some inquiries."

Her handsome dark eyes travelled over me. She still looked anxious. "I'm sorry. I know I shouldn't have said that. But it's years since Colonel Powell sent, and the last time . . ."

I said: "I'm not one of Colonel Powell's staff."

She left me then, but I'd only time to move to the window before a small car came along the road to the bungalow and swung round the front with a scrape of tyres to disappear into the garage at the back. The door of the car slammed and a door of the house opened and shut, and after that there was the murmur of voices. On a table by the window was a letter addressed to Commander Martin Coxon, D.S.O., M.A., and a pretty good and business-like sketch of a racing yacht with all dimensions marked. Beside these was a tin of El Toro cigars and a copy of *Les Liaisons Dangereuses*, by Choderlos de Laclos.

The door opened and a man came in. "Mr. Turner? I'm Coxon. You wanted me?"

"Colonel Powell gave me your name. He said he thought you might be able to help me."

"Powell? Well, it's a long time since I heard from him. What does he want?"

I told him. He was a handsome-looking chap of medium height. For the lean strong lines of his body his face had a delicate look because of its pallor under the thick dark hair, and also perhaps because of its expression, which was sensitive and introspective and mobile. I don't know what I'd expected but I hadn't expected this—certainly not anyone so young looking; someone perhaps with a more obvious tang of the sea. There really wasn't much of the seaman about him at first sight in spite of his clothes, which were a sort of freehand adaptation of the old Navy battle-dress carried into civilian life. And with it went a very fine-tooled leather belt with a broad silver buckle. While I was explaining I took a cigarette he offered me, and he pushed some books aside and sat

24

on the window-seat, tapping a cigarette sharply on the side of his case but not lighting it. Only once he lifted his head and stared at me. When it was finished he said:

"I remember reading something about your brother's death in the paper. . . . But I haven't even seen Buckingham since nineteen forty-eight. How does Powell suppose I can help you?"

His voice wasn't a bit like his mother's; it was cultured and easy on the ear. I said: "I'm going to Holland to-morrow and I want all the information I can get before I start."

"I'll give you what I can about Buckingham, of course; but it's precious little. And why the emphasis on Buckingham? I should have thought the girl who wrote the letter would be able to tell you more."

"She might if we could find her; but we don't even know her surname. And I've a feeling that if I trace Buckingham I shall find the girl too."

Coxon put the unlighted cigarette between his lips. There were rings under his eyes, and at times his mouth had a wry disappointed twist that somehow made you personally concerned for the cause of the disappointment. It was easy to understand his mother being worried over his health; yet there was far too much vitality in him for real illness.

"Have you been in the Navy?" he asked.

"Yes. Why?"

"I don't know. Something about a man's trim. I can usually tell. What were you in?"

"Destroyers. Only two years."

"I was R.N.V.R.," he said. "No right to the rank now, but it clings. I had a minesweeper at the beginning of the war, but the bloody little tub sank under me. A corvette after that. What were you, a lieutenant?"

"Eventually. By painful stages."

He finally lit his cigarette. For a few seconds while he was talking about it you could catch the authority in his voice that a man gets after a command at sea. "I suppose you were barely fledged when it was all over. One can hardly believe it was so long ago." He might have been remembering an old love affair, part pleasure, part conflict.

I said: "Well, you can have been barely fledged when it all began."

"Oh yes, I was. I'm thirty-nine, though you might not think so. . . . What did you want to know about Buckingham?"

"Anything you can tell me. What does he look like?"

"He's about five foot eight or nine with a short beard and brown eyes rather narrow; and a strong aquiline nose. Dark greying a bit. If you still believe in things like good and bad then maybe you'd call him a bad man, because he doesn't conform to any recognisable code of ethics. But he's a thoroughly clever fellow, intelligent and subtle, and that's precisely why no one knows much about him. He lives his own life and makes his own terms, and when he does anything on the shady side of the law he's done it and gone long before anyone can touch him."

"Did you like him?"

"Like him? No."

"Why not?"

Martin Coxon pushed back his hair with two parted fingers. "Why does one like or dislike a man? Glandular secretions? Planets in opposition? For one thing I prefer my fun a bit cleaner."

"If you can tell me, how did you meet him?"

"Oh yes, I can tell you. He was running Jews into Palestine, and I navigated his ship for one voyage."

"Were there any women with him then?"

"Not belonging to him. There was a little Rumanian Jewess of about nineteen that he invited into his cabin one evening. He tried to board her but she cleared decks and fought it out. There was a hell of a fuss when her family got to know. But of course that was all six years ago. Will you have a whisky?"

"Thanks."

He got up and went to a cupboard, brought out a bottle and two glasses. "Tell me more about your brother. What was he doing in Java? How did he actually come to meet Buckingham?"

I told him, and he nodded and listened carefully. Once he smiled, and it was queer the way the dark look left his face. While I was speaking I was sizing him up, trying to decide whether to follow up a sudden impulse. He asked me quite a lot about Grevil's death, and when I couldn't answer his questions I said that that was what I was going to Amsterdam to find out. His attitude was entirely different from Powell's this morning. He seemed interested, his mind ready for new impressions. It was a tremendously refreshing change. There were no closed doors here.

At length I decided to risk it. "You tell me you don't like Buckingham?"

"I didn't when I met him. He got up my nose more than once. Why?"

"You wouldn't, I suppose, care to help me find him?"

He was pouring whisky into a glass. When he finished he held it up to the light. "I'll swear some of this modern stuff's been taken out of bond too soon. Very different from what we got in Scotland before the war. . . . What use would I be to you?"

"You'd at least know Buckingham if you saw him."

"He's probably hundreds of miles away by now."

"Perhaps. But it's slightly less unhopeful with you than without you. Actually Powell rather hinted at the idea; but at first I thought he was trying to attach some detective to me to see I didn't get into mischief. In any case I'd no thought of suggesting it when I came down. It's simply that I—like your approach."

"Thanks." Martin Coxon hesitated, then he shook his head suddenly, with nervous emphasis. "Sorry, but I can't see it as a reasonable proposition."

"I didn't suppose you would, but I put it to you. Naturally the expenses would have come on me."

The door opened and his mother came half in. She began to speak but then stopped and flushed. "I was going to ask if Mr. Turner would like a cup of tea. . . . I see I'm too late."

"See what you've escaped, Turner. Or perhaps you'd have preferred it?"

Mrs. Coxon said: "I really do feel it's too early to be drinking, Martin. Mr. Turner will think——"

"I used to know a man who always had a tumbler of whisky sent up with his shaving water. He said it gave the razor a finer edge." Coxon squirted a dash of soda into my glass. "Join us, my dear. It'll do your nerves less harm."

"Thank you, no," she said distastefully. "You know I wouldn't consider it."

When she had gone he wrinkled his forehead at me apologetically. "My mother has never quite grown up. Forty years ago she laid a duck-egg by mistake, and ever since she's been worried about me being in the water. Psychologists would have a name for it, if one bothered to look it up."

I said: "I've never been to Amsterdam. Do you know it?"

"Yes, it's a good city. The Dutch aren't stolid in their enjoyments. That's just a popular misconception. On the wall behind you there's a photograph of the *Winterhude*. I first saw Amsterdam when I was eighteen. I landed there off that old windjammer—a hundred and twelve days from Melbourne. Sixteen weeks of celibacy and then one glorious burst. I couldn't stick it now. I don't mean the profligacy, I mean the celibacy."

"I shall be flying to-morrow afternoon if you change your mind and decide to come."

He had got up, and he thoughtfully tilted the amber-coloured whisky in his glass. I might not have spoken. In

28

profile he had a distinguished head—the small hollows in his temples gave him a sensitive look.

"The last time I was over there was just after the war on a piece of cloak-and-dagger nonsense for Naval Intelligence. I was in Holland for three weeks, mainly in Amsterdam and Rotterdam. . . ."

"All of which would make you of more use to me than you think. It's an enormous advantage when someone knows the ropes. But of course I understand how you feel. Even if you had the time, why should you waste it on a complete stranger?"

He said pleasantly: "It isn't that I mind helping a stranger. But I'm recently home from Ireland and have work to do. And I've a series of three articles to finish for *The Yachtsman*. If I go with you for even a week, that's twenty guineas down the drain."

"Naturally I could make that up."

"A lot of things seem to come naturally to you." He pushed back his hair with a sharp irritable gesture. "I don't see what you're *driving* at. Supposing you found Buckingham—and this girl. The utmost that can happen is that you find both of them. Then what? What does it lead to?"

I stared at him. "I knew Grevil, and simply don't believe that he committed suicide."

He was a long time before speaking. "Ye-es. I see some point in that. But there are only two alternatives, aren't there?"

"That he fell in or . . . yes, I know."

"Could he swim?"

"Very well."

Coxon said: "Then you think he was murdered."

I said: "I want to find out."

Chapter Three

I could tell he was more interested then, but I wasn't at all sure how far it would go. He was obviously a man with a liking for anything out of the common run, and I guessed by his expression that the temptation was there. But I also guessed that he was the sort of man who by nature gives his whole attention to whatever is in front of him, whether it's an uncharted channel or a chess problem or a girl; and it just depended in this case whether the thing was big enough to keep his interest after I was gone.

So when he phoned early next morning to say he would come with me, I felt I'd done something worth-while. Going at all was a pretty wild throw in the dark; the only thing you could say was that it was slightly less so with him than without him.

We left London Airport at three and landed at Schiphol at twenty-past four. I expected to stay three days. To say the least, my firm didn't look with a lot of favour on what I was doing. To drop an important assignment and fly home seven thousand miles because of a brother's death was in itself quite a pill. A couple of sympathetic letters would have paid off most such relationships. Neither Hamilton in San Francisco nor Withycombe in London saw eye to eye with me, though I tried to explain. Now to ask for more time to go to Holland on business hardly clear to myself was stretching their patience past the safety-point.

While we were over the North Sea Martin Coxon told me more about Buckingham. It didn't help much in the way I wanted it to help, but it did begin to build up a picture of an active ruthless man who was ready to risk anything for the whim of the moment. I got the impression too that perhaps Martin Coxon had some old score to pay off that he wasn't telling me about, because there was more in his voice to-day when he spoke of Buckingham. Perhaps since yesterday he had been remembering. Perhaps that was behind his decision to come.

Then he asked me about my family and myself, and I told him what I could, and about my job with British Turbo-Jets, and my ambition once to paint and my failure to make the grade and . . .

" Are you married?" he asked abruptly.

" No."

Just saying that must have conveyed more than I thought.

" Going to be?"

" No. I was engaged a couple of years ago, but it came to nothing." Not easy to explain about Pamela and the way things had gone adrift. Anyway, I didn't want to. The conventional thing is to go off the rails when a love affair misfires. Mine had had the opposite effect. It was as if a cold blast of common sense had blown over me, removing illusions I had held too long.

" And you?" I said to him.

" Me?" He shook his head. " The German word for marriage, *ehe*, sums the thing up : two vowels united in a sigh of boredom. As for the rest, well I had a good many years before the war that you didn't have; and I suppose I made the most of them. *Wer nicht liebt Wein, Weib und Gesang. . . .*" The stewardess brought him some cigarettes he had ordered and he smiled his thanks. I saw her face as she turned away. " Looking back it seems a little futile now—but perhaps nothing very much matters once you've done it. All that counts is the next step." He offered me a cigarette.

I said : " If I thought that I shouldn't be bothering to fly to Holland to-day."

After we'd lit up he was silent for a time, reading the

thing he had brought with him. I saw it was Housman's preface to Book One of *Manilius*. In the bright light the lines showed on his face for the first time—the sort of lines that come only to a man who has seen action in war.

I thought of my first aeroplane flight sixteen years ago, and that again brought me back to Grevil. It isn't many young men of twenty-four, flying to Paris for a scientific conference, who will go out of their way to take along a schoolboy of fourteen. I remembered that he'd asked special permission before the plane left the ground so that I could spend a few minutes of the flight in the cockpit—a terrific thrill at that age. I remembered too that he had somehow managed to make time to show me things in Paris —the artists' quarter and the house where Oscar Wilde died, the blood-stained sites of the French Revolution, the Ile de la Cité and the hill of Montmartre. . . .

"Tell me again," Coxon said, putting down his book. "What makes you so convinced your brother didn't commit suicide?"

"Knowing him, that's all. He was a clever man but a perfectly natural and normal one—full of good spirits and excessively generous. He wasn't faultless and he was certainly no prig; but he had pretty definite views about some things for these days. And if there was one thing I should say he believed in more than any other, it was in the value of the ordinary individual—very much the Christian outlook: the worth of one's personal spirit, or whatever it's fashionable to call it now. A man with those ideas doesn't generally snuff out his own life. If he does, he's ramming a hole through the beliefs he has always cared most about."

Nine thousand feet below, through a thin roof of mackerel cloud, the coast of Holland was coming into view.

"The other thing," I said, "is what happened to my father. It hasn't been a thing ever talked of in the family, as you'll understand. Father died when I was seven. That's the way it's put. Well, so he did. How he died isn't referred to. But of course you can't live as a family without its coming up some time, and whenever Grevil has said anything about it to me I've always got the impression he felt the way I did. With that example before him, it would be the last thing he'd do himself."

Martin nodded sharply. "What persuaded me to come to-day was the hunch that when anyone feels anything as strongly as you do about this, he's probably right."

"I'm glad."

We were silent for a time. He said: "But I'm still sailing without a chart. What do you propose to do when we get there?"

"I shall see Tholen first. Then if he——"

"That's the man in charge of the case, is it? Does he know you're coming?"

"No. I've a letter of introduction."

"You'd do far better to give it to the seagulls. If you invite police help over this you might as well be back selling jets."

"I don't see why."

"Well, it's obvious the police have already made up their minds in this case. If you go to them you'll get *their* facts presented in *their* way. The Officer of Justice—or whatever he's called over there—has made his findings, and the thing's fixed so far as they are concerned. If you go along and start making the motions of unfixing it you'll find someone blocking your approaches. I've been on their side once or twice, and I know how their minds work."

I thought of Powell's attempt to put me off. "I'm open to suggestions."

He pushed back his black hair with that horizontal victory sign of his. "Not easy, I know. But I've one or two contacts dating from my last visit. Have you booked a hotel?"

"No."

"Then I suggest we stay with a man called Boets, if he's still there. He keeps a little place off the Heerengracht—not luxurious but clean enough; they all are. The point is that during the war he ran part of the underground. He knows everything and everyone. I think it would be worth while."

"The first thing I want to do is trace this Hermina Maas. I want to talk to her about what she says she saw."

"Boets should be able to fix that."

We were losing height now, and the plane lurched disconcertingly as we hit the first cloud.

"Whatever he can fix," I said, "let him fix."

Christian Boets fanned himself with a menu card and said: "There will be no difficulty over that, please. It is in the newspapers of two weeks since, an account. I know a man who keeps the back papers. My son will get them. But for the rest, if the police fail . . . I am out of touch. In Holland when the war is over, we drop the war. We have better things to do. For years now I keep this hotel, nothing more."

"I'll write the names down for you," said Martin Coxon, tapping his fingers on the table. "Jack Buckingham. And Leonie. Just Leonie. I see it's hard and we shall have to pay."

"Some things you cannot buy, for no one has them to sell." Boets eased his great tight stomach against the table. The table creaked and the top of his trousers bulged over the rim like a meteorological balloon. "I will do what I can, please, but that is very small. You have others also who would help?"

"No one except the police," I said.

Boets winced and Martin said sharply: "Of course there are others I can try, but I'm relying chiefly on you, Boets."

When he had waddled out Martin said: "He's always

34

like this; pay no attention. It's his way of putting up the price."

A few minutes later when we were on the terrace taking coffee and *verkade*, Boets came in with a few crumpled copies of the *Handelsblad* and read the brief account to us in guttural English that at a distance of a few yards would have sounded exactly like Dutch. There appeared to have been no formal inquest on the lines usual in England. Hermina Maas of Zolenstraat 12 had reported to the police that on the night of . . .

"Zolenstraat," I said. "Where is that?"

Boets blew out a breath and his eyes closed as if the fat had squeezed them from below. "It is near the Oude Kerk in the district of the docks, perhaps a kilometre from here. It is a part of not good repute, known locally as De Walletjes. As you will turn over a bridge Zolenstraat is upon——"

"De Walletjes," said Martin. "Isn't that the red-light district? But of course it will be. This girl . . ."

I was trying to read what it said in the newspaper under a photo of Grevil. "How far is this street from the Hôtel Grotius where my brother stayed?"

"Oh, something less distant than from here. See." Boets took up three coffee spoons. They looked like matchsticks in his fat fingers. "This for us. That for Grotius. Here for Zolenstraat. Seven—eight hundred metres—or a little more. But it is not a place the visitor finds, nor even the resident, if you understand me, but except he knows the way."

Martin was staring at me. "It's not a dainty district, Philip. I've been there once. Would your brother go there of his own accord?"

I looked at the photo. Would Grevil go there of his own accord? I said: "You could find your way again?"

"It's years . . . But Boets can brief us."

"I will tell you," said Boets. "But I do not wish to go with you."

35

"We'd better try this evening," I said, "as soon as it goes dark."

Martin Coxon snipped the end off his cigar and flipped it over the edge of the bridge into the canal. His lighter showed up the long barrel of the cigar and his pale, thoughtful, disillusioned face. Then a cloud of blue smoke drifted before him in the gentle breeze. We had left the shopping streets behind—though not very far behind —and now were walking beside a canal lined with chestnut trees. It was quiet enough, and behind the gables, roofs and towers broke the edge of the evening sky.

He said: "I was in this part on my first visit in '33, but I don't recognise it yet. I remember the Zee Dyk and the Oude Zijde cabarets. When you're eighteen you've got more appetite than discrimination."

There was a barge moored against the side, and I looked down and saw that the walls of the canal were straight and brick-lined.

"Not easy to get out if one fell in here," I said. "And no railings."

"Did he drink much?"

"No."

As we came round a corner, light flooded from a cheap café with a striped awning, wrinkled across cobbles and fell on the face of the dark quay. Martin stopped and asked the way. The respectable burgher who directed him looked a bit peculiar as he walked on.

Martin said: "If his wife had been with him he'd have said he didn't know where it was."

"De Walletjes. . . . I wonder what it means."

"The Little Walls, according to Boets. It's not an official name, but it's a typical expression of the town. I don't know what the significance is—if there's any at all."

"You sound depressed."

"No." He was silent a minute. "But I suppose coming here—to this district—is rather for me like trying to return to my lost youth. I wonder if when I was eighteen it occurred to me to suppose I should be back here twenty-one years later—with all that means in terms of waste and unachievement. Maybe from childhood one carries one's middle age and one's old age about with one, like a parcel not yet ready to open. . . ."

Now we were coming into the oldest part of the town. Narrow canals were bordered by sloping cobbled quays overhung by derricks, with twisted alleys leading off between crooked gabled houses like London before the Great Fire. At a street corner a crowd of young men argued in loud voices over some pigeons in cages.

"We're not far away now," Martin said.

In two or three minutes we turned out upon a wider canal with a quay on either bank. Tall old gabled houses flanked the canal. By now it was dark, and many of the lower windows of the houses were lighted, much more obviously lighted than any we'd passed up to now. Most of them had flimsy tattered curtains drawn well back, and only here and there a blind was down, showing the light through. All the blinds were red. In the distance someone was playing a mandolin.

"This is it," Martin said gently. "But we're a bit early. Business isn't very brisk."

As you walked along the uneven cobbled street you could see into the rooms. Most of them were little bed-sitting-rooms with shaded lamps and a few cheap mirrors and cushions. A woman sat in each window. They were of assorted ages and variously dressed according to their estimate of what would be most likely to appeal to the passer-by. Some combed their long hair and pretended to ignore us, others adjusted their garters or beckoned to us as we went past. One or two called after us, trying Dutch and English and German.

The light glimmered on the dark water, reflecting only innocence. The mandolin player was on the first floor. I drew back to look up, but a figure brushed past me and

37

went in at the doorway. Presently the instrument stopped and someone pulled down the blind.

"Maybe they're moral walls," Martin said. "The average Dutch burgher must have a lot of them to climb before he leaves his spotless shiny home and comes here for the first time."

I said: "I shouldn't have thought the average Dutch burgher comes here any more than the average married man of Highgate visits the ladies of Frith Street."

"Perhaps you're right. That girl isn't bad, you know, if one were not so far past the stage of liking the obvious. . . . Now that fat one; if you launched her in a beam sea she'd be pooped in no time."

"Zolenstraat 12," I said. "Which way did Boets say?"

"Farther on, I think. You know how it is—like Harley Street. All the specialists can't get rooms there so they overflow into Wimpole Street."

At the bridge crossing to the other side I asked a young man in a reefer jacket. By now I was getting used to the idea that everyone spoke English, but he was an exception. It took a minute or so for him to understand what we wanted, and then he pointed and hunched his shoulders and passed on.

We came to the corner on the other side of the bridge, but instead of turning back along the opposite bank of the canal I walked over to the corner house whose windows were lighted both overlooking the water and looking upon the narrow alley continuing the road from the bridge. On the brick wall *Zolenstraat* was painted in black.

So Hermina Maas was not far away. If this was the corner from which she had seen Grevil—if she *had* seen him—then near this bridge somewhere he had met his death. I went back to the corner of the bridge and looked down into the water. All along, the canal glimmered with the reflected lights from both sides of the stream. We might have been east of Suez. Perhaps the long Dutch tie-up with the Far East had first brought this district in this way to their land. And Grevil—what had Grevil been doing here? To-night was overcast and a chill air blew in from the sea. Three weeks ago on this spot. . . .

Behind me I could hear Coxon in talk with one of the ladies. Presently he joined me. "She says over there, that dark woman on the first floor."

I didn't answer for a minute and he leaned on the parapet beside me. I said: "Now I see the place I can make sense of it less than ever."

He looked at me. "It's always hard, however well you know a man, to measure up the motives for his actions. If he did come here for some special purpose, then maybe it was because some of *his* walls had gone down—unexpectedly. It's what happens."

"The metaphor's a bit deep for me. Anyway, assuming he didn't come here for the obvious purpose, what other could he possibly have had?"

"I don't *know*. I'm only speculating. He was a man of integrity, wasn't he? Capable of doing rash or dangerous things if the situation seemed to justify it? You remember that thing from Horace: "*Hic murus aheneus esto; nil conscire sibi, nulla pallescere culpa.*" Who knows what may happen to a man in a district like this in the dark hours of the night."

I stared at his shadowed face and wondered if he was reading into Grevil an attitude of mind more likely to be his own.

He said: "Anyway, we're theorising out on a limb. Your brother may have come here out of curiosity, have stumbled on a stone and died without a thought in his head." He flung away his cigar. The end spluttered when it hit the water. "It's over there on the first floor. Let's go."

"I'll try alone first."

"I shouldn't. There's safety in numbers."

"I want to try. Sometimes these things come off better alone."

"She'll be liable to misunderstand your motives."

"Perhaps that'll be an advantage. You don't mind being left?"

"Oh, God, no. I was only trying to help. But if you want it that way I'll sit on the bridge and keep watch."

"Yes," I said. "Keep watch."

Chapter Four

She was dark with a streak of hair dyed blonde like a caste mark, and big ear-rings that clinked. For her type she wasn't bad looking and not as bold as some. She was wearing a shabby purple kimono, stockings that didn't match and tarnished gold slippers. She yawned when she saw me and got up, stretching till you saw how tall she was; then she said something in Dutch and lifted a hand to the tassel of the blind.

I said: "Do you speak English?"

"O.K. Sure. I speak English fine. Come in, big boy. Glad to know you." She welcomed me like a dance-hall hostess towards the end of the evening.

I said: "Are you Hermina Maas?"

"Sure." Then she looked at me more narrowly. This wasn't quite the usual lead. "You been recommended?"

"No."

She fastened the blind down and turned again. "Hang up your coat. It is a peg behind that door. You got a cigarette?"

The room was like a decorated cell, with too many brown flowers on the wallpaper and pink art-silk hangings round the bed. A cheval glass, cracked at one corner, reflected the springs that were sticking out of the bottom of the red plush couch, and on the dressing-table were a few bits of bric-à-brac like trophies of a chase that never achieved the dignity of a chase. In a saucer were about a dozen cigarette butts, stained pink, and there were three empty Pilsener bottles. A single-bar electric-fire grinned beside the mirror, and on the wall above was a calendar with a snowy picture of a girl skating and the words: *Vroolijk Kerstfeest*. Somebody had pencilled in a moustache.

I lit the cigarette for her. As the light flickered over the mascaraed lids and the plucked eyebrows I said: "My name's Philip Turner."

"O.K. That's swell. Now we're——" She stopped and lifted her head. "Turner?"

"Yes. It was my brother who was drowned in your canal."

All the sketchy welcome went away from her face as quickly as my lighter snapped out. She said: "That's over and finished, see? I quit. You go to the police. Maybe they tell you something. Not me."

"I don't want you to tell me anything. I came to thank you."

"What is it you say?"

I sat on the stronger end of the couch. "You did your best to save him, didn't you? Everyone would not have done that. Certainly not everyone in your job. You must have known what it meant—coming before the police."

"Huh! I did *not* know! If I had known——"

"I think you would have done the same."

Her eyes were narrow and cautious through the smoke. "Anyway, it is over. And it did not save his life."

"I was in America when it happened, when he died, so I couldn't be here for the inquiry. I flew home last week. That's why I'm late in coming to thank you."

She shifted a bit, drew in smoke greedily, didn't speak.

I took out a hundred guilder note. "Perhaps you'll

41

accept this—with my gratitude for what you did—even though in the end you couldn't save him."

She watched me put the note on the dressing-table. She watched it very closely as if she expected it to move, and then she looked at me again. "What else is it that you want?"

"Nothing."

"Then why do you give me this?"

"I've told you."

"But what for? Do you want me for all to-night?"

"I came only to see you. It isn't that in other circumstances—you understand. . . ."

"Ah, so." She shrugged indifferently. "It is not many good-looking ones that we get here."

"My brother was the good-looking one. Don't you think so?"

"I did not see him real close. He was out by the bridge. But he was much older than you, isn't it? And thinner, not so strong, I guess."

"He didn't come in here, then?"

"Oh no."

"We have not been able to trace the other people who were with him."

She flipped off the heel of her slipper and tapped ash into it. "What other people?"

"The man and the girl."

"I saw no girl."

"She may not have come this far. But the man was with him surely."

She said: "Look, mister, I tell the police all I know. See? For nine hours they ask me questions, this way and that, all because I try to save a man's life. You do not know our police. Since the war they have learn too much from the Germans. I wish to have never set eyes on your brother. I wish to have kept my big mouth shut. I am sorry for you but I cannot help you now."

"I'm not going near the police," I said. "It's the

last thing I want to do. I want to settle this in my own time and my own way."

"So."

"And now that I have seen you I want next to see the man who was with my brother when he died. The man with the little beard, I mean."

She said: "I thought you came for nothing. I thought you give me a hundred guilders for nothing."

"So I have. Don't tell me anything that you don't want to."

She smoked for a minute or so. Then she pushed back the sleeve of her dressing-gown to scratch her elbow. "If you think it is only the police I have to be afraid of, then you are not born yet."

It was quiet round about. The whole house seemed suddenly very quiet. She said: "I am not old—I mean I am new—round here. Two, three months, that is all. Soon, when it is safe, I shall go back from here, back to Utrecht. But yet it is not good to go too soon and so I stay. And so I keep my mouth shut, for it is safer that way."

"All right," I said. "We'll leave it. I'm sorry."

"It has not been a good experience for me. It is bad, this part. They say they will grill my face. And it is true. They tell me of a girl . . . I did not know that this is a bad house, that I should not ever remember what I see here. To me when I came it is like any other. I did not know until your brother dies. Then when I run out and call the police, they tell me they will spoil my face."

"Who are they?"

Upstairs a door banged and then a window screeched on its cords. She listened. A nerve in her cheek twitched twice.

"That night your brother I first see standing by the bridge at an hour before midnight. It is a good moon that night, but low and there are shadows. He has just

43

come, I think, for he strikes a match to light a cigarette and twice the match goes out before he can light it. Like others, I think perhaps here is a man, see; but he pays no attention and stands smoking and throwing away cigarettes and then smoking again. He walks across the bridge and back many times."

"What is he like?" I said.

"Your brother? High and thin, and broad long shoulders and the little stoop of the neck, so."

She bent her head forward in an attitude so exactly right that I nodded, instantly satisfied. "Yes. Go on."

She picked up the hundred-guilder note, stared at it, folded it twice, tucked it rapidly into the top of her stocking.

"It is not safe for you to be here," she said. "If they knew. . . . It is not safe for me."

I said: "That money will pay your fare to Utrecht. Go to-morrow. Once you're out of this district no one can touch you."

"No? I am not so sure. Thirty kilometres is not enough."

"You were saying about my brother. . . ."

She shrugged. "After he had been there some time the man came out of here. He was to walk away, but your brother stops him."

"What is he like, this man?"

"How do I know? He has not been visiting me. Less high than your brother, and a small beard, like you say. I do not see him come in here but I seen him once before on the last night before. They stop and speak. Soon it is a quarrel or an argument. . . ."

From where I was sitting the long glass reflected the door. As I glanced in the glass I saw the door shift. It moved so slowly I thought it was just a flaw in the mirror. Then I saw her face and knew it wasn't. I looked again. A man was standing outside the door.

"Another cigarette?" I said.

44

"O.K. Thanks." She took the cigarette out of my packet. The varnish had chipped on her finger-nails. Her hand wasn't steady now.

I said casually: "A fellow recommended me here. He said there was nowhere like De Walletjes. He said he'd been here often."

Her eyes met mine. "So?"

"Yes. He used to put in to Amsterdam regularly. About once every three months when his ship docked. Perhaps I'll come again. That's if you'd like me to."

"Sure," she said. "Sure. Come any time."

The door opened and the man came in.

I got up. He was a big man, middle-aged, with a stomach. His hair was of a faded fairness without being quite grey, and he wore octagonal rimless spectacles. If it hadn't been for his clothes and his eyes he would have passed for a schoolmaster or a respectable clerk.

He shut the door and said in fairly good English: "What are you doing here?"

"What business is it of yours?"

"Some business of mine. This is one of my girls. I want to know what you are doing asking her questions."

I stared at the watch-chain with the lucky charms, the green silk shirt, the red-dot tie. That was what let him down, the look of too much money wrongly spent.

He said: "What is your name?"

"Turner."

"Mine is Mr. Jodenbree. I live in these parts."

I said: "Say what you have to say and then get out."

There wasn't much colour in his eyes at all as he stared at me: pupil and iris the same. I'd seen that look somewhere before. "What I have to say? It is that we don't want trouble round here. We like it quiet. Mina is a good girl when she is quiet. But she is not used to being quiet, see."

"I say nothing to-night, Joe. Nothing at all."

"Oh yes, you say nothing because there is nothing to say.

But we do not like snooping and prying. It is time that you go, Mr. Turner."

"I'll go when I'm ready," I said. "Wait outside for me if you want to."

He said gently: "Perhaps you think I am a bluff. I am Mr. Jodenbree. If that does not mean anything to you, then that is a happy innocence. You can only keep that innocence if you very quickly go."

I said: "I don't *want* to bring the police in again. We might make a deal."

With one plump freckled hand he fumbled in the pocket of his gaberdine coat. He got out a silver whistle. "Once I was a trainer of dogs," he said. "Once I learned a dog to switch on a light when it came into the room and switch it off when it went out. Once I learned a dog to dance. That is why I am patient. With fools I am very patient. But if a dog is a fool too long I beat him. It is the same now, only now I no longer have to do it myself."

You could see he had done this sort of thing before, by the timing, by the inflexion of his voice; it was all there, the shabby technique of terror. Looking back, I've wondered if I was afraid. Fear disguises itself as anger so that you can never be sure.

I reached a hand across and let the window blind go. It went up with a rattle, and the woman jumped as if she had been shot.

Mr. Jodenbree said: "You think that will help you? That will not help you. Leave the blind, Mina. It is no matter."

I said: "Don't you think we're both rather old for that schoolboy stuff? And we both stand to lose by it. I proposed a deal. The offer's still open."

"What offer? What is it?" This was appealing to something older in him than the gangster; perhaps he had begun life as a street-trader, they were words he recognised and understood.

"Certain things I want to know. When I know them

46

I'll go and trouble you no more. Chiefly I want to know about Buckingham."

At that he began to laugh, soundlessly, his mouth open a little. He looked quite jovial. Yet the whistle was taut in his fingers, making a lie of the rest. "Buckingham? I do not know the name. Who is he?"

"The man you were with the night my brother was killed."

I knew now where I'd seen those eyes before. During the war there was a morphine addict in the hospital at Gibraltar. "I do not think you are clever to say that. It is clear that patience with you has a very poor reward. In two minutes——"

As he spoke the door behind him opened again and Martin Coxon slipped in.

Jodenbree turned and hesitated. He licked his lips. There was nothing sensitive or sympathetic in Martin just then. He didn't say anything.

"Ah, so," said Jodenbree, and blinked. "So this is how it is." The new arrival had put him off-balance.

"This is how it is," Martin said.

"I hoped you'd come up," I said.

"I thought it was time."

Jodenbree said: "You have a friend. That is interesting. I too have friends. It is quite simple. . . ." He made a movement with his hand.

"Don't use that whistle," Martin said, " or I'll stretch you out."

The girl was trembling. I could see her hand as she tried to put her cigarette down. Perhaps it was seeing the way she was that came back on me. In the last few minutes the tension had built up unreasonably. I felt myself to be in the presence of evil, real evil for the first time in my life. It was unexplainable, but it was there, and I didn't know quite how to deal with it.

I said to Jodenbree: "I've told you. I'll leave if you tell me where Buckingham is. Is he still in Holland?"

The girl gripped my arm. "Get out of here *now*! Go home. Go from Holland!"

I turned on her. "Was my brother murdered? Did you see him murdered from here?"

"No, no, no, no!" she said vehemently. "I saw nothing! Please to go at once."

Jodenbree's face twitched angrily. "You see what she talks. If you wish to go back to England you will go right now."

As he turned Martin hit him. I don't know if it was all good judgment or partly luck, but it was as vicious as a snake. Jodenbree was hard enough for all his stomach, but his head jerked back and he went down like a folding umbrella. Things were clawed off the dressing-table as he fell.

The girl screamed. "You fool! You *damn* fool! He'll get you for this! and me! He——"

Coxon pushed her back. "Shut up or I'll put you out too. Shut up and sit down!" He turned to me. "Now ask her your questions."

I pulled Jodenbree away from the electric fire. He was right out, and there was a trickle of blood from his lip where his teeth had come together. His spectacles were hanging off one ear. After the awful clatter the place was suddenly quiet again; it was like brawling in a house of death. The girl fumbled, finger-nails scraping, picked up her cigarette. Her breathing was checked and noisy.

Martin wiped his hand across his nose. ". . . Petty hucksters crowing on their own dung-hills. I could put *him* in the canal. The right place . . ."

The girl was swallowing the smoke, drawing it in and swallowing it and staring from one to the other of us. She looked sick under her make-up.

Martin turned on her. "*Listen*—what did you see that night Dr. Turner was killed?"

She said hysterically: "Why do you come here to do

this? Why do you come here? They will think it is my fault!"

"We want the truth about Turner's death. We're not the police; we can't be fobbed off with any damned story! He was murdered, wasn't he? *How?*"

"I tell you I see nothing more! Nothing——"

"Was he pushed in? Was it this fellow who did it or one of his rotten diseased friends?"

"I want a drink," she said. "I think I shall be going to faint."

Martin rubbed his knuckles and jerked angrily round. "There's a gin in the corner, Philip."

I slopped some into a glass and handed it to her. After he'd tried one or two more questions I put my hand on his arm. I said to her: "You're tired now. Is there somewhere we can meet to-morrow, away from all this? Somewhere where it's safe for you to talk?"

"Nowhere is safe for me to talk! And nowhere is safe for you. Go home, you fool."

Martin watched her drink and then glanced at the figure of Jodenbree. He said in an undertone: "I doubt if we shall get more out of her to-night."

She had drained the glass. I said to her: "Can't you help us? Won't you help us?"

She seemed to be listening for something outside. Certainly she was not paying much attention to what I said. Then with an effort the hysteria cleared and she focused her eyes on me. "Take your money and go home before you are in the canal yourself."

Martin opened the door an inch or so. We glanced at each other, weighing the advantages of staying and the risks.

"All right," I said. "There's no more point in this now."

He opened the door wide. His knuckles were bleeding. I said: "But we can't leave this fellow here."

"Why not?"

"He'll blame her."

"He'll blame her anyway."

"We can carry him down into the street. Get hold of his knees."

"Even touching him makes me want to spit."

We carried him down. She slammed the door the minute we were out and we had to grope our way down the stairs. Jodenbree got bumped about a good bit. At the bottom Coxon said: "This is far enough." He dumped him on the bottom step.

We went out into the street. The mandolin had begun again. The sound blew upstream in the cold air from the North Sea. The lights reflected in the canal were like drowned faces, shivering where the breeze touched them. Nobody stirred on the empty cobbled quays. Martin gave a hitch to his tooled leather belt.

I said: "Thanks for helping out."

"Not very tactfully. But a man like that . . . it's the only thing to do. . . ."

"Well, it's one thing to do."

He glanced at me and sucked his knuckles and spat. The blood from his hand had smeared his upper lip.

"Don't expect wisdom from me, Philip. I do what I think when I think. Anyhow, he wouldn't have let us get away—not in front of the girl. He'd soon have brought his friends. I'm not fond of being beaten up, are you? Let's go."

I was wakened next morning by the buzzing of the telephone at my bed. It was late because we'd stopped out late. Martin, obstinately intent on dredging the memories of his youth, had refused to go home and had wandered from place to place trying to find the old haunts he had visited years ago.

At one place, in a cellar decorated with modern murals which would have left Freud practically nothing to interpret, Martin had borrowed an accordion and sung half a dozen songs—queer songs, not sea-shanties or jolly choruses. Two by Schumann, "*Du bist wie eine Blume*" and "*Hidalgo*", and some by Fauré. When he sang was like when he smiled: the darkness left his face and he looked about twenty-five and happy and free from disappointment. I reflected that he was the type that perhaps only the English breed truly—the man who will fight a modern guerilla campaign on the principles of Hannibal or lead a last-ditch boarding party with a volume of Livy in his pocket. He seemed to me the classic man of action, whom only discipline might defeat.

For me these later and milder adventures of the evening had had the effect of making the first one seem less tense and perhaps a little less important, so that when at last I got to bed I had slept soundly for several hours.

I lifted off the telephone.

"Mr. Turner?"

"Yes?"

"This is Inspector Tholen speaking. Good morning. I do not know you are in Holland. When do you arrive?"

"Only yesterday. I hope I may come to see you some time." Get it in first.

"But of course. What I was about to suggest. Colonel Powell mentioned you may come."

Did he indeed. The voice went on: "To-day perhaps? Let me see. . . . Not this afternoon. For lunch perhaps?"

"Thank you."

"The American Hotel at one? Good. You are alone?"

I hesitated. "No, I have a Commander Coxon with me. I don't know if you have met him."

"No. But please to bring him also if you will like him to come."

Ten minutes later Martin came into the room and sat on my bed.

"Have you had your breakfast yet?"

"No."

"It's nearly nine-thirty. I've been up since six."

"For some reason?"

"It's a habit one gets. I don't sleep long any time."

"Were you trying to make me drunk last night?"

He vee-d his hair back and smiled. "No, but you were keyed up after the first part of the evening. It was high time you took your foot off the pedal. That was the only way I knew of getting you to do it."

"Thank you. Well, it worked."

I told him of Tholen's call. He said: "Confound the fellow. I've been trying to find another man who might be able to help us, but if he knows we're in touch with the police. . . . You've accepted for me?"

"Tholen must know I've a friend with me, or he soon will. But please yourself whether you come."

"Oh, I'll come. I want to hear what he has to say."

Chapter Five

Inspector Tholen tapped the ash off his cigar, and a fog of smoke drifted across the table. "I wish you have come to me yesterday, Mr. Turner. The visit that you have paid is very unwise. It is good that you come to no harm."

I said: "If you suppose we were in some danger last night, why are you so sure there was no foul play in my brother's case?"

"Foul play," said Tholen, "leaves foul marks. The medical evidence is for you to see."

"Were there no other witnesses besides Hermina Maas? In a place like that surely——"

"In a place like that witnesses are hard to find. All say their blinds are drawn. But we are still trying."

Van Renkum said: "Was your brother a man liable to nervous exhaustion, Mr. Turner? Did he ever take stimulants or sedatives, do you know? Phenobarbitone is the universal cure-all of to-day. It's prescribed for every Tom, Dick and Harry, and is not hard to obtain."

"He wasn't either a drunkard or a drug addict, if that's what you mean."

"No, I don't at all mean that. But the more brilliant a man is the more highly strung. The danger of the barbiturates is loss of memory which can perhaps lead to an overdose. . . ."

I was still trying to get used to the idea of being entertained to luncheon at one of Amsterdam's best hotels by an Inspector of Police. It couldn't happen in England. Probably it didn't happen here except when a man like Grevil Prior Turner came to a bad end and was esteemed as he had been esteemed. Perhaps that too explained Van Renkum, a very superior Dutchman who spoke English with a purer accent than I did, and seemed to be here in no official capacity. Martin made a silent fourth, his handsome pallid face closed up, secretive, thoughtful.

We'd already put away enough for eight : an enormous chicken mousse in aspic, stuck about with truffles and pimento; great steaks dressed with foie-gras; glass after glass of neat Bols. Tholen, who looked like a working framer, ate at a great rate and smoked between mouthfuls. After he had drawn in, the smoke seemed to come out of everywhere, nose, mouth, ears, even, you imagined, his pockets.

I said: "Have you any more information about Buckingham?"

"We have had much communications with Jakarta, but there is still some difficulty in the way of full co-operation." Tholen looked uneasily at his companion.

Van Renkum frowned at his cuff-link. "What Inspector Tholen means is that the feeling between our country and Indonesia is not yet all it should be. *We* feel that the full independence of the Dutch East Indies was seized from our hands while we were in bad straits after the war—a blunder made by the United Nations, because the Indies were not ready. Leave a tottering child without its reins and it will fall—no doubt into the arms of Communism. *They* feel, the Indonesians feel, that what we gave we gave grudgingly and with ill-will. So if we ask co-operation on internal matters we do not always receive it."

Tholen nodded vigorously. "But now one of my men to Jakarta a week since was sent, to look into this for us. Yesterday he leaves on his way home, so to-morrow we shall know more."

Martin at last broke his silence. "We know about Buckingham in Java. What we want to find is where Buckingham is now."

"Yes. But in police work it is often what-has-gone-before which tells what-is-to-come. We hope for a full description of Buckingham to add to yours, Commander Coxon; perhaps some sure means of identification, perhaps, who knows, a photograph. Already our man has cabled news. We know how Buckingham meets Dr. Turner. In three, four months of late last year and early this a ship, the *Peking*, has been running arms from the Philippines. There is a port in Java held by the Dar-ul-Islam. These are Moslems in revolt against the central Government. This Buckingham owns the ship. But in February she is holed by a Government plane and beached. Buckingham loses everything." Tholen turned his hairy face on me. "Your brother is a very kind man, helps the down-dog, is of a strong and charitable friendship. His assistant is fallen ill. This Buckingham makes himself useful. So. No doubt this Buckingham has no money and Dr. Turner pays his fare home. But in Amsterdam Dr. Turner dies and this Buckingham disappears. It seems that he does not fly on anywhere else. Perhaps yet we shall find him."

"And the girl Leonie?" I said.

"No foreign-born woman enters or leaves Holland with that name. It is perhaps a pet name. If of course she is Dutch that is a difference. Among Dr. Turner's friends here there have been many inquiries and about his two other visits last year, but so far nothing."

The cheese was brought. After a bit I gave up, but the other three persevered to the end.

Van Renkum said: "There is one other matter, Mr. Turner. How far did your brother go in the first atomic experiments? I hesitate to mention it, but these days the strangest things can happen. Diplomats disappear and your best friend takes a plane to Russia."

"He's been out of touch for twelve years. Anything he knew then would be practically prehistoric. But of course his sort of brain would be an asset to any country if he chose to use it."

"That's what I wondered—whether any pressure could have been brought to bear on him to do something that he was not prepared to do."

Martin accepted the cigar offered him by Van Renkum. "Do you know a man called Jodenbree?" he asked.

There was a flicker of a glance between the two Dutchmen. Tholen said: "A man who lives in the Oudekerksplein? Do you meet him last night?"

"Yes."

"He is not a good character. He has influence in all that district. Do not accept his friendship."

"I don't think it was being offered."

Tholen said: "To-morrow you must meet my man coming from Jakarta. You must also see the evidence. I will have an interpreter for you."

Martin persisted: "What *about* this man Jodenbree. Have you questioned him?"

"Yes. But of course he has witnesses that he was far away on that night."

"Which suggests that he was not."

"It does not follow. If there is ever trouble, Mr. Jodenbree has the witnesses that he was elsewhere. On his part it is just an insurance."

"How does he live? Does he draw money from those girls?"

"He has property there."

Martin lit his cigar. He shook the match out impatiently. "I'm only an observer, as you know, trying to help Mr. Turner. I've no axe to grind. But the more I see of this the less I'm sold on it. If Grevil Turner had shot himself in his hotel bedroom . . . suicide, yes, you'd accept it there. But not how it happened and where it happened. Not in that district. Not among men like Jodenbree. Turner's death has been rigged to look like suicide. Somehow, for some reason, he was killed. If that woman hadn't seen it happen and called the police, he'd have disappeared altogether. Weeks later he'd have been 'found drowned' and the verdict would have been death from misadventure. . . ."

"But the testimony of Hermina Maas is that——"

"She was fool enough to talk when everyone else was afraid to talk. But she realised in time that she was in danger and made up the suicide story. Even now she lives in terror of her life."

"And the letter found on him?"

"It doesn't convince me of anything."

"And the manner of his death?" said Van Renkum coldly.

"God knows. God knows. Held under water perhaps. There are ways that will fox the pathologist even yet."

A gleam of sun fell on the tree-lined canal outside.

Tholen said: "It may yet be as you have said. I do not think so, but we may find it so. In the meanwhile I think there is much danger if you, either of you, act on your own. You understand me?"

"Oh yes."

"It would give me pleasure to have the promise from you not to act on your own."

I said: "I don't feel I can give that."

Tholen looked at me. It was a careful look, weighing up. "I am sorry, Mr. Turner."

"I'll not look for trouble," I said. "But my time is short. I feel I must use it as I think fit."

As we left the restaurant Van Renkum drew me aside. "I have word from Count Louis Joachim that he'd like you to dine with him before you leave Holland. Would to-morrow evening suit you?"

"Thank you," I said. "I shall look forward to it."

Martin and I strolled back up the Leidsestraat among the crowded bicycles and the noisy trams. He had become uncommunicative again, and all the food and drink had sapped me of initiative.

When we were nearly home he said: "Well, that doesn't leave us much sea-room, does it?"

"You mean Tholen's attitude?"

"Yes. Behave or I take the necessary steps."

"What steps can he take?"

"Probably he'll have us tailed. This is Powell's doing. There simply wasn't any point in our coming over if we have to be in leading-strings all the time."

"I'm sorry you feel that way," I said.

"Well, don't you?"

"What I mean is, I should be sorry to feel you were losing interest because we were now in the eye of the police."

"I'm not losing interest in the very least," he said. "Rather the opposite. But I'm losing a belief that we shall do any good this way."

"Then what way is there?"

"I don't know."

"Boets has got nowhere so far?"

"No, but he's our best hope."

"Anyway, there are only two more days," I said.

"And then you'll go back to America?"

"I suppose so."

"At least you can't reproach yourself with anything left untried."

"I can't congratulate myself on anything worth-while done."

"Did you get the impression that Tholen and Van Renkum were being particularly frank with us?"

"No. It seemed to me that they headed away from your questions about Jodenbree. I suppose he couldn't have some sort of protection, could he? That sort of thing doesn't happen in Holland?"

"Well, I don't know. I suppose it can happen anywhere."

We walked on for a time in silence. He said: "If you do go back to America with this thing unsolved it will still mean a lot to you?"

I shrugged. "It's not a matter of choice."

He nodded. "I know; that's the trouble. One isn't always able to choose."

In the early evening Martin had a cable from his mother. There had been a burglary at their bungalow. It was a long cable and he smiled sourly.

"My mother occasionally still sees herself as the helpless young bride needing seomeone to depend on, and me as a husband-substitute. But she'll get over it."

At dinner he told me more about himself. His father had been the younger son of a Scottish peer and Lottie Bernstein, the actress, and had himself become a theatrical producer. "He did very well for himself and was quite a hit with the ladies. Too much of a hit, because his constitution hit back and he died at thirty-five. I don't remember him much, but I used to go up and stay with the old man, my grandfather, Lord Callard, in Fife. He was an old devil but a blue-blood to his finger-tips. My mother was a teacher at a kindergarten when Dad married her."

Towards the end of the meal he reverted to the cable

he'd had, and decided to wire telling his mother to phone him in the morning. She could do this from a neighbour's house.

While he was sending this I walked round again to the Hôtel Grotius to see the receptionist who'd spoken to Grevil's woman caller. I'd been once before but she was off duty. This time I found her. Grevil's friend, she said, had given her name when she called, because it had had to be phoned up to his room; but she hadn't the least recollection of what it might be, or whether it was even a married or an unmarried one. She'd a vague idea that it was a foreign name and short, possibly English. The lady she said was pretty and seemed to speak her English with slight difficulty.

"Do you mean that she spoke it like a foreign language?"

"Well, I think several times she hesitated over a word."

Another receptionist remembered Grevil coming into the lobby the day before with a fair girl and a man, and they had gone into the bar for drinks, but the bar-tender didn't remember them.

I walked home feeling that not one fact of any value had come out of our efforts so far. Trying to discover what had happened three weeks ago was too much like clutching at a part-deflated balloon—no sooner did you grasp it than the surface slipped away. Even the police were shifty. And time was running out.

The following morning while we were at breakfast Mrs. Coxon rang, and Martin came back after speaking to her to say he thought he should go back after all. The old lady wasn't so young as she used to be, and there was some trouble over the insurance. I suggested to him that a couple more days wouldn't make much difference, but after a certain amount of hesitation he said he felt he should go.

I half wondered if he was using the cable as an excuse

to drop out. You could see he was a man of impulse, and he had probably made up his mind quite suddenly to take the trip to Holland, certain he could do something fairly impressive for me. But his nine-year-old contacts hadn't come up to scratch, and his enthusiasm had begun to run out. And the moment Tholen came into the picture, Martin saw his own uses as limited.

It isn't an unusual experience to meet people who promise—in all good faith—more than they can perform. Anyway, I could hardly blame him, for the responsibility for his coming had been mine.

He got a seat on the twelve-thirty plane, and I went with him to the airport. Before he left he said, seeming to see into my thoughts: "I'm sorry that I haven't been able to help more. Believe me, it hasn't been for lack of the wish to. Perhaps you would have managed better on your own."

"How could I have? It was a forlorn hope, anyway."

"There may be developments yet. If for any reason you *don't* come home—if anything turns up here and you need me, do wire me and I'll come back...."

"I will."

He stared at me steadily for a second. "Whatever comes out of this, I think it might be worth our keeping in touch. What do you say?"

"By all means."

"Let me know before you go back to the States. And if you have any thoughts after you go back there and think I can help you, write me. I still think the suicide explanation is a phoney one, and I should still be glad to help you prove it."

"Thanks," I said. "I'll remember that."

When I rode back from Schiphol I felt rather lost, missing his companionship. I'd known him only a few days, but from the beginning knowing him had meant something. Perhaps, I thought, I should have been prepared to throw the thing up at this stage and go home too. Perhaps I *wasn't* quite normal on this issue at all. I was still letting the thing mean too much to me, but what I'd told Martin was the absolute truth. I wasn't able to choose. That much was a legacy of the past, of all the past, right from being a kid of seven.

In the city again I called on Tholen. He had a disappointment for me. The man they had sent to Jakarta had cabled that he needed three or four more days. Now he would not be home until next week. Tholen seemed rather more agreeable this morning. If I had to leave when I said I must, he promised to send me the report by letter.

I spent a good bit of the day having the full police and medical evidence read to me by a polite young policeman with blue eyes and a baby skin. I got back to the hotel early and wrote a letter to Dr. Pangkal whose address I'd had from Tholen. Grevil usually made personal friends of his assistants, and it seemed to me that Pangkal might be more willing to give his confidences, if he had any, to Grevil's brother than to a Dutch police official. Then I began to change for my dinner with Count Louis Joachim.

I was half through when Boets' wife came upstairs and, as far as I could understand it, said there was someone below for Commander Coxon. She only spoke about six words of English and Boets was out; but I signed for her to bring the caller up.

I put on my jacket as a young man was shown in. He was pale and thin, with very thick rimless spectacles and a look as if he hadn't ever seen a joke or been at ease in company. He wasn't badly dressed and looked like a junior clerk or something.

" Commander Coxon?"

I hesitated. " Well?"

" You are Commander Coxon?"

I nodded.

The young man looked round the room as if he expected to be stabbed in the back.

" Sir, a Mr. Lowenthal informed me that there was

information you wished to purchase. Sir, you know him?"

I nodded again.

"You wished to know about a certain lady who left the country on the thirtieth of March."

To hide my expression I bent to pick up my cigarettes. "Yes, I do."

"Well, I have it. I was promised two hundred guilders."

I would have given a thousand. "Yes, I'll pay that—if the information is what I want."

"May I have the money then."

"When you have told me what you have to tell."

We looked at each other, but I stared him down. After a minute he fumbled in his pocket and fished out a piece of paper.

"She left Holland on March the thirtieth at 21.15 hours in K.L. flight No. 341 for Rome. Her address is Rome was given as Hôtel Agostini, Via Quirinale 21."

I offered him a cigarette but he shook his head. "Thank you, sir, I do not smoke."

"And is she still in Rome?"

"That of course I do not know."

I lit my cigarette. "And her name?"

He stared at me through his thick lenses. "Her name?"

"Yes, of course."

I thought he was going to ask me for more money, but he didn't. Instead he glanced at his piece of paper again. "Helen Joyce Winter."

"Mrs. or Miss?"

"Mrs."

"British?"

"Yes, sir."

"And the man?"

He blinked. "The man, sir?"

"Wasn't there a man with her?"

"I do not know, sir. To the best of my knowledge she travelled alone."

62

I thought: Helen, Helena, Eleanora, Leonora, Leonie.

"Have you any other information?"

"No, sir."

I took two hundred-guilder notes out of my pocket-book and handed them to him. He blinked at them with his head bent over them suspiciously, then folded them in his quick narrow nervous fingers. The notes crackled as they disappeared.

I said: "Would you like a drink?"

"Thank you, sir, I do not drink."

I didn't want to let him go, but when I questioned him he didn't seem to know anything more at all. He'd come to sell one definite piece of information, and if he'd had more it seemed pretty certain that he would have been willing to sell more. As it was, his only interest now was to escape with the money. As we went down the stairs Boets mountainously shuffled in with an inquiry and perhaps a protest on his lips; but I made a face at him behind the young man's back and saw the fellow away.

Martin Coxon's inquiries, it seemed, had not been useless after all.

Chapter Six

Count Louis Joachim lived in a very simple way, and was courteous and kind to the brother of his old friend. The room we ate in was full of the things of their common interest: a Hittite clay tablet, a framed papyrus from the tomb of Weserhet, a twelfth-dynasty gold mask, decorated pottery from Phylakopi.

He spoke of his long friendship with Grevil stretching back almost twenty years and of their last meeting before he left for Java. They had talked all that evening about his purpose in making the excavations, and Grevil had told him then that he felt he was groping his way towards a new conception of man's origins. If his findings in the next two or three years confirmed his present impressions, he thought he could see his way to a complete regrouping of anthropological dates.

"Young men of promise—there are plenty of such," said Louis Joachim. "Your brother was that much more important thing, a mature man of promise. There was no staling in him—along with maturity there was this constant renewal, so to say. Nothing of his youthful approach had been lost. He was ripe for big things. That is why it is so tragic."

"And inexplicable."

"And inexplicable." He was silent for a time.

I said: "Do you attempt to explain it, even to yourself?"

"Only by the recollection that Grevil Turner was a good man and a very unusual one."

"I don't see what follows."

"No. Nothing follows. It is just the feeling that one has to strive to see through this veil that his death has cast. One turns this way and that. . . ." Louis Joachim frowned at me thoughtfully. "Always your brother was a man to set himself the almost impossible task. How would he, I have been wondering, tolerate failure, from whatever source it came?"

"How does anyone?"

"Yes, that is so. But the ordinary man surely does not risk as much to begin, or feel as much to finish. His standards, let us admit it, are flexible; they adapt themselves more quickly to the need of the hour. Whereas the man of high ideals, with the great capacity for goodness, such as your brother, sometimes has not the spiritual ambiguity to compromise. He cannot or he will not. They must conquer or die who have no retreat."

It struck me again that in all these speculations about the mystery of Grevil's death, every person, Arnold, Colonel Powell, Martin Coxon, and now Count Louis

Joachim, really only imagined what *they* might or could have done themselves, so that instead of a projection you got a reflection. Each one put himself in Grevil's place and interpreted or speculated according to his own temperament. None of them really knew or understood what Grevil had thought. Perhaps that was impossible. Perhaps that pretty problem was mine alone to solve. And I could do it not by any mental acrobatics but by deep affection and understanding—or not at all.

Towards the end of the evening I noticed Louis Joachim twice emphasised his country's debt to Grevil because of all the kindness and help he had given to the Royal Family between 1940 and 1942. He was sincere enough in saying this, but he said it as if it needed to be mentioned. I wondered if he was more in the confidence of his police than I was.

I left about ten and was back in the city by ten-thirty. A feeling had been growing in me all day. Before I left, before I was finished with this visit to Amsterdam, there was still one thing. I wanted to see Hermina Maas again.

De Walletjes wasn't easy to find even at this second visit. I took two wrong turnings and eventually came on it from the other end, which at least saved the walk beside the lighted windows.

A light rain was falling; the cobbled bridge glistened as I crossed it. In the distance a man was shouting a drunken song; instead of sounding jolly it sounded lonely and lost. These little lighted rooms might be sarcophagi, the bodies inside marking the final corruption of the flesh. However you dressed it up, vice fundamentally was shabby and depressing. The sexual act can be all that the poets sing of; or it can be just what's written on lavatory walls.

As I came to the end of the bridge I thought I heard a footstep clink on the cobbles behind me. I swung round. Nothing stirred. Then a man came out of the house opposite and came towards me. He was a buck negro of the type you don't often see outside the cosmopolitan ports of the world, a fine tall fellow of six feet three or four with an ebony face, in a light-coloured jacket with the sleeves much too short and a grey felt hat with the brim upturned at the front. The set of his head and the sway of his shoulders told you a lot. I stopped and waited for him to catch me up. He looked at me with a glint of white in his eyes, and opened his mouth to say something, but then went on past and up the street and disappeared round a corner.

The first-floor window of Zolenstraat 12 was in darkness and the blind of the lower window was drawn. I wondered if Mr. Jodenbree was waiting behind it. I went in and up the stairs.

The upper landing was in darkness, and I had to grope my way to the door of her room. My fingers touched the handle and then I knocked. There was no reply. My foot was on a loose floorboard, and I shifted it to stop a further creak. It seemed suddenly important that I should make no more noise. Upstairs someone had a wireless on, and in the street beyond a dog was yelping as if it had been trodden on. I tried the handle of the door. It turned and the door opened.

I didn't at once go into the room but felt up and down the wall inside for the light switch. After a bit I found it, but it was already pressed down. I flicked it a couple of times but nothing happened. Half in the room, I tried to remember last night. The room had been lit by a table-lamp. Probably there was a second switch there. The blind wasn't drawn, and as my eyes got used to the dark I could see the sharp corner of the cheval glass and what looked like the rounded silhouette of the lampshade.

I haven't thought of myself as a nervy type, but it took an effort to go into the room. A voice was nagging at me to skip it. After all, I had the other girl's address; that was enough; what did I need here?

Only one thing, but that the most important.

I got as far as the lamp without falling over anything and my fingers travelled energetically down the stem to the button at the bottom. The light came on.

After the darkness of the last ten minutes it looked too bright, too obvious, too public. I reached quickly to the window, pulled down the blind.

I don't know what I expected to find in the room. My eyes have never travelled quicker round anywhere. The ruptured settee, the soiled pink hangings to the bed, the brown flowers on the brown walls, the calendar, a pair of laddered stockings, a dress with green dots and a stain down the front, a lipstick, hair-pins, cigarette ends.

She was not here.

Still feeling a need for getting on, I opened one or two drawers, lifted the coverlet of the bed, picked up a scrawled envelope but couldn't read it. The door was still open and I thought it time to leave. I went to it and flipped the switch, but the light didn't go out. I had to return to the table-lamp, plug it out there and then grope my way back to the door.

Once I was out on the landing I remembered the blind was still down, but I didn't feel like going back. I shut the door and groped by way down the stairs. I thought of knocking on the lower door and asking for information, but when I got down I knew I shouldn't be able to do that because two men were standing waiting for me on the threshold of the outer door.

There wasn't any other way out, and they'd heard me come down the stairs. I wished Martin Coxon was with me then. But to-night there was no convenient friend on the bridge.

And these men weren't Jodenbree. These were his professional thugs, warned probably by the buck negro, ready with cosh and razor. At least I couldn't see myself ending up in the canal unmarked.

" Mister Turner," one said.

" Well?"

"It is necessary that you come with us."

So perhaps this was to be the subtler method after all. Perhaps I would learn by personal experience how Grevil had died.

I took a step. Break through? But help wouldn't be easy to find outside.

The man said: "Inspector Tholen has instructed us. You must leave this district with us and return to your hotel."

My knuckles were hurting. I slowly relaxed them. I tried not to make much noise with the breath I let out.

"Inspector Tholen sent you?"

"Yes, of course."

"Have you been following me for long?"

"Since yesterday."

I felt thin round the knees. "I came to find Hermina Maas."

"She is in protective custody. Now come at once."

He spoke sharply, and it occurred to me that they weren't feeling too secure themselves.

I went with them. "Why have you taken her into protective custody?"

"Should you not suppose it best for her after your visit and your friend's visit on Tuesday?"

I said: "And Mr. Jodenbree?"

There was no reply. On the bridge three men were talking. The rain had come on harder, but they didn't seem interested in that. As we passed I saw that one of them was the big negro. There was another negro as well, and a white man in a heavy sailor's jersey. They stopped talking and watched us past.

The man with me said: "It is as well that we followed you, Mr. Turner."

Arnold said: "What will you get out of a visit to Rome? I don't understand."

"Nor I yet."

68

"You don't want to tell me what you've discovered?"

"Practically nothing—so far."

"Your firm will have had something to say about this, won't they?"

"They'll have something to say when they know. As yet they don't know."

I could see Arnold's brain moving round it. The fact that I'd travelled up to the Midlands to tell him so little had been a surprise perhaps. Then the thing suddenly worked itself out.

"They may cut up rough."

"I should in their place. Things in California are in a very crucial stage. Having me drop out just isn't a business proposition for them."

"And you?"

"I shall ask them to send someone in my place. How they'll react I don't know. They may be nice. Or they may take it as a sign of the family insanity."

Arnold blew his nose. He was thinking out his words carefully. "I know you're not a person who *needs* security, Philip—not perhaps as an ordinary person does. You've proved that by refusing to draw more than a pittance from us all those years you were trying to paint. But you must know that if anything goes awry between yourself and B. T. J.'s—especially over this—there's still a position for you here, either temporary or permanent."

"I suppose I ought to know. But I don't take it for granted."

Arnold got up and flattened out the dog-ears in the telephone book. "I've been thinking a good deal about this, Philip. Much more since Grevil's death. That sort of thing makes one. . . . I'm anxious to link you to this firm, and it's occurred to me that hitherto my approach perhaps hasn't been right. I'm sure if we sat down to plan the thing we could block out something more congenial for you than sitting behind an office desk. There are opportunities for—for initiative, for travel."

"Yes, that could be."

"What I'd like to see is someone of the same name. We've not been a prolific family in this generation. Myself without children, Grevil one daughter, you, after the break with Pamela, showing no serious signs of settling down. There's no one coming on. Of course I know" —he stopped—"I know you and Grevil have always felt I attached too much importance to the firm."

I said: "The money we've had from it has kept us all—Grevil when he dropped his physics, I when I monkeyed about after the war. We'd be pretty ungrateful to despise what gave us that or to feel patronising towards the only one of us who has kept his head down and made the thing go. Grevil was a man apart and had to be treated as such. I'm not. I know I've always been restive under the bridle, but it may work off with age."

Arnold went to his desk. He wasn't a man to hang his feelings out for anyone to see, but I thought he was satisfied with this as far as it went. And in a queer way, although I'd been fighting against this happening all my grown-up life, I was not unwilling now to leave the offer open. With that at my back I was better set to do whatever I wanted to do. And perhaps Grevil's death—or the gap left by his death—had brought us closer together than we'd ever been before.

All the same, that was in the future, the very much unspecified future. Until Grevil was off my mind—if he ever could be—there didn't seem to be any settled future at all.

"By the way, Philip, there's one other thing I should mention. I expect you know, don't you, that the stuff Grevil was bringing back, the results of his excavations —or such of them as were portable—were mainly for the Rijksmuseum of Amsterdam. But a few things, at his own discretion, were to come with him to England. All these were flown back in the plane with him to

Amsterdam; four small packing-crates for the museum and one for himself. Well, when he died, the Dutch police impounded his belongings—temporarily you understand —in order, they said, to help them in their inquiries. These have now been released to us. His ordinary things came to our house—where luckily I was able to head them off before Grace saw them—but the case went to Professor Little at the British Museum. Well, I've had a letter from Little to-day, and he says the case was two-thirds empty."

"You mean the Dutch had lifted the rest of the stuff?"

"Apparently. Why, we don't know, unless the Dutch archæologists felt that Grevil's death put an end to the arrangement and so they were entitled to help themselves to everything of interest. It was queer keeping all his personal belongings until now."

"What does Little think of the stuff that's eventually arrived?"

"In the crate? Not much. But he's forwarded on to me Grevil's notes, which are in that shorthand of ours. I shall find it tedious work because it's years since I did any. I wondered if, in view of what you intend to do——"

"Yes, of course," I said. "Where are they?"

Father, among his other diverse activities, had invented a shorthand of his own, which he had failed to get taken up in a big way but which he had passed on to his sons, the elder two direct and me at one remove. Grevil had always written to me at school in it and kept his own notes that way. He'd often said it was useful to have a langauge no one else could read without preliminary effort.

Arnold had fished a couple of loose-leaf note-books out of his drawer. "Little would like a full transcription if you can manage it. And it's just possible the notes may shed some light on the situation before Grevil's death. At least it will give us an indication of what the Dutch have chosen to keep for themselves."

71

"Yes," I said. "I'll take it with me to Rome."

I didn't see Martin Coxon before I left. I should have, because it was entirely his doing that I had what information I had; but I badly wanted to take the next step on my own.

Withycombe was very stuffy about my wanting further leave, and I didn't at all blame him, but there was not much he could do except emphasise the difficulty they'd be in to find another man to fly to California at once. At least I didn't get the sack, and I didn't feel compelled to resign; but I came away knowing I hadn't improved my prospects in the firm. It was a pity because I liked the job, and I flew to Rome feeling rather down-in-the-mouth about the whole thing.

In one way Withycombe was helpful, and that was in agreeing to have my last month's salary cabled to me in dollars abroad.

It was impossible at this stage to make an estimate of how long I should be away or what money I should need.

I took the night plane, slept a little on the way, and had breakfast in the noise and the hot early sunshine of the Piazza Colonna. By eleven I was walking up the steps of the Hôtel Agostini. Somehow I hadn't expected the search to end here, and it did not. Mrs. Winter had stayed two nights only at the Agostini and had then left for Naples. My troubles were only just beginning. However, I walked up to the station and found a train just leaving, caught it without a ticket and was within sight of the Bay by a little after two o'clock.

Naples is a big city to search, and there were only two ways of going about it. I either spent a week going the rounds of the hotels or I went to the police.

I went to the police.

I told them Mrs. Helen Winter was a very old and dear friend of mine, and I'd heard she was in the town but not where she was staying. I was most anxious to trace her for personal reasons, etc. The man I interviewed was sympathetic. He agreed to do what he could. Information regarding the registration of aliens was naturally for police records only, but—he would do what he could, and in the circumstances . . . I caught his eye and smiled apologetically. I made it clear that this was almost a family matter, and if it was not already that I wanted it to become one. He nodded again, fully understanding, and said it would take a little time. In the meanwhile if I would give him an hotel where he could get in touch with me. . . .

Next morning, having heard nothing, I went round again, but my friend of yesterday was not there. Instead a tougher looking man greeted me and asked me to wait. I waited for an hour. Then the first man came in with a slip of paper. I was glad to see him.

"This is the information you want, *signore*. Mrs. Helen Winter spent the night of the fourth April at the Hôtel Vesuvio."

"Only the one night?"

"Yes. She left for Capri the following day and registered there at the Hôtel Vecchio."

Mrs. Winter was a restless mover. "And from there?"

"We have no notice of her having left. But of course it may not yet have come in."

I thanked him adequately. The police I said had been very kind, and he saw me out. Then I caught a taxi down to the docks. A boat I found was leaving at 2.30. I took that.

Chapter Seven

As I walked through the main square of Capri the hollow bell of the town clock was striking twenty-seven, though the fingers pointed to ten past five. I'd been here once before, in 'forty-six, when the island was still shaking itself out after the war. That was August and a crowded one. To-day there weren't many people sitting in the square, and a good few of the coloured umbrellas had been taken in against the threat of wind. The Hôtel Vecchio was up one of the narrow slits running off from the cathedral, an alley no wider than an arm-stretch with arches propping the opposite sides three stories overhead. Following the usual job lot of people: bowed natives carrying wood, foreign residents in beach hats and blue jeans, old men with donkeys and young men with girls, I came to the end of the cobbled alley and climbed the slope to the hotel.

From what the policeman said I'd expected and hoped that this would be the end of the road, but when I asked about Mrs. Winter the receptionist shook his head. Mrs. Winter had stayed only one night. He didn't know where she had gone. She had left no forwarding address. I felt rather desperate at this, because it looked as if I was getting nowhere at all. I asked to see the manager. The manager was out. I asked for the under-manager. A dark young woman came out fastening a cameo to her blouse and I said I wanted a room. (I certainly did, for there was no way of leaving the island to-night.) The woman showed me up to one, and there I tackled her about Mrs. Winter again. I said I had information that she was still on the island, and I really must ask them to co-operate in helping me trace her. After a bit of fencing the woman, to my great relief, gave in and admitted that in fact Mrs. Winter hadn't gone far and was staying with friends. She specially asked that her new address shouldn't be given away to casual strangers. It seemed that Mrs. Winter was anxious to avoid some sort of publicity and she did not wish reporters. I said I was not a reporter and would treat any confidence with the greatest discretion. I could still hardly believe that the bluff had come off. The dark young woman pulled back the shutters of my bedroom, showing the sea going cobalt with the approach of evening; then with a little look under her eyes at me she said the address was care of Mme Weber, Villa Atrani.

Sometimes you follow a trail so closely that the trail becomes an end in itself and your mind doesn't go beyond. This had happened to me now. I had been so full of the need to trace one of these two people who were bound up with Grevil's death that, now I had apparently caught up with one, I was at a loss as to the next move. The first thing was to make sure there had been no mistake in identity. After that. . . .

All through dinner I thought round it, and then after dinner I went for a stroll.

Going out in Capri after dark is always a secretive business —that's if you get away from the few main "streets" and the square. It's all as badly lighted as an early English film, and the lanes and alleys bend and twist and climb and fall on half a dozen different levels between the blank high walls of houses or private gardens which cut off a view of where you're going or where you've come from. If you do meet a Capriote, the chances are he'll hurry past with a half glance or a muttered good evening, or sometimes within a fan of light thrown by one of the infrequent street lamps there may be a group of young matrons sitting and gossiping with their children beside them; and then they'll stop talking and watch you till you're past. There's a quietness about it all, a feeling of having to do with things which have no business with the superficial world of the tourist and the foreigner.

I went in the direction I'd been told, and after losing my way twice came on a couple of stone gateposts and a wrought-iron gate with a crest worked into the middle. On one gatepost was *Villa* and on the other *Atrani*. You couldn't see the house—at least you couldn't in the dark; only two big tree-ferns and some yuccas and a curving path.

The narrow lane I was in went down some steps farther on and disappeared into darkness. The only light came from the back top window of an old house on a lower level. In the garden of the Villa Atrani it looked dark. I opened the gate slowly, and it made a noise like a soprano from the Scala, Milan. I went in.

You soon saw the lights of the house. It was a big place but built low, with a flat roof. At the front there was a long shallow verandah supported on baby Corinthian pillars. The lights were at both ends of the house. As I went up, the gravel crunched under my feet so I stepped upon the grass verge.

The blinds of the drawing-room hadn't been let down, and I could just see in, though on a lower level. There was a tall heavily-built woman moving about, and once she came close to the window to pick a dead petal off some flowers in a vase. Then I saw a man, a dark handsome chap probably about forty. He was wearing a reefer coat and a polo sweater, and beside him was a tall thin woman with an enormously long cigarette holder between her teeth. They were looking at something together out of my sight. Then the first woman bent down and a dog barked.

I heard something else too: the shrill creak of the gate behind me and the sound of footsteps coming up the path.

It was too late to move far into the undergrowth; the sort of foliage round me would make a lot of noise if shoved quickly aside; I leaned back against a palm tree.

Three people; they went past very close; a slim fair girl in a scarlet blouse and dark slacks, a young very dark man with a hooked nose and a limp, a plump girl in a white sweater and jeans. They were talking together. The man said in English:

"That is putting temptation in the way of me. You are very rash. You are both very rash."

The fair girl said: "I don't believe you ever thought of it before. Did he, Jane?"

"Well, I guess he never thought of it in *my* presence."

As they went up the steps the man said something more to the fair girl that I couldn't catch and she laughed.

The door of the house opened and they went in.

Perhaps I should have taken that interruption as a warning, but I didn't. I thought if I could get up near to the window I could see right in.

A firefly darted across the path as I moved up it. I had gone perhaps a dozen steps when the door of the house suddenly opened again. I backed into the shrubbery. The big woman I had first seen in the room was silhouetted against the light. She walked with a stick, and after a second two great dogs bounded out from beside her. One gave a deep throated bark and came straight down the path. I saw it was a mastiff.

"Macy!" the woman shouted. "Macy, don't you dare go out of the grounds, dear!"

The dog came straight for me. I backed an inch or two, but it was no good. He came off the path and stopped about a yard away. He opened his mouth and gave off a noise that was half a bark and half a cough.

I muttered to him in a low voice: "Good dog. Good dog."

The mastiff made no move but just looked at me as if waiting for me to start running. That was when the fun would begin. There was a trampling in the undergrowth as the other dog came at me by a less direct route.

I put out my hand.

The second mastiff pushed his way through some decayed canna lilies and also saw me and stopped. He growled, low and deep. Mastiffs have big heads. This one was dribbling at the sides of its jowl.

"Macy! Gimbel!" said the woman. "Don't you dare go out of the garden!" She began to come down the steps.

The first dog moved a few paces nearer and sniffed at my hand. He didn't look as if the smell pleased him, but at least it was a sign of hesitation. I didn't move. The second dog growled again.

"Gimbel," I muttered.

"Who's there?" said the woman. "Is anyone there?"

After what seemed a very long time Macy turned away and began sniffing at some leaves. I wasn't sure but thought there was a movement of his tail. The other chap now came over and examined the leg of my trousers. I should have been a lot happier if his tail had moved too.

The woman was at the bottom of the steps but didn't come any farther. She had stopped to light a cigarette. I took my life in my hands and patted Macy's head. He shook it, and a tiny bell rattled round his neck. Gimbel was now making extraordinary inhaling noises as if the smell of me was giving him asthma. Macy stretched up, and his head came level with my top waistcoat button.

The woman called to them again. Slowly, with obvious reluctance, Macy detached himself and ambled up the path. Gimbel, later here, was later going.

The fair girl came to the door. "Are you all right, Mme Weber?"

"I hope I am, Leonie darling. Gimbel and Macy are being very naughty. They know they should stay with me and not go off into the overgrown part of the garden. Provokin'. One never knows, one might meet a snake."

I couldn't hear the girl's reply because at that moment Macy came into Mme Weber's view and went wuffling and wagging up to her, and she immediately rounded on him, calling down the wrath of God on him in such honeyed tones that he thought he was being praised.

Jealousy was stirred in Gimbel, and he abruptly left me and went off up the path. Presently the two women and the two dogs went in and the door closed. I wiped my hand, which was wet with Macy's saliva, on the leaf of a convenient banana tree, and made a move to leave the

78

garden. Before I did so a light came on in one of the bedrooms upstairs and I saw Leonie Winter lean out and pull the shutters to.

I walked back to the hotel and had a few minutes more conversation with the manageress. Now that she had given way on the first point, she seemed quite willing to talk. She told me that Mme Weber was a well-known personage on the island and fostered local painting.

Later I spent an hour deciphering and writing out the first pages of Grevil's archæological notes. On the fifth page there was a reference to Buckingham. "Authority in this district scarcely exists—planters cannot live on estates but come weekly to inspect, under convoy. Even Indonesians do not venture out at night for fear of bandits. Rubber trees cut down for firewood in their thousands. No wonder we were attacked. Buckingham's behaviour then is in keeping with his general attitude towards this state of affairs, which he argues is the most natural in the world. Civilisation as we know it, he says, is a glacial condition preserving what is dead and done with and preventing true development which occurs only in flux and thaw. Absolute moonshine, I tell him. We wrangle amiably long after dark. Have decided to check up on his report of fossils in Urtini river bed and we shall leave Djandowi to-morrow. He's very knowledgeable on archæology—apparently would listen to me all night if I would go on—but what his practical experience is am not at all sure; no doubt shall know more by Thursday!"

A couple of entries later come the first one headed "Urtini". "This location not dissimilar from ancient terraces of Solo below first Trinil site, and the resemblance is the more encouraging, even though all finds so far of undoubted Pleistocene date—probably Chellean. The two teeth dug yesterday much worn and their nature inconclusive. The trace of an expansion of the pulp cavity, but their transverse diameter is significant. Am sure Pangkal is wrong in attributing to orang-utan.

"Shall probably stay here several weeks, Buckingham having certainly justified himself. A man of many talents, but with a philosophy at once egocentric and destructive. Of course it's very typical of the age but carried farther than I like to see it carried. Irritating to find it in so worthy a man and on one's own doorstep so to speak!"

My eyes skipped hastily along, trying to find the name again. But it didn't turn up in the next few pages so I came back and went on with the deciphering.

The following morning was brilliantly clear and fine, one of those magic days that you see at their best in Italy when the world looks as if it has been re-created while you slept. There's an innocence about it that wind or cloud may probably soil later, but to begin with even their existence isn't to be thought of.

I did not know the plans at the Villa Atrani but I'd a good idea what most people want to do on a morning like this, so after breakfast I walked into the noisy square, bought myself bathing trunks and rope-soled shoes and took a bus.

I got down to the sea and swam straight away. The water was cold and tonic and very buoyant. Afterwards I hired a canoe and paddled round the little beaches, keeping close in-shore. On the western-most and most unspoiled I saw four people lying in the sun and thought they were the likeliest. I paddled in between two rocks and took an interest in the sea bed until they moved. Then I recognised the dark man and the shape of Leonie Winter's head.

As I turned the canoe and headed away, a very handsome motor yacht entered the bay and came close in-shore. Leonie Winter waved and I recognised the man at the wheel as the man in the reefer jacket who had been in the Villa Atrani last night.

When I got in I took up a position between the sunbathers and the motor road. Whatever their means of transport, they must come this way.

By now it was noon. I smoked and lay in the sun beside a pool. There were not a lot of people about this morning, and I felt myself likely to be conspicuous as a newcomer. At twenty to one the two girls came past me. The men, it seemed, were staying down. A crowd was gathering for the quarter to one bus. The girls joined it. I did too.

So I got my first real look at her.

She was wearing only a blue linen blouse cut sailor fashion, and brief blue linen shorts with a white stripe down the side and scarlet rope bathing shoes.

People don't queue in Italy. First come first served is an axiom foreign to their temperament. When the bus arrived there was an unprincipled scramble, and as I was chiefly interested in being near the two girls I wasn't lucky over a seat. Instead I stood close beside them, straphanging immediately over them while a tall Italian woman elbowed my ribs from behind.

The other girl was doing all the talking, with an American accent, about a flirtation she was having with someone called Nicolo. Leonie Winter only nodded her fair head occasionally in an absent-minded way. Her shortish hair looked casually untidy but in fact it had been cut that way by a first-rate hairdresser. In the bus her legs were golden with the sun, and the tiny hairs on them, that you couldn't see except in sunshine, gave them a polished golden sheen. They were a very good shape, you had to admit that.

The bus palpitated into life, the door concertinaed the last struggling people in and the driver started off with a jerk. We rounded the first hairpin with a lurch and a swerve. I was carrying my rope-soled shoes, which were very wet, and I now changed hands with them and saw the first drops fall on Leonie Winter's leg.

They'd been buying ice-cream, Nicolo and Jane, and Nicolo had said if you put brown ice-cream against white . . . and Jane had said . . . Leonie Winter moved her right leg. I shifted my arm and the drops of sea water began to fall on her left.

" So I said to Nicolo, ' My dear, you can't suppose, you just can't suppose that I mean *that* . . .' "

The second hairpin. The bus accelerated into the first straight climb. A hand touched my arm. I looked down. It was the plump girl, staring at me with pleasant friendly eyes.

" Do pardon me, but your shoes are dripping on to my friend."

I looked at Leonie Winter. She had tried to move her legs out of the way but hadn't quite made it. She wasn't looking up or looking at anything in particular.

" I'm sorry." I moved the shoes into the other hand. " I'm very sorry indeed. . . ."

The American girl smiled nicely enough; the other girl didn't stir. I looked at her legs and fished a clean handkerchief out of my breast pocket.

" It was very careless of me," I said. I bent and dabbed her legs with the handkerchief. I dabbed them both a couple of times, and then she moved them. Still she hadn't looked up.

I put my handkerchief away and smiled back at the plump girl.

She said : " It's these buses. They're *quite* awful. One never knows how they're going to behave."

" Or the people in them."

She laughed. " Oh, I don't know. You take it as it comes."

" Fine if you have the right temperament."

She said : " Everyone develops the right temperament in time."

I said : " You've evidently been here some time."

The bus lurched to a stop, throwing everyone more or less in a heap. Round a bend two donkey carts were stopped abreast while the drivers talked over the municipal elections.

" Mother of Heaven," said the Italian woman. " Your pardon, *signore*. That was your toe?"

The bus ground its way past the carts with an inch or so of the road to spare. We went on and up. A few hundred yards from the terminus we stopped at what I recognised was the back entrance to the Villa Atrani. The two girls and some others fought their way out.

Leonie Winter looked at me for the first time. She got down. Jane smiled and nodded a friendly good-bye.

That afternoon I had a stroke of luck. I walked down to the square and passed near the bank, which had just reopened after its siesta. Outside the door, tied by a lead to a stone post, were two small yellow-brown lion-cub-like puppies.

People were milling around and I could see the bank was crowded. I strolled over and bent down and began to stroke one of the puppies. I was in no danger of losing a couple of fingers or half a leg to-day. They were nice little brutes, these two, and fell over each other making friends with me. They climbed over my shoes on wobbly bow legs, and bits of tail waved in the air. They sat and scratched themselves and shook their muzzles and then came back for more. I was pretty sure it was her feet and rubber-tipped stick before she spoke in Italian.

I straightened up quickly: "I beg your pardon. They looked lonely."

She was in her late fifties probably, not exactly stout but big. She'd thickened in the body but retained the quality of ankle and wrist. She looked ill, her skin yellow under the make-up.

"You're English." She smiled at me absently. "I might have known by the back of your head. Interestin'. I shouldn't have brought them; at the bank it always takes time before I'm through. Civil of the gentleman to entertain you, darlings."

"They entertained me."

"I do hate performin' dogs, don't you. Going through hoops and balancin'. Unsuitable." She looked me over.

"I never go to circuses. You're interested in mastiffs?" She pronounced it maystiff.

"I used to have one."

"Very few do now; I suppose it's the feeding. And they do take up room. Like grand pianos. Was yours a dog or a bitch?"

"Dog."

"I have two at my villa. Very difficult exercisin' them. The island's overcrowded." We talked for a minute or two, she leaning heavily on her stick while people went in and out of the bank and the puppies rolled over in a mock fight. Then she separated them with the point of her stick and turned to go. "Maybe we shall meet again, Mr. ——er——"

". . . Philip Norton is my name. Yes, I hope so."

"Everybody meets everybody on this island sooner or later. It's like a Paul Jones. A lottery that dance, I always thought. No hand-pickin' at all. Are you staying long?"

"About a week, I suppose. I want to do a little painting."

"Oh . . ." She looked at me again with a glimmer in her bloodshot eyes. "You're an artist?"

"Only in my spare time now."

"People do come and go. Irritatin'. The island's a magnet. Do you know Langdon Williams?"

"I've met him."

"He may be here later in the month. Landscapes. Cezanne and water I always think. But he's esteemed." She took another step and then stopped again. "I suppose you're not free this evening? A few people are coming to my villa for drinks. It'll be very dull and I've forgotten who's invited, but I'd like you to meet the maystiffs."

I said I'd be charmed to meet the maystiffs.

"Careful now, Bergdorf, you're bitin' too hard. A joke's a joke. I'll expect you around six to six-thirty then, Mr. Norton."

I said: "I'm afraid I don't know your name or where to come."

"Mme Weber. Villa Atrani. Just on the edge of the town. Anybody'll tell you. It'll be English gin, anyway."

Chapter Eight

At six twenty-five I put in to the Villa Atrani for the second time. In the daylight you could see that a good bit of the garden was overgrown; but the house itself was well kept, and I should think had been refurnished just before the war in modern Italian fashion, the furniture and decorations being the work of men who still knew how to use their hands. There were about a dozen people in the big white living-room when I was shown in; but I noticed at once the dark man in the reefer jacket, and that he was talking to Leonie Winter as if they knew each other well.

First I had to meet the dogs.

Mme Weber was impressed by the way Macy and Gimbel accepted me. "Usually they're so slow to admit people to their friendship. Startlin'. Vermouth, or do you like it pink? I give up gin every year, the way one gives up the carbohydrates. Of course it's perhaps having had one of your own. Maystiffs are such reliable watch-dogs, aren't they. Macy and Gimbel would simply tear the throat out of anyone who broke into this house or this garden.".

I patted Macy's muzzle. "But one always feels they know just where to draw the line."

"Oh, Leonie darling, let me introduce Philip Norton. This is Mrs. Winter. Looking very summery in spite of. Mr. Norton is a distinguished artist staying for a few days. Breeds dogs. Macy practically fawned. And Captain Sanbergh, a very old and dear friend."

I said to Sanbergh: "But of course I remember seeing you this morning in a fine motor yacht at the Piccola Marina."

Sanbergh was taller than he looked, with the broad shoulders and lean hips of a younger man. He'd a handsome raffish face, a capable look; eyes vigorous and alert but thickly lashed, the mouth wide and Pan-like when he smiled.

He said to Mme Weber: "You see, Charlotte, we've become notorious, I and my *Sappho*. Already I'm a marked man."

Mme Weber said: "It's Charles's new love-life, Mr. Norton. Quite awful. I christened her two weeks ago in *asti spumanti*. She doesn't live up to her name; it's the men she's after."

"Well, she's been waiting for me since January."

"I hope you'll let me see her some time."

His eyes travelled over my face, incuriously but expertly; summing me up. His expression wasn't particularly friendly. "But of course."

"Charles is taking some of us out to-morrow afternoon," said Mme Weber. "Let's all be sea-sick together."

"I'd like to. If Captain Sanbergh. . . ."

"But of course," said Sanbergh again.

Leonie Winter hadn't spoken through all this, and I hadn't looked at her.

I said to Sanbergh in a conversational tone: "You've been away?"

"Away?"

"You said your yacht had been waiting for you since January."

"Oh—yes. I ordered her last year. I've been out of this district for a time."

I was going to add something more but Mme Weber was plucking at my arm. "Do you know Mr. Norton? This is the Master of Kyle. You're lookin' downcast on this lovely evening, Mr. Kyle. Isn't the Scotch right? Berto has the bottle. I'll get him to bring it over."

A bald elderly Scotsman acknowledged me with a sour, uncommunicative face. I tried to talk to him for a minute or so, and then was taken over to meet the other three who had been on the beach that morning: Jane Porringer, the American girl; Nicolo da Cossa, the man with the limp, who in close-up was less young than I thought; and an American lawyer called Hamilton White, a tall thin man getting on for fifty with white skin reddened by the sun. I didn't like da Cossa. His club-foot was like an outward sign of something warped inside.

I neither looked at nor spoke to Leonie Winter throughout the party. Once I saw her looking at me through one of the Florentine mirrors, and much later I watched her, reflected in a picture, talking energetically to Captain Sanbergh. I looked at him and thought, what was the description? Dark with hair greying at the ears (easily dyed), a short beard (easily shaved), medium height, brown eyes rather narrow, strong aquiline nose.

"Admiring my picture?" Mme Weber came up behind me. "Nicolo painted that. Technical achievement, I think. Fireworks. My first husband had a passion for fireworks. In real, I mean. Used to subsidise the fiestas. Nicolo's very talented, don't you think? Do you work in pastel, Mr. Norton?"

I saw the picture behind the glass for the first time. A bit flamboyant as Mme Weber said, but impressive. "It's very good indeed. No, I generally use oils."

"For landscape work?"

"For all work. Portraits as well."

"You should paint Leonie, Philip. May I call you Philip?"

I said I'd like her to.

"You should paint Leonie, Philip. Fairness is so often insipid. But it's ice and fire with her."

87

" I've noticed the ice."

" Her skin with those quite dark lashes. Nicolo wants to try."

I finished my fourth drink. " If I were to paint anyone I've seen so far, it would be you."

Charlotte Weber gave me a look. It was a sophisticated glance or was meant to be, but somewhere behind there was a glint of coquetry. It was like a young woman making use of an old woman's eyes.

" Dear boy, that's quite the nicest thing. . . . But I'm a sick woman—have been for years. D'you know that just before the war they gave me only a few months to live. It was practically melodrama. I came here to *die*. And I've been here ever since. You don't want to paint a woman who's been living for sixteen years with an anti-climax."

" How do you know what I don't want to paint?"

She sighed and fumbled for a cigarette. I lit it for her. "Vermeer, Van Gogh, people like that, were always paintin' women seven months along. Must have seemed indelicate to the Victorians. My father called it paradin' and perpetuatin'. Are all artists specially interested in women when they can't pretend?"

" Most painters like qualities that *need* no pretence. Don't you? Lines of distinction, and the marks of knowing about life and how to live it." I passed her an ash-tray.

" Philip, how nice you are. Leonie hasn't been without experience, of course. I'll tell you some time. Nicolo, we've been admirin' your picture."

" That is too kind," said Nicolo. He had big sombre eyes, like dates, that made you think he'd been hurt when a boy and never got over it. But the hammer-beam nose and the sharp little teeth suggested it was probably some-one else who'd got hurt most after all. " It is of course the Faraglioni Rocks seen from near the Certosa monastery. The purple morning-glory brought me the inspiration. That is so necessary, that first impulse, as you will agree."

88

I noticed while we were talking that Charles Sanbergh's eyes were on me. I wondered if Leonie Winter had said anything to him. They could hardly have any suspicions of me yet. But I certainly thought there was a flicker of hostility and suspicion in Sanbergh's eyes when I saw him before I left.

As I walked home to the hotel I wondered if a half-joking arrangement between Charlotte Weber and me would really come to anything.

It was getting on for three years since I'd touched a brush. My last thing had been one of Pamela and had been a total loss. It had probably reflected something in our relationship which just then was drifting on the rocks. Perhaps it had also put a finger on the wider issue, because everything had seemed to be breaking up in me just then, the inspiration that da Cossa talked about so glibly—which anyway is always mainly perspiration—even the urge to sweat any more. The thought of buying paper, holding a pencil in my hands again, even disingenuously, gave me a bit of a fright. It would be like digging a part of myself up out of the ground.

When I got home I began on Grevil's notes again, but although I found one or two references to Buckingham, there was nothing important in them. So after ploughing through about five pages I gave it up, and just lit a cigarette and sat there watching my own smoke.

Reading Grevil's shorthand like this made me think of the letters I'd had from him regularly when I was a kid at school—in this shorthand—joking and chatty, but with long-headed bits of good sense thrown in like currants in a cake. In many ways he had been responsible for a sort of heightened appreciation of ordinary things that was probably my chief asset when I eventually began to make the motions of expressing myself on canvas. It was he, for one thing, who had first put me in touch with people like Traherne and Blake and Jefferies and Whitman and Rilke. He'd always shown impatience with anything that seemed to him half-hearted or lacking in guts. He never had any room for people who didn't know their own minds. I remember him saying to me once, quoting Ben Johnson: "I will not be a parasite to time, place or opinion"; and in fact he'd followed that precept all his life.

Just after his twenty-fifth birthday he'd written to me telling me he was getting married the following week and that he wanted me to be the first to know about it—me at fifteen; And I remember that along with feeling gratified at the compliment I'd been surprised because I'd been home the week before and apparently nobody knew anything about it or had even met the girl. (Nor had they.)

In a friendly way he'd always been rather up against the family—and up against Arnold in particular over me and my wanting to paint. There might at a later date have been a set-to about it, but Hitler saved that war because by the time I was seventeen he was established in Paris and not encouraging art-students from England.

I thought of this to-night because along with Grevil the thought of painting had come up in my mind again. It's one thing, perhaps, to be kind and encouraging to a boy you're fond of and to take him about and get pleasure out of his pleasure, it's another to keep up that interest in a man in his middle twenties making heavy weather of the job of coming to terms with his own ambition.

In the middle of all his own preoccupations Grevil had never wavered for a second, and almost the only row I'd ever had with him had been when I told him I was throwing it all up and taking an ordinary job. At first he'd absolutely refused to admit that there was any justification for doing that. He blamed it on the break-up with Pamela and said I'd feel differently in six months. Then when that didn't work I remember he said: "I could understand it if you were starving"; and I replied: "That's just it. With this small income from the firm

I haven't even the merit of failing the hard way. Grevil, I want to *earn money*, live on what I make myself; it's more overriding than *any* other need I've ever had in my life, even the need to paint. Very few people have the luck I've had to be able to go on so long. It's a matter of self-respect now."

After that he more or less accepted it, but never with a particularly good grace.

But I'd never regretted the change.

Chapter Nine

However you might feel inside about things, there was an "atmosphere" here that began after a day or so to have its own effect. Grevil's death meant every bit as much to me as it had ever done, but the site of it was nine hundred miles away. The beauty of Amsterdam I had seen against a backcloth of vice and half-masked terrorism.

When I got down to the cove the following afternoon the *Sappho's* two tall masts were doubling their length in the olive-green water. Every now and then a stray breeze stroked the surface and cork-screwed them out of shape; then the dinghy was lowered to bring me off, and broke the reflection up into mosaics of sunlight.

Rather to my surprise I was the first aboard, and as soon as I went below I knew that the next move was on. Sanbergh's expression hadn't changed since yesterday except that it had got more so. If I felt suspicion of him, he felt suspicion—on some grounds—of me.

After we'd seen what there was to see—and she was a lovely yacht with all the refinements and graces that the Italians can produce—we went into the tiny cabin and he offered me a drink. We made conversation but it was formal stuff. I stared at his books; they were in Italian, English and French, and no language had a working majority over the others. It's not exactly usual to see Karl Marx sharing a shelf with St. Thomas Aquinas or Hakluyt with Machiavelli.

I noticed Sanbergh's beautifully manicured hands as he gave me a glass. "You are Italian, I suppose?"

"What makes you ask?" he said.

"Oh, idle curiosity."

"Do you think curiosity is ever idle? I've always doubted that."

"It hadn't occurred to me. You speak English almost without accent."

His glance flickered over me. "Perhaps I belong to no country entirely. I am my own country, and make my own laws and rule over myself. My kingdom is forty feet of deck and my frontiers are the horizon."

I sipped the drink. "Do you issue your own passports?"

Something moved in the depths of his eyes. I was being refocused. "You don't appreciate figures of speech, Mr. Norton."

"Oh yes, on the contrary. The idea sounds good and I was thinking of the practical obstacles."

"Obstacles are made to be overcome. Buy yourself a yacht and see."

"Find me the money and I will."

"Ah yes, the money. But isn't that only another obstacle? If the need is sufficient——"

"The way can be found? Does it follow?"

"Usually. One contrives. One takes special measures, however unpalatable."

"In what way unpalatable?"

With a cocktail stick he dabbed at the lemon peel in his glass, drowning it and then letting it surface, drowning it again. "All work is unpalatable to me, Mr. Norton, as it is to any civilised human being. Otherwise it wouldn't be work but play. That's the definition."

"Most civilised human beings would agree with you. But they don't know how to avoid it."

"Why should they? If they did they would be miserable for lack of contrast. Balance and proportion are the things that matter."

I didn't know whether he was being subtle or sententious. In profile against the porthole his face looked larger than life and angular. There was no up-curving of the wide mouth to-day. "And what of yourself?" he said suddenly.

"Of myself?"

"Do you find painting profitable as well as palatable? I should have thought not."

I said: "You thought right."

"Though I imagine as a hobby it can be—useful at times."

He seemed to have seen through the ruse before it was practised. I said: "Everything is useful in its proper place."

"And where is your proper place, Mr. Norton? Not on Capri."

"Only for as long as I choose to stay."

"And then?"

"It rather depends what happens while I'm here."

"I thought it might."

Hiss glass was empty and he went to fill it. "May I offer you a word of advice?"

"I can't stop you."

He came back. "Don't stay too long. The climate is enervating. A week at most should be enough for a conscientious artist. No more."

"You seem to have survived for longer than that."

"I'm not an artist, Mr. Norton; and possibly not conscientious."

"I can believe that."

"I hope during this week you will come to believe many other things. Among them. . . ."

"Among them?"

"That Mme Weber is given to foolish friendships."

"I should need very little convincing of that."

He said: "Be convinced of it but don't trade upon it."

We stared at each other hard for a second or so, and I nearly forced the whole thing out into the open. Then there was a footstep on deck and it was too late. His eyelids drooped. "The others have come. Shall we go up?"

Leonie Winter pressed the lighter. It came on, but before she could put her cigarette to it the breeze blew the flame out. She tried again and the same thing happened. It seemed a good opportunity and I moved up beside her.

"Perhaps mine will work."

I flicked my own lighter open for her, and she nodded and lowered her head to the flame. The wind puffed it out. I shut it and flicked it open again. This time it didn't light at all. I tried a couple more times but it only sparked.

She said: "It doesn't matter."

"Sorry. Lend me yours, will you. At least I can keep the wind off."

She handed me her small gold lighter, and I opened my coat and lit it in the shelter. She put her shiny head forward again and lit the cigarette. "Thank you."

When the first smoke blew away she looked at me, which was only the second time ever. I'd heard somebody once talk about sandy-green eyes, but I didn't know what that meant until I saw Leonie Winter's. They were thickly and quite darkly lashed, as Charlotte Weber had said. I've seen that colour in a sea pool, but not in Italy where there's too much rock and the sand isn't bright enough.

I said: "It's draughty for smoking. The wind has had most of mine."

"Yes, so I see."

I threw my cigarette over the side, and then, to have something to do, got out another. I tried my own lighter and this time perversely it lit quickly enough.

She turned away to stare over the rail. Behind us the Bay of Naples drowsed in a haze of peacock blues, and on the port side the Sorrentine peninsula raised its improbable cliffs like a back-cloth painted by Verrocchio.

I said: "Where are we heading?"

"This afternoon? For Amalfi, I think. Mme Weber has property near there."

"I've not been in the Gulf of Salerno since 'forty-three."

"Nineteen forty-three? During the war?"

"I was in one of the destroyers covering the landings."

"Oh, I see. . . ."

"Anyway, I didn't get much of a view because I was in the engine-room most of the time."

She had very fine skin on her face but tiny lines at the sides of her mouth. They looked as if they'd come with smiling. I wondered how much laughter she'd got out of Grevil's death.

For the first time in that minute it came to me to question the thing I'd been so certain of all through. Up to now I'd been absolutely sure that Grevil wouldn't commit suicide for *any* girl. . . .

I said: "Tell me, what does it feel like to be a beautiful woman?"

Her eyes flickered up to my face again. "What do you mean?"

"Well, perhaps you'll think this is impolite but—you give me the impression of being—unapproachable. Is that what you really feel, or is it something put on more or less in self-defence?"

She looked at her cigarette. "If you tell me what all the other women say, I'll t-try to keep in step."

"I've never asked anyone else."

"Then don't you think you should try?"

"No, seriously, as a point of interest. You must be so used to admiration. . . . You give that impression, anyway."

95

She said swiftly: "Do I? When have I?"

"I thought on the bus."

"On the bus. Oh, that was different."

"How different?"

"Well, it was."

"You think I gave you cause to be uncivil?"

"It's a matter of opinion."

"Yes," I said.

A seagull came down near us and planed along without moving its wings; then suddenly it changed direction and disappeared to leeward as if blown away.

I said: "What I mean is, I wonder if people who are so very good to look at realise the pull they have all the time, everywhere, practically all through their lives. Wherever they are they start off a step ahead of other people; there isn't the same need to exert themselves, to build up a relationship, to impress, because it's done for them. It comes as part of their birthright. Even when they more or less set themselves to throw it away, the —the insignia is left. It's practically the last form of privilege."

She glanced at me again. The wind blew her slight fringe across her forehead and she pushed it away. "Well, it's an interesting point of view."

"It wasn't meant to be only that."

"Are you a communist?"

"No." I wasn't sure if she was serious or poking sly fun. "Why?"

"You spoke as if you didn't like privilege."

"No; I only don't like the misuse of it."

She said coolly, candidly: "And you think, supposing that I've got any, that I misuse it?"

"I didn't mean quite that. I was only wondering how far your use of it was instinctive and what it must feel like to have it."

She said: "I still think both questions are assuming rather a lot."

"Yes," I admitted pleasantly, " perhaps they are."

As I turned, my cigarette caught on the rail and the wind blew the ash in my face. I didn't say anything for a few seconds because a speck of ash had gone into my eye. I took out a handkerchief and rubbed a corner under the lid. She saw what had happened but didn't speak. Then when I'd groped for a bit she said : " Perhaps I can get it out for you."

I gave her the handkerchief and she put her finger-tips on my face. She was very slight when she stood up beside me, but quite tall.

" Is that better?"

" Thank you." We separated. " I think it's gone."

She said quietly : " Do you mean the ash or the prejudice?"

" I hope there wasn't much of either."

Behind us, near the wheel, Sanbergh, looking like a dark Viking, was talking to Mme Weber, who had come aboard in bell-bottomed navy blue slacks and a large blue hat suitable only for the gentlest breeze. She had also brought the two puppies, Bergdorf and Tiffany, and one had already been sick. The other one, who seemed to be enjoying his sail, now came wobbling across and collapsed at the girl's feet, rubbing his nose against her ankle. She picked him up and settled him in her lap.

Presently we began to talk a little more easily, desultorily but without obvious stress; and while we talked the yacht drew nearer to the great cliffs guarding Positano and Amalfi. As we came into the bay of Amalfi a church bell was ringing, at first sedately enough, then suddenly urgent, clamorous, more like a fire alarm than a call to prayer. The sun was past its height and moving towards the precipice behind the harbour, and parts of the little white town climbing the hillside were already in shade. Sanbergh and Mme Weber were met by an elderly car which took them off round the corner of the coast-road and out of sight. I wondered if in some way I should have contrived to follow them. Sanbergh had carefully ignored me since the conversation in the cabin, but I could tell he was very well aware of me.

Nicolo da Cassa had brought his easel with him, and as soon as we landed he set it up on the quay and went on with a half-finished painting of the town. He wasn't bothered by the local interest, and Jane Porringer squatted on a stool beside him and ate *nespoli* while she watched. That left Leonie and myself and Hamilton White.

I'd hardly exchanged a word with the tall American lawyer so far, but it looked as if he would be with us for the whole time ashore. Then by luck we came on a wood-carver who interested him, whose masks and faces seemed to stem more from Easter Island than the Mediterranean. White went into the shop, but Leonie Winter wandered on and I followed her.

The main street of Amalfi, starting in the square beside the cathedral, tapers off as it climbs, and a few larger shops at the beginning become dark little one-room places with their owners sitting at the doors gossiping in the sun. In a few yards you pace out the eternal contrast and the eternal problem of Italy. From the opulence and cheerfulness of the seaboard you step up into the grinding poverty of the hinterland, into the dust and the heat and the loneliness.

There wasn't much worth buying here, but the girl, a few paces ahead of me, ducked into one shop, and after waiting for a bit outside I followed her in and found her looking over some head-scarves. Serving her was a fat old woman nursing a tiny black-eyed infant very new to his surroundings, and three children from about seven years old down. Over the sale, and in a hotchpotch of English and Italian, it turned out that the mother of the child had died at its birth and grandmother was keeping the shop open for the time being. This wasn't of course poverty as understood in Italy; those with a shop were well off; but misfortune had come on them and they were taking it with dignity. In a short time, apart from the mere business of selling a scarf, they were chattering with Leonie Winter, staring grave-eyed at some snaps she showed them, accepting sweets from her with natural grace, growing more and more friendly but never lowering their standards. Her glistening fair head looked odd among all the dark ones. I didn't actually join in, but I watched it all with interest. There was an obvious misunderstanding about my presence, but she soon put that down. After a bit we were out in the daylight, she folding some dirty notes and with a twist of amusement at the corners of her mouth.

Daylight but not sunshine. In the interval the sun had slipped behind the cliff, and in a few seconds Amalfi, even seashore Amalfi, had lost all its gaiety and colour. The yacht still sunned itself, but fleetingly, like a butterfly on a wall, while the dark line crept out.

I said: " You have children of your own?"

"No."

" Those photographs. . . ."

" They were my younger sisters—my half-sisters."

" May I see them?"

" Some other time perhaps."

We walked back a few yards, watched by the inhabitants sitting quietly in their doorways. In the square Leonie Winter turned to go up the great flight of steps to the cathedral and the campanile. I went with her.

" Where is your husband now?" I said.

" Which one?"

I watched her, still not sure of her. " The current one."

She wrinkled her brow. " I haven't a current one. Sorry."

We got at last to the top of the steps, both a little out of breath, but not entirely with the climb. The face of the cathedral was brilliant with light.

I said: " Of course you know you were right about me in the bus."

99

She glanced at me startled then, but after a minute her face clouded. " I w-wonder if I was."

I caught an undertone of other-meaning, but pretended not to notice it.

I said : " Have we time to go into the cathedral?"

She pushed open one of the doors, and at once we were in cool gloom lit by a fiery sort of light from the west windows. A shadow broke away from a marble pillar and came across to us, welcoming us, offering to show us the beauties of the building, but I waved the ragged little man away. In the central nave she stopped; and her eyes caught the reflected light as she looked at me.

" I'm trying hard but I still don't think I'm quite keeping up with you, Mr. Norton. D'you mind telling me just what you really want?"

" Well, I should like to know you better. Do you find that very surprising?"

" Yes—in a way. In your way."

" Why in my way?"

After a minute she said : " What do you want to know?"

" . . . the bones of St. Andrew, the Apostle of Fishermen," said the little man, who had followed us. " Also these great columns, borne here from mighty Pæstum . . ."

" That's much more interesting than anything I can tell you," she said. " Look at those mosaics. . . . Have you ever seen the mosaics at Ravenna? I went there three years ago. The town is dull, dusty, depressing; not like Florence. Florence is the happiest town in Italy. I'd like to live there, wouldn't you?"

" May I call you Leonie?" I said.

" I thought that would be taken for granted. Everything else has."

" You think I'm rushing my fences?"

" Don't you?"

" Yes," I said.

" But then I suppose this is so much a normal routine

that you don't see it in the same way. What is the name for those pulpits. Is it ambos? If——"

"Ambos," said the little man, following encouraged. "Very ancient, on both side of the high altar, see? When the cathedral first was built in 1203, these ambos . . ."

"Would it surprise you," I said, "if I told you I've never made this sort of approach to a woman before?"

She was silent for a while. "I believe we should go back. Charles said they wouldn't be long."

On the opposite hill a church bell was ringing again, strident, scolding; another began nearer at hand, then a third.

"Amalfi," said the little man, "one time a great maritime republic. Ninth, tenth centuries, defeated the Saracens. As great as Genoa. Then alas in 1073, a great tidal-wave demolishes the town. Others, too, there have been since. So this cathedral . . ."

I said: "Charles Sanbergh's a lucky man to own such a fine yacht."

"He is, isn't he."

"You're old friends, I suppose."

"No."

I watched her face. "Are you staying long in Italy?"

"I haven't decided. And you?"

I said: "Well, I don't know how long I shall be *able* to stay. I have some business commitments."

"Here?"

"Not here."

She hesitated. "Don't they include painting Charlotte Weber?"

"Who told you I was going to?"

"A friend."

"Well, it isn't at all decided."

"I'm told you like to paint women who show the lines of gracious living, and that you're not interested in flat insipid faces like mine, with no character or breeding about them."

We got to the door of the church.

"The cloister," said the little man despairingly. "Chiostro del Paradiso. Gothic arches of thirteenth century. A small fee only . . ."

I gave him two hundred lire. "Your friend da Cossa," I said to Leonie, "has all the talents of a back-stage gossip. I wonder what Jane Porringer sees in him."

We were out in the daylight again. Below us, as siesta time was over, the shadowed town was coming to life. Leonie Winter stared across at it, her eyes wide, alert, extra brilliant.

"What does anyone see in anyone? If you look for an explanation, you flounder."

"No doubt you're right."

"Right and trite. . . . Are you married?"

"No."

"Not even once?"

"Not even once." Something made me add: "I did intend to be, but things wouldn't work out. . . . So my record is most modest compared with yours."

She blinked then, as if coming out of a deep and unattractive memory. "Oh . . . yes. My record. Dossier perhaps. Is that the better word?" She turned the focus on me again. "What went wrong?"

I shrugged. "I don't know. She was wise enough to see the red light. . . . But it was all very ordinary. Its only uniqueness was that it happened to me."

"Surely that's the only uniqueness of anything. Dear, dear, how pompous that sounds."

We came to the head of the great flight of steps. Two young Italians coming up the steps stared avidly at her. Overhead, in the high sky, some birds were twittering. The bells had stopped.

She said: "They'll be waiting for us." And began to patter quickly down the steps. I found however hard I tried I couldn't keep up with her, and when she reached the bottom she was two dozen steps ahead. She stopped and looked at me and smiled. It was the first time she had smiled at me, but her eyes were only flecked on the surface by amusement. Underneath was something deeper, and I thought rather unhappy.

We were back before dusk and landed at the Marina Grande. My feelings were a bit off-key. I'd set out at the beginning to get to know Leonie Winter, and I had certainly done just that. But I wasn't at all sure now that the rather clumsy way I'd gone about it was the right one.

Because if I'd come out to-day with any preconceived ideas about Leonie Winter, the afternoon had killed them stone dead.

I felt out of patience with myself generally. Could Grevil really have got so enamoured, in so deep. . . . In my early thoughts the woman in the case had been a shadow, unpersonal, conventionalised. She was anything but a shadow now.

After dinner I wrote to Coxon.

"Dear Martin,

"Thanks to some part of the 'underground' you stirred up in Holland, I have located the Leonie of Grevil's letter —and, I'm almost certain, Buckingham with her. But before I make any further move I must have your identification. Without it nothing can come to the boil.

"Can you fly out or train out one day this week? I should be so grateful if you could. I'm enclosing a cheque which should pay expenses and enable you to pick up your foreign exchange.

"Regards,

"Philip."

Chapter Ten

On the way home Charlotte Weber had casually mentioned the sketches I proposed to make of her, so it was only necessary for me to suggest I might go round the following morning and begin. She'd spoken in front of Sanbergh. Da Cossa was there too, and though I didn't know quite where he fitted in, it was plain that he didn't propose to fit in with me. I looked on him rather as Sanbergh's jackal and, if anything, more full of enmity than the lion.

If I hadn't altogether forgotten how to draw, then I felt like making a good job of this or dying in the attempt. It was queer in this business—and disconcerting—to find already how many things initiated with only one purpose, begun cold and with no thought in my mind but the inquiry into Grevil's death, had already come to catch at my personal life and my own private feelings. It was damned unsettling.

After breakfast I did some more of Grevil's notes. The shorthand was very rough, and here and there he used abbreviations of his own, so that it all took a considerable time. But I came on one interesting entry right away.

" Heard Pangkal no better. Much miss his painstaking efficiency, all the peculiar merits of the studious Asiatic. Buckingham no substitute, though he handles the diggers well. This not always easy because the fossiliferous stratum is below the low water level and liable to flooding . . .

" Have never met anyone like B, and he says same of me! Used to think he put on this pose of representing the new morality. Now I wonder if partly sincere. He argues that what is called crime is as biologically natural as birth, death and procreation, and that in the near and enlightened future it will no longer be forbidden but will be recognised and renamed as an integral part of human behaviour. Honesty, he says, will then be regarded as never having existed except as an imaginary barrier to defeat natural enterprise. Truthfulness will be a convenience used only when the facts can't be denied. Uprightness will be seen as another name for stupidity.

"I tell him he's still in intellectual rompers, that these arguments he advances are as modern and progressive as Nineveh and Ur. Every tyrant from Sennacherib to Hitler has used them. I tell him he's not ahead of the times but behind them.

"In fact, he's nobody's fool, and I sometimes wish I could feel more convinced of my own arguments . . . not that they're right—I know that—but that they're powerful enough and urgent enough. Vitally important such views as his should be discredited because it's becoming less and less safe for humanity to breed the renegade and the tyrant. So much harder—and slower—to impose upon the human spirit by example what the scientist can now impose upon the human body by nuclear fission.

"*Much* quality in B. though. We have tremendous conversations. Have talked more to him than to anyone before about this new theory I have denying man's catarrhine affinities and placing his antiquity as a distinct primate from the first interglacial. Jack's keen alert brain is quite admirable foil. He's no archæologist in the strict sense. What he does do is bring to everything he tackles intense intellectual curiosity that for a short time sweeps everything before it. Flaw is in the word short. With his talents he should have got anywhere; instead nowhere. His brain is much too good to be running the way it is. Somewhere he went off the rails, and if one could find that point . . . Of course the way to put him right is to prove him wrong!"

"You should be out swimmin' and divin'," said Charlotte Weber, fiddling with the scarf round her neck. "Wasting the days on me. Make hay, etc. Last April we had seventy-two hours of thunders. All through it I read *War and Peace*. I felt I was at a celestial movie and God had written the background music."

"I was in California until the beginning of the month, so missing a day's sun won't hurt me."

"In California. I surely love the beaches there. Not that I've ever been, but the postcards one's friends send. What were you doing?"

I told her while I began to get the first rough lines on paper. The challenge in this job was not merely in the hate campaign of some of Charlotte Weber's peculiar friends, but in Charlotte herself, in the personality behind her big dark bloodshot eyes and sagging heavily powdered face and large tolerant undisciplined mouth. I was surprised how important that had become.

I said: "Tell me about Leonie Winter. You promised. Have you known her long?"

"Oh, dear Leonie. Oh yes. Yes, I met her first at Cannes just after the war; that is, the season when things began to start up again. I remember the collaborators were still being sorted out. Like laundry that's got mixed. But even that was better than the year before. The year before, you'd call to see your old friend Raoul and find him hangin' from his chandelier. Embarrassin'. It always upsets me to see my friends in trouble even when they've been naughty."

"You met Leonie?" I prompted.

"She was representing Great Britain in some swimming contest. She was seventeen or eighteen then, I suppose. She was like a beautiful fair bitch maystiff just growing out of the puppy stage. I'm simply livin' for the day when Tiffany and Bergdorf are that age. Didn't you ever hear of Leonie Hardwick? I've seen her once or twice since and kept *pressin'* her to come and stay, but she never would or could. Life's so complicated for the young."

I stared at the line of her nose. It needed no over-emphasis.

"Maybe she was busy with her various husbands."

"Husbands?" Mme Weber turned her head and spoiled the line altogether. "No, I'm the one with the husbands, dear. Overwhelmin' when one thinks. Girls should be warned when young. Marriage is habit forming. But Leonie's only had one so far."

"She was talking about several yesterday."

"You must have provoked her. She's quick with her tongue when provoked. It's a good failin'. You didn't believe her, did you?"

"What happened to the one?"

"He died. Such a nice boy, and money in the family too. D'you ever read Tennyson? My mother did whenever she was *enceinte*. I don't know what the significance was. Maud, Maud, and the rest. Don't thou marry for money but marry where money is."

"Is that what Leonie did?"

"No, they were devoted. It was that bad summer for polio in England. They all caught it. Leonie got over it quickly—just left her with that slight stammer—but Tom Winter and the baby both died. I felt very angry when I heard."

"Angry?"

"So many scoundrels left in the world. Deplorable. Fate should know its business better."

I stared at the sketch and then slipped it quietly behind and began again.

"D'you mind bringing your head up. Thanks. Not too much. Right."

"She gave up serious swimming when she married, and never took it up again. Just as well. Competitive sport is fun for the teenager, but after that you begin to wear it on your face. I rather lost sight of the dear girl until she wired me to know if she could come and stay. Why is one flattered by the attentions of the young?"

"And Captain Sanbergh?"

"Can I move my shoulder? I'm having cramp."

"Of course. We'll stop for a few minutes. Get up and walk about."

"No, really very comfortable. This chair is Venetian: I like to think one of the Doges sat in it. Or Titian. His girls are overrated. What were you telling me about Charles Sanbergh?"

"I wondered if you'd known him long?"

"Oh, God, yes. A lifetime." She sighed. "Dear Charles. So kind, so reassuring. A man like that. One forgets one is more than half a hundred years old."

I sketched for a while.

"Does he live here all the time?"

"Who, Charles? I'd say not. He's been away all winter. . . . Have you ever done a self-portrait? Must be interesting."

I saw that she was not prepared to talk about Sanbergh. "No," I said after a second. "I don't think it would be very interesting."

"What? Not with a face like yours? *I'd* want to. Sincerity, insight, steadfastness of purpose; they're all there —and eyes, restless but *very* seeing. Should say you were bitter but soft-hearted. Interestin' disharmony. Well worth a pot of paint."

I smiled but didn't reply. Presently I said: "You're not an American are you?"

"Do I look it? Improbable. What makes you ask?"

"Some turns of speech. And then——"

"I'm part Italian, part Danish, with a lot of other things in back. One grandmother was a Scot and the other a Serb. No chance at the Kennel Club. Have you noticed the Continental European, if he's over thirty-five he talks English with an English accent; if he's under it's with an American. Signs of the times." She pulled her scarf round. "My last husband was an American. Dear Sam. He spelt his name with two B's, but when he died I dropped one and pronounced it the European way—I hope he doesn't mind."

"I wouldn't if I were he."

"It's queer, you know, him dying so much before me when I expected to die so much before him. Downright confusin'."

There was silence for a time. I said: "Tell me, when you heard—when you were told you hadn't long to live, did it ever occur to you to take your own life?"

"No. . . . No, I don't think so. I was too busy. Think of the arrangin' to be done. Tidyin' up. Codicils. If you're going to be cheated of twenty years, why give up the last twenty months?"

"Provided there's any part of it you can enjoy."

"Well, yes. There nearly always is. I thoroughly enjoyed mine. Why sulk?"

I worked for about another hour, and by then had made a fairly satisfactory sketch. At least it seemed satisfactory to me. I suppose I was like someone who hasn't played tennis for years; you go on a court and are pleasantly surprised you can still play at all.

By now it was past noon and the sun was creeping round to the loggia where we'd been sitting. The four mastiffs were admitted and came lurching and snuffling in, making a great fuss of us both. Mme Weber invited me to lunch but I refused. I didn't want to sponge more than necessary.

So she excused herself. Before lunch she wanted to see Louise Henriot, the Frenchwoman with the long cigarette-holder, and it would give the dogs exercise. Leaning on her stick, tapping across the tiled floor, with a shuffle of paws following her, she left me, having told me to take another glass of sherry before I went.

I leaned on the balcony. There was more wind this morning; the leaves of the palmettoes and the tree ferns fluttered and rustled in the garden like old men reading newspapers. Overhead was high cloud and the smear of an aeroplane. Mme Weber's footsteps receded into silence. The house was very quiet.

She had two servants, I thought; an elderly woman who had once been a local beauty and dancer, and a slim cheerful young Roman called Berto, who did all the waiting at table. I wondered where they were now. I picked up my sketch and stared at it. I laid the other sheets on top of it and rolled them into a funnel and put them in my pocket. I could either leave by way of the loggia and the front garden or through the house and out of the back gate.

I went through the house.

In the white hall shallow stairs with a square stone balustrade led up to the first floor. I picked up a copy of the *New York Times* and stared at the headlines. Now, very faintly, one could catch the sound of voices. They came from the kitchen. The two servants were in there. And the four dogs were out.

I went up the stairs.

The window at which I had seen Leonie was the end one above the drawing-room. The white passage had flush doors with brass lever handles; this all looked now as if it had been redone very recently. I tried the last door and went in.

To begin ransacking a strange house at midday is probably not the most cautious of moves, but all day to-day I'd felt the need to force the pace. Yes, it was Leonie's bedroom. That very faint scent, and there were sandals I recognised, and a scarf, and on the lower half of the shutters a green strapless swim-suit. On a folding rest of canvas and wood was a Rev-Air suitcase. I went to it and saw the K.L.M. label still tied to the handle, Amsterdam to Rome. With a feeling as if I were doing something really unpleasant, I flipped back the catches and lifted the lid.

The case was about a quarter full, some underclothes, nylon stockings, a beret, a girdle; in the pocket papers; I ran rapidly through them, map of Rome, a few receipted hotel bills, among them one for four nights at the Hôtel

Doelen, Amsterdam; passport. Issued four years ago in London. Helen Joyce Winter; maiden name Hardwick; profession married woman; born Cambridge, 1st March, 1929; residence 9, Granville Gardens, Maidenhead. Height 5 feet 7 inches; eyes hazel; hair fair; special peculiarities, none.

She'd lost weight since her photograph, changed. Her face looked rounded, girlish, the expression unformed, innocent, secure. I looked at the embossments; she had been to France twice, Italy once before this time; not apparently to Holland before; there was nothing else to see.

As I was going to close the case I saw three or four unlaundered handkerchiefs at the bottom, and one looked bigger than the rest. I picked it out. On the corner was a familiar monogram, G.T.

I glanced quickly at my watch. Twenty minutes after twelve. The dressing-table.

Here all the usual things. Nail varnish, cigarettes, scissors, hairbrush, a freckle of spilt powder from a Lanvin box, that was the scent; needle and a reel of silk thread. In the drawers a gold bracelet, a garnet necklace, a flimsy nightdress—a writing-pad with a letter unfinished in it.

"Dear Mummy,

"So glad to have your letter—I've been intending to write every day. I have been here a fortnight already and am feeling so very much better, more relaxed, able to let go, and I think, I believe able to see things straight for the first time. One good thing—Holland ended everything. Although it didn't seem so at the time, perhaps it was better that way, the way it worked out. Nothing could be more final. Now perhaps I shall be able to plan again.

"Thank you for not giving away my address. I think I shall stay here just as long as Mme Weber will put up with me. I've done more swimming these last weeks than since before I married Tom, and the weather has been perfect. Last night I slept seven hours. It's a completely feckless life, everybody lazes about and eats and drinks and smokes and gossips. There's no *point* to it—it's not going anywhere, but that suits me just now. One has ample time to think—and just doesn't want to. So stop worrying about me. I'm really all right.

"The broom is coming out and the slopes of the island are yellow with it. There are geraniums in flower all the way beside the funicular. Very few tourists yet. If there should be a sudden influx next month——"

The letter stopped there. One good thing, Holland ended everything. Perhaps it was better that way. With Grevil's swollen body floating in a canal? With his wife and daughter bereaved and all the promise of his career flung away?

There was a movement by the door. I turned sharply. Nicolo da Cossa was standing watching me.

Chapter Eleven

He said: "I fear Leonie has little valuable jewellery. Perhaps I can direct you to Mme Weber's room."

"Has she something better?" I said. "Of course you'll know about that."

The shock was running out to my hands now. It left me feeling boneless.

He smiled spitefully: "I know about it, but I am not a thief. I do not abuse the hospitality of my friends."

I looked round. "Well, I've finished here. Let's go down and drink a sherry while we discuss it."

"There is nothing to discuss, *signore*. Except how quickly you can get off this island."

I shut the drawer. "What are you doing in the house yourself?"

"You thought I was on the beach? Sometimes I have migraine. Now please to go down and I will follow."

I went to the door and out. He followed me down. I turned through into the big drawing-room and picked up my glass.

"Sherry?"

"Thank you." I could see he was enjoying this. "I shall tell Mme Weber, of course, as soon as she comes in. I think perhaps I shall leave it with her if she tells Leonie."

"You're not going to call in the police, then?"

He limped across and took the second glass from me. "Why be vindictive?"

"Especially when you've no proof."

"That is so."

"In fact, it's only your word against mine in telling Mme Weber."

"She and I are old friends. Besides, what have I to gain?"

"You might think you had something to gain."

He stared at me with his big sombre eyes. "Tell me what?"

"You might be uneasy over my friendship with Charlotte Weber."

"With an old woman? You must be insane."

"A wealthy woman who regards you as her pet artist."

He showed me his teeth. "You flatter yourself, *signore*. I have not seen your work, but you are a confessed amateur, a Saturday-painter. Charlotte is too wise in her judgment not to know shoddy stuff when she sees it."

Glass in hand I walked over to stare at his pastel of the Faraglioni Rocks. "I should have thought her very liable to be taken in by the fake and the sham."

Outside there was a sound of grinding gears as a bus drew away from the gate. A few moments later there was the pad of quick feet, and Jane's voice and then Leonie's and Hamilton White's. They were back but did not come in here. We heard their feet on the stairs.

Da Cossa had come over to me. "I should be happy if you would explain what you say."

A few years ago I felt he would have used a dagger. "That isn't your picture, is it."

"'Look for yourself," he said. "It is signed. What more is it that you want?"

"To have seen you paint it."

"I'm sorry. I can't oblige."

"Nor could you ever have. The thing's a bit florid for my taste, but it's painted by a man who knows every trick in the trade. It's thoroughly expert."

"Quite so. I——"

"I saw you painting on the quay yesterday. You just haven't the technique to do a job like this. I'd stake my life on it."

"Yesterday I used oils—an unfamiliar medium. And——"

"The medium doesn't matter—not that much. Be sensible; we're both of age."

He stared up at me. He was near enough for me to smell the scented oil on his hair and to see the black hair curling like a mat on his chest under the open silk shirt. I said: "In the ordinary way it wouldn't be my business, but I should guess you wanted to impress Mme Weber, so you bought this from some down-and-out artist and . . . Perhaps others too. Are there others too?"

In the garden there was the gruff coughing of dogs.

He said: "And the proof?"

"Your word against mine. But I could sow the doubt."

"What were you doing in Leonie Winter's room?"

"Not stealing."

He smiled again, nastily. "Fetishism, perhaps. I knew a man once. . . . For my part now, I am only interested in underclothes when there is someone in them."

"I'm glad you have some natural instincts," I said.

"More, I am certain, than you have, *signore*."

We faced each other like two bristling dogs, each waiting for the other to bite.

Then we heard the tapping of a stick.

"Well, that's fine, you've stopped on, Philip," said Mme Weber. "We need another man for lunch. There's baby octopus, d'you mind? I've a weakness. You two artists been exchangin' trade secrets, no doubt? Nicolo, is your head better?"

In a minute the room seemed full of people and dogs. Just as Charlotte Weber and Mlle Henriot came in from the loggia, Leonie and Jane entered by the ordinary door. Leonie looked surprised to see me, and just for a second not too sure of herself. I thought: so far I understand nothing about her at all. "One good thing, Holland ended everything. It was better that way, the way it worked out." An accidental combination of skin, bone and flesh—attraction she hadn't earned, power she didn't deserve. . . . Yes, but it wasn't just that, it was more than that.

It was all very well to kick myself for being unable to approach her as I would an ordinary woman. I wasn't detached enough on either count. Grevil got in the way of normal friendship. *She* got in the way of normal antagonism.

Before lunch she kept out of my way, but at it we were put together so there was no escape. Towards the end I said: "I think I started off on the wrong foot yesterday. D' you think we might scrap the record and begin again?"

"And the day before?" she said pleasantly, after a moment.

"And the day before."

". . . Very well. If you feel that way."

"I wondered if you would come a walk with me this afternoon."

I watched her long clear-skinned fingers as they broke a

stick of bread. She hadn't looked at me during this. "A walk?"

"Yes, I thought it might be pleasant as there's a breeze to-day. We could start off and see where we should get to."

"I can tell you. Into the sea. The island is only four miles long. There are very few level places at all."

"Then let's climb."

She looked at me then with her sandy-green eyes, thick-lashed, cool, unsmiling. "Should that follow?"

"I don't know."

"Is that the first doubt you've had about me since we met?"

"You don't really believe that, do you?"

She looked down. "Well, walking wouldn't help."

"Talking might."

"That's a doubt *I* have."

"Then maybe we can help each other."

The young manservant tried to refill her glass with Orvieto, but she waved him away.

"Will you come?" I said.

We climbed up to Anacapri and then took the path to La Migliari. She was in a frock to-day, with green suède sandals, and a wide-brimmed beach hat rather like the one Mme Weber had worn yesterday; but on Leonie Winter it looked different. Having seen that four-year-old photograph, I saw she was fine-drawn now. You could understand the sentence in her letter about having slept seven hours. It must have been quite an achievement.

And why?

After a time she mentioned her husband, and I said: "And what did your second husband like?"

She didn't answer for a minute, and I went on: "Tell me, *was* it photographs of your half-sisters you were showing that Italian family yesterday?"

116

She stopped to pick a sprig of broom. "I rather supposed you'd ask Charlotte Weber."

"She told me without asking. Anyway, if you've had one husband only, and a child, and lost them both in that way, why put on such a terrific act for my benefit?"

She sniffed the broom delicately. "It wasn't an act. I didn't think you really wanted to know."

"No," I said. "I see that. I'm sorry."

She glanced at me. "Thank you for saying one sincere thing, Philip."

"Am I such a rotten actor?"

"I don't know. I don't know the play."

We were walking now across open land, having done all the climbing necessary. If you blinkered your eyes you could have thought yourself on Dartmoor.

I said: "There's no play. One ad-libs as one goes along. That's life."

She said quietly: "Oh, I grant you it all. You say your lines, and what does it matter if they're messy and meaningless? Nothing at all."

"Well, it can matter."

"When?"

"When it cuts in on someone else who's had the wit or the luck to contrive a pattern that makes sense."

"Are you thinking of a special case?"

I didn't answer, and we walked on until we came rather unexpectedly to some bars across the path. There the path ended, and so it seemed did the earth. We'd come to the edge of a sheer cliff that fell away about a thousand feet into the sea.

A sudden eddy of wind met us, and she put up a hand to her hat. "This is the end of our walk."

The world felt very empty, standing there, and two sea-gulls wheeling and crying didn't help to fill it. The sea was finely wrinkled, like thumb-prints under a magnifying glass. There was a fishing-boat and two men in it, one with a red handkerchief round his head.

She dropped the sprig of broom. At first it seemed to cling to the ragged cliffs among the other wild flowers, but then it went circling down, getting smaller until it reached the sea. She turned away. "Phew! That makes me dizzy."

After a few seconds I followed her and sat about a yard away on the springy turf. I thought of the letter of hers I'd read this morning. And the handkerchief lying unwashed in the bottom of her case.

She took off her hat and put it beside her and shook her hair. The bit of light fringe fell back provocatively over her forehead. "How long have you been painting?"

"Oh . . . pretty long."

"All your life?"

". . . Until these last few years."

"And then?"

"Then it didn't add up any more."

"You don't do it for a living?"

"No, that's the point."

"What's the point?"

For a second or so I examined in my own mind whether I wanted to explain anything more about this to her. I came to the conclusion I didn't. But confidence might breed confidence.

"Well, you play about with a thing for a time and think, fine, I'm coming along nicely. And then suddenly you wake up to the fact that you're a big boy now and nothing really important is coming along after all."

She tucked her legs under her with a sliding movement and pulled her skirt into its proper fold. It had been tight about her thighs. "D'you judge that by whether you make money of it or not?"

"No—that's only one of many ways. The important thing is when you realise inside you that it never is going to amount to anything—even to yourself."

She shook her head. "I don't see how that can be."

"Why not?"

"Well, I don't see how something you create yourself can be a dead loss to yourself—however good or bad it may seem to other people."

"That's true only for someone who hasn't the intelligence to criticise his own work."

"No, surely. . . . No, I don't agree."

I said: "Perhaps I wanted too much."

"I can certainly understand that," she said.

"Oh, you mustn't judge everything by yesterday."

She smiled. "Talking of yesterday. . . . Tell me one thing."

"If I can."

"Did you—well, try to rush things because of your opinion of me or because of your opinion of yourself?"

"Neither, as it happens."

She waited. I said: "Where do you live in England?"

"Mainly in London."

"With your father and mother?"

"No. My father was killed in the war. My mother has married again, and I have two half-sisters in spite of your mistrustful mind. But I work and have my own flat."

"And you swim."

"I hate to think how much you'll know by the end of the portrait."

"You haven't the arms one expects of a swimmer," I said.

She put one hand up to cover the other arm above the elbow. "You've old-fashioned ideas in some things—if not in others. Would you ever like to jump over a place like this."

"Not much."

"I used to love diving, and it would be that sensation you'd get, wouldn't it, only a hundred times more so? Like an arrow falling."

I said: "It might be worth trying some time when

you're tired of life. It would certainly be more dramatic than dying in bed . . . or for that matter in some back street or dirty canal."

There was dead silence for a bit. I hadn't meant to blurt it out. She slowly took her hand away from her arm. "So that explains everything."

"Explains what?"

"You *are* a relative of his."

It's queer how the exchanges of a dozen words can make and break something so quickly. "His brother. Did you suspect it?"

"Of course, to begin. You're so like him—younger, broader; but the same *shape* of shoulders, your eyes, voice. And then I thought it was just nerves, imagination." She stood up. "Well, tell me what you want to know, and then I can go."

"How he died."

"I know nothing about that."

"You mean you don't know how it happened."

"I mean I know nothing about it."

The breeze was blowing one lapel of her frock covering her throat and then uncovering it again.

I said: "Sit down. We can talk about it quietly."

"No, thank you."

"Don't you think I'm entitled to ask?"

"I don't think you're entitled to go about it the way you have. If you wanted to know about Grevil, it was less than ever necessary to—to——" She stared angrily at the sea.

I said: "How was I to know what you'd be like? He'd never even mentioned you to me."

"He didn't have much chance."

"When did you first meet him?"

She shook her head but didn't answer.

"Leonie, you must tell me. When did you first meet him?"

"In Holland. A month ago."

I got up too, stood beside her. "You're telling me you met Grevil for the first time only a few days before his death?"

"Of course I am! What did you think?"

"I think it's impossible——"

"Well, you're perfectly entitled to——"

"No," I said, catching her arm as she was turning away. "Listen. How can you expect me to swallow that? How do you explain the letter?"

"What letter?"

"The one that was found on him—that said everything was over between you."

She got her arm free and stared at me. "I didn't know any letter *was* found on him. . . . Do you mean"—her eyes changed—"the one I wrote?"

"Didn't you leave it for him before you left?"

She had gone very white. "No. . . . Oh yes. But—was that how you traced me?"

"Partly."

"So you thought—is that what you think?"

"What do you suppose I should think?"

She took a breath. "But it—it's beyond belief that . . ." She stopped again and didn't seem able to go on.

"It's beyond belief to me," I said. "I don't see why it should be to you."

"And how has that. . . . Do the police know about it?"

"Of course."

"Do they think it had something to do with his death?"

"If you were the police," I said, "what would you say?"

Chapter Twelve

She had dropped her hat, and now she picked it up, dusting bits of dry grass off it. I watched her mouth. As I was going to speak she said:

"Give me a minute. I have to put this straight in my own mind."

I stood and waited. Due west was the lighthouse on the extreme promontory of the island. Between it and us in a direct line were the monstrous profiles of the cliff.

She said: "Tell me exactly what the police think."

"That Grevil committed suicide because of his love affair with a woman called Leonie, which she ended by writing him that letter."

"And do you believe that?"

"No, I never have. At least, knowing Grevil, I didn't believe it possible, until I saw you."

"What difference did that make?"

"It occurred to me that over a woman like yourself it was just on the cards."

She looked thoughtfully at me. I said: "You don't deny having written the letter?"

"Of course not."

"Why did you write it?"

"If I told you, you wouldn't believe me."

"Supposing you try." She made an impatient gesture. I said: "You must tell me. It's vital."

". . . I knew Grevil barely two days. I'm certain when he died he'd not even read the letter."

"Yet you believe he killed himself."

"Isn't it for the police to say?"

"If they can. It's still more for the people who were on the spot."

"I wasn't on the spot—or near it. If I had been——"

"Why didn't you go to the police and make a statement as soon as you heard—if you've nothing to hide?"

"I didn't hear of it until I was in Naples. And I didn't say I had nothing to hide."

I said: "Look, my dear, we've got to get this straight. If you don't answer me, you'll have to answer the police."

"Do they know where I am?"

"Not yet."

"But you're going to tell them?"

"It depends."

"I couldn't help them, Philip."

"We could decide that better if you told me what you know."

"I . . . don't think I can. It involves someone else and I——" She stopped.

"It involves someone else?"

"Yes. I——" She glanced round as if trying to see a way out. "Philip, I *can't* say much now. I've got to have a few hours to see round it. I'd no idea, honestly I'd not the ghost of an idea . . . certainly not that the police had found my letter. Well, you may think, that's all very well but they did, and now it's time for you to tell what you know. I know it is, and if it was the police asking me I'd have no second wind at all. But Philip, you're *not* the police, and I want to ask you . . . perhaps till to-morrow. If you called in the police they wouldn't be here till then, so it won't be much delay. . . ."

She turned her eyes on me, and we looked at each other pretty straightly for what seemed a long time. I knew I was going to think badly of myself if I gave way.

"Yes," I said.

She smiled a bit then, doubtfully, but not at all with the look of yesterday. I was going to say something else when I heard a dog barking.

In the distance, along the path we'd followed, a man was coming our way. Among the rough stones two big dogs were rooting about, waving their tails, making the most of their freedom. The man was Charles Sanbergh.

I wondered if she'd seen him before I did. I came to the conclusion that she had.

I knew I'd been a fool to spring this on her and then give her breathing space to recover. Before he came up she got her compact out and made some repairs, but she couldn't hide the look in her eyes, and that, I think, warned him we hadn't been discussing the scenery. We walked back together making heavy weather of it. The ill-feeling between him and me could hardly have been more obvious.

Somehow we began to talk about the Blue Grotto; perhaps she'd been looking for a harmless topic; and when she asked me I said I hadn't seen it, because I always fought shy of the accepted wonders of the world.

She said: "Well, it's often overrun with tourists, but it's impressive at the right times. Charles was saying —weren't you?—that a good time is in the very early morning just as the sun comes up."

Sanbergh said: "I should have thought it would have appealed to an artist interested in colour. You should take the opportunity before you leave. It may not occur again."

"Perhaps I will, before I leave."

"And that, I imagine, will be soon."

"I've no idea."

"I think we should go one morning," Leonie put in.

I said to her: "We must try it together."

Sanbergh picked up a stone and threw it for Gimbel. It was a good throw but a trifle vicious, and Gimbel went ploughing in among somebody's vines. "And how is the portrait of Mme Weber coming along? We've seen nothing of it yet."

"Did you expect to?"

"No, frankly I didn't."

Leonie said: "Philip has only had a couple of hours so far."

"And I shall probably need at least one more morning before I do any painting at all."

"Mme Weber is an extremely busy woman," said Sanbergh.

"I can wait."

"I always think," he said, "that patience is an overrated virtue."

"It depends how you exercise it."

Sanbergh stared at his manicured right hand, making sure it wasn't soiled, then he pushed it into the pocket of his reefer jacket. "I would rather say it depends on what we exercise it. I wouldn't deny there's virtue in being patient with that which is worth-while, with something which gives a high rate of return. But to waste it on the worthless, the meretricious, the bogus, the impudent . . . that I'm just not willing to do."

I said: "Is that how you see it or is that how you'd like to see it?"

He turned on me softly: "I think we must talk of this some other time, Mr. Norton."

There was dead silence for a bit, except for Macy who was making friendly chewing sounds at my heels.

We went on down the hill.

When I got back to the hotel the expected telegram was waiting. "*Arriving Naples to-morrow at thirteen hours. Noli irritare leones. Martin.*"

I thought it was typical of him to make a pun even in the cable. The following day I went over by the morning boat and was at the Capodichino airport to meet him. He came through the customs looking as sallow, as dissipated, as handsome and as distinguished as I remembered him. It was the first time I had seen him in an ordinary grey suit, and I wondered if he had not bothered to bring his battledress. We shook hands warmly and he said: "I wonder what happens to air-hostesses when they get old and wrinkled."

"They don't," I said. "They marry and bear other air-hostesses; it's a special breed. Is the burglary cleared up?"

"Three-quarters of the stuff was recovered the following day where it had been dumped. Either the thieves got windy or they discovered the silver was electro-plate. But they didn't return my El Toro cigars, blast them."

I took his case and the book he had been reading. It was a privately printed edition of *Novelas Exemplares*, by Cervantes. When I glanced up he said gently: "So you've found both the girl and Buckingham?"

"Yes. I know I owe you an apology for carrying on on my own when it was entirely the result of your contacts that I got a lead at all. But I thought it might well be a complete fiasco—someone getting an easy two hundred guilders out of me."

"You're sure it isn't?"

"Certain about the girl. Reasonably sure about Buckingham; but I need your identification." I told him all that had happened, the way I had traced them to the Villa Atrani, and what I had done so far. He listened intently. He was a good confidant—not one of those men whose eyes stray over your shoulder while they listen. "I hoped to hold everything up until you came, but—it didn't work out."

"She's given you no explanation of why she wrote the letter?"

"Not yet."

"That's rather trusting of you, isn't it? Surely the first thing she'll do is tell Buckingham."

"I don't think it matters about me. Only you can identify him, and they know nothing about you."

"Is she very attractive, this girl?"

"Yes, but not so that I'd lose my sense of judgment." I wondered if that was true.

The dark look lifted from his face as he smiled with that unexpected yet compelling gentleness. "I only asked. Wait a minute, I must wire my mother, tell her I got here safely."

When he came away from the telegraph counter he said: "I wonder how they traced the right woman in Holland when the police failed. Lowenthal's a queer bloke —I only approached him on the off-chance."

"D'you mean the little clerk?"

"No, no; Lowenthal's a big shot." He rubbed his chin. "These early starts; I shall need another shave before the day's through. . . . Afraid I haven't the same contacts here. What sort of course are you going to set?"

"I'm going to run you across Buckingham's bows and see what happens," I said, using his phraseology.

"And if it isn't Buckingham?"

"I shall be damned disappointed."

We got on the air transport bus. He pushed back his lank dark hair with two fingers. "Tell me again about Holland."

I told him of my second meeting with Tholen, of my dinner with Count Louis Joachim, of my failure to see the detective coming from Java, and of Tholen's promise to write me if the man brought any news.

"I've yet to meet a policeman who ever wrote letters." Martin stared broodingly at the airport as it slid away. "I've a feeling you'll have to go back there in the end, tackle them afresh."

"You mean you think the real solution is there."

"Yes. Yes." I didn't speak. He added: "I've no good reason to say so—it's just one of those hunches."

"In that case you think neither Leonie Winter nor Buckingham is at the bottom of this."

After thinking for a minute he gave his shoulder a hitch. "Explain a thing like this and it becomes nonsense. I don't know. . . . How am I to meet this fellow Sanbergh —Buckingham? Have you that fixed, too?"

"Yes. Mme Weber is having some people in for drinks to-night—she does that every two or three days. Sanbergh is sure to be there. I asked her if I might bring a friend."

I was on edge about the meeting—a lot more so than I admitted even to myself. It might have been more to the point if I'd bought a gun in Naples that morning instead of a canvas and a stretcher and some brushes and paints.

Of course it might all yet fizzle out. It was a game of bluff. If the surprise failed, then we were back at Square One. But I didn't see how the surprise could fail.

I'd booked a room for Martin at the Hôtel Vecchio, and it was queer to see how quickly he had the dark young manageress fluttering around him, and the rest of the staff ready to help. It wasn't anything he particularly said or did; in fact he looked rather depressed and disillusioned about things. It didn't matter. Indulgence was extended to him before he demanded it.

The short twilight was nearly over as we made for the Villa Atrani. Martin walked by my side, for once without anything to say. I don't know if he was feeling some of the tension I was feeling or whether it was just that we had talked ourselves out. Anyway, there was nothing more to do at this stage but light the blue touch paper and stand well away.

As we got to the gate I said: "Do you think Buckingham will recognise you?"

"He isn't likely to have forgotten."

I glanced at Martin in the half-light. "I've never asked you, but have you some private score to pay off against this fellow?"

He hesitated. "What makes you ask?"

"Well, as a stranger in this case, you've been very patient and very interested."

He smiled slightly, but it didn't lift his brooding expression this time. "It's only as things have gone on that I've come to realise what I've had against this man. Some day I'll tell you about it. Even now, thinking it over, I'm not sure how much I owe him—any more than you do yet. Perhaps when you find out, I shall find out too."

We went up the path.

At the door the dogs met us, fawning on me, getting Martin's wave-length as quickly as if they had been human. Mme Weber in an odd-looking sack-like pink dress and with far too much mascara on her eyelids, waved an impaled cherry on a stick in welcome and led the way into the living-room.

Many new people to-night; my eyes flickered past them to the known faces: Nicolo da Cossa, with Jane, Hamilton White, Mlle Henriot, Signor Castiglioni, a tall, stout Italian shipowner who'd been at the luncheon yesterday.

The buzz of voices, introductions forgotten as soon as made, remarks which meant nothing drowned by others which meant less. "Is he here yet?" Martin said. "No," I said; "nor the girl." Half a dozen other people came, then some more. The room would soon be crowded. This was a much more ambitious party than the last. Half the exhibitionists of the island. A man in shorts with a red beard, a woman with a hat with big tin animals stitched to the straw as ornaments. A fat middle-aged woman with incredibly tight yellow jeans.

"Dear Philip," said Mme Weber speaking suddenly in my ear, "the Master of Kyle will take nothing but Scotch; it's his signature drink; could you be an angel?" Her eyes glimmered approvingly over Martin. "Good of you to come and see us, Commander Boxer. We're dishevelled. *Far* more people than I ever invite. Flatterin' but a strain on the gin."

"Where's Leonie?" I said to her.

"Upstairs lying down. She hasn't been well this afternoon. But she promised to look in later. Dear Mr.

Weekley, how good of you to come. You'll take a Manhattan?" Mme Weber was swept away on an eddy, and I was left holding an extra glass.

"Kyle?" said Martin. "Did she say Kyle?"

"Yes; that bald old chap by the window."

"By God, yes, it's the same. I used to know him well. I thought he'd been cremated long ago."

"Well, come over with me and see. We'd better keep together."

We went across, edging along with muttered apologies and a couple of bumps. Not only Martin but Macy, snuffling, followed me. The old man was rubbing his bald head and talking resentfully to Mlle Henriot. I gave him the whisky, and he eyed me with the same expression, as if he expected a confidence trick somewhere. Then I introduced Martin Coxon.

"Coxon?" Kyle peered cautiously from under his eyelids at the man beside me. "What *Martin* Coxon, Lord Callard's grandson? Why didn't ye say so? It's a decade and a half——"

"More," said Martin. "I didn't suppose you could still be alive."

Kyle said stiffly: "Then you supposed far from the truth. I was ten years Callard's junior, and he would not have been beyond eighty if he'd ha' lived. What are you doing now? I trust ye've settled down since the war. Didn't I read you were up for the D.S.O.?"

"Yes, up before the beak. It seems half a century since I climbed on your roof and tied a pair of the cook's drawers over the kitchen chimney-pot."

"Well, it's a quarter anyway. Aye, ye were a wild lad, and ungrateful forbye. I mind well the time when Callard came to me and said, John, that boy, there's no training him. . . ."

Over the heads of the milling people I saw Leonie come into the room. She was very pale, and her make-up couldn't hide it. She looked sharply round. I wondered if she was looking for Sanbergh. She saw Mme Weber and moved towards her, asked her a question. Then before the reply came she saw me. Mme Weber caught her arm and said something, and Leonie nodded and half smiled in a strained way, before she began to push nervously through the crowd.

". . . what's more," said Kyle. "And although neither the island nor the queer cattle living on it please me and I sigh for the manly scenery of Scotland, the soft sickly climate here suits an old man. . . ."

Leonie came up and gave me a queer cold look that I'd never seen on her face before. A complete change from yesterday.

"I'm sorry you're not well," I said.

"Only a touch of the sun. . . . I don't need your sympathy." She glanced at Martin as he turned.

"This is my friend, Commander Coxon, Mrs. Winter." My voice was half lost in the din.

I saw Martin's dark eyes on her. "Philip has been talking of you, Mrs. Winter." He didn't say any more because that was enough. Then after a sufficient pause to give it air, he added: "I've been admiring your lovely island this evening. That comes up to expectations too."

"It isn't my island, Commander Coxon; we share it between us, but the title deeds go back to Augustus."

"Who knew what he was about. One of the great men of the world, in spite of Voltaire. A pity Gaius didn't live to succeed."

He went on talking, and by the time he'd finished he'd taken Leonie in, deferentially but pretty thoroughly, and her own colour had come at last. Once again he was getting away with it, and I felt a queer twinge almost of resentment that it was so easy. After a while Leonie turned to Kyle and Kyle began to speak, but his words were drowned in a burst of laughter from some people near. I didn't take my eyes off Leonie. She turned to me. "Could you get me a drink, Philip? I need one badly."

"Of course." There were plenty on a tray near, and when I came quickly back with one Martin and Kyle were wrangling over some reminiscence of the Scottish moors, and Leonie was half leaning against the wall behind her, staring across the room, a frown of pain between her eyebrows.

I said: "Where is Sanbergh this evening?"

"He went out in his yacht fishing."

"I hoped he'd be here."

"Does it matter? He hates cocktail parties." She took her drink quickly, nearly spilling it.

I said: "They're the nadir of social life, no doubt. Conversation pumped out as the gin is pumped in. Raised voices and fallen arches. What do you think of my friend?"

"Very charming. Have you invited him here to help you search the bedrooms?"

"Should I have?"

"No. You do that so tactfully yourself."

"I'm sorry I had to."

She fumbled with her glass, put it down because a drop of the liquid had run down the outside, dabbed at her hand like a child with a cut. "Why had you to? What compulsion was there? Is that why you came here under another name? What *difference* could it have made?"

"It'll make none at all if you raise your voice a bit more."

"I can't help but think you must see yourself as one of those private detectives who risk their lives and their virtue for ten dollars a day and expenses. I suppose you expected to find the dead body of a girl in black nylon pyjamas and—and. . . ."

I said: "All right, have your fun."

She didn't say anything more. She was as taut as a bow-string.

I said: "I think you let this bit go by; but as it happens there is a dead body among our stage properties. Only this one wasn't in black nylon pyjamas. It does make rather a difference. Anyway, if you believe that by registering contempt at what I've done you can head me off from anything I intend to do . . ."

The Italian boy came round and refilled our glasses. Leonie gulped at hers again. Catching a glimpse of her eyes then, I saw it was no longer just physical pain. They brimmed for a second or two, then she blinked it sharply away.

Martin turned back and began chatting to her. Charlotte Weber bore down on us, her eyes and lips fatigued with smoke and noise but herself undefeatable. I saw her as a sort of sick bird dragging one wing, determined to flutter and be gay just as long as she could. She took Leonie away, and then I somehow got separated from Martin. Still more people were crushing in at the door, and I'd have left but for the hope of seeing Sanbergh.

I wouldn't take more drink but kept chewing unrecognisable bits of food that found their way into my hand. I got people's elbows in my back and women's buttocks shoving against me and odd scents of Schiaparelli and Gauloise and a few more earthy odours. The dark woman with the toy hat eyed me with some speculation, and then decided that I probably wasn't worth the effort of pushing through the crowd. A tall baldish man with a thin nose stopped by and began to ask me about the literary situation in Italy. It took five minutes to convince him that I knew nothing whatever about it.

After another half hour, while the battle was still at its heights, I beat a retreat into the loggia. There were one or two others out here who had fallen by the way. The air was cool and scented. Beside the balustrade a lemon tree grew with flowers and fruit hanging together. I fingered the lemon and then sniffed my fingers gratefully. In the distance the northern arm of the Bay of Naples was winking with lights. I rubbed my eyes which were smarting with the smoke.

A man came into the loggia from the room and looked round. When he saw me he came towards me. It was Hamilton White. "I thought I saw you slip out, Norton. Are you coming with us on this trip to-morrow?"

"What trip?"

"To the Blue Grotto. I've never been, you know, and I should never hear the last of it in the States if I spent two weeks on this island and didn't see its most famous sight."

"Oh. . . . No, I hadn't heard about it. Who's going?"

White stared at me rather foggily. "Leonie and Jane and Nicolo. Sanbergh's lending us his small boat, and we figure on starting at dawn. There was some talk of inviting you to be in the party."

At that moment there was a sound like angry bees as the door opened and Leonie slipped out. She didn't see us, and looked as if she were going into the garden.

White turned and called to her, and she saw us and slowly came across. Her eyes were big and very dark, and there was still that stretched paleness in her face.

White said: "I was asking Philip for to-morrow, Leonie. I don't know if he wants to be included in."

"I've only just heard," I said.

Leonie said: "I'm sure there won't be much in it for you, Philip. Perhaps you could stay behind and question the staff."

"What's that?" White interrupted, looking from one to the other of us. "Question the—I don't quite get it."

I said: "Oh, it's just a low-spirited little joke we have between us."

"Well, if you make up your mind——"

"I have. I'll come."

"Good. That's fine. We've all agreed to be down at the Piccola Marina at five-thirty prompt. By the way, I noticed you have a friend with you this evening. I don't know whether there would be room——"

"There isn't," Leonie said. "Charles advised us against taking more than five."

"Martin Coxon won't mind," I said.

Chapter Thirteen

I was bitterly disappointed at the way the evening had gone, and on the way home I told Martin so.

He didn't speak for a while. When he did it was almost to himself. "Queer how one gets tensed up for a thing. I thought I was too seasoned for that." He looked at me. "Well, Buckingham's absence made a damp squib of it, but we can wait. Leonie Winter is certainly a high-octane number."

"She was hard going to-night."

"These pretty girls usually are."

"I don't mean in that way. Da Cossa had been talking."

I told Martin of the arrangement for the early morning. He said rather irritably: "Mme Weber has invited us both to dinner to-morrow night, did you know? I wonder *why* she's entertaining these people? I don't like women over fifty. They're like floating wrecks, water-logged, drifting; you're liable to run foul of them at any time."

"My feeling is she knows little or nothing about it. I think Sanbergh is simply making use of her home until this blows over."

He stopped at a wall, part lit by a window near, and picked a couple of wild flowers. "Some of the real aristocrats of the island," he said. "Probably they were blooming here before the Phœnicians set foot on it. I wonder which is the end-product nature's most interested in—us or them." His long elegant face was preoccupied as he put the two flowers in his pocket-book. Then he said: "What do you intend to do to-morrow after this early rise? Didn't she promise to explain her letter to-day?"

"Yes," I said. "To be fair I haven't given her the opportunity. One thing I'm worrying about is whether Sanbergh has taken fright and already gone."

"Left the island? Why should he? No one knew I was coming. No one knows that I knew Buckingham."

Before going to sleep I did the last big piece of the diary, but for the most part there was little beyond a day-by-day record of the excavations. I'd almost decided to give it up when I came on an entry dated ten days before they left.

"Up for the first time to-day and feeling pretty seedy. Distinguished it by my first row with J.B. Ungrateful I suppose in view of all care he's taken of me while ill—certainly couldn't have been in better hands. For four days had hell of a time—must be less resistant than used to be. Came on very suddenly, one hour well, the next shivering so badly could hardly stand. Temp. 104.3. 20 grains quinine. Jack up most of first night constantly refilling hot-water bottles at my feet and back. First morning clearer in head and less thirsty, but at it again before midday. From then on very confused memories, chiefly of head flaming and body and legs of ice, of trying to get up and being kept in bunk by force or persuasion, of Jack pressing more quinine on me, or drinks, or relighting fire. He tells me in my delirium I solved all the problems of phylogeny of man. Wish I could remember how! I doubt if he got much rest any night. All the same while I've been ill he has catalogued and crated most of our finds to date and has kept the men at work on the diggings. Invaluable fellow.

"Row started to-night somehow over discussion about slave labour and concentration camps and the possible defeat of the human spirit. He contends that no human will can stand up against the scientific degradation which can be so easily switched on in such places to-day. That merely by the applied technical tricks worked out in last generation any man of whatever spiritual calibre can be reduced to primitive animal crawling in the primeval mud, that such tricks are being and will be more and more applied in the modern world, with mass propaganda the first step and individual coercion the last. The individual is lost and his cause is lost.

"This an insufferable contention. If it were true I think one would be capable of that desperation absolute and complete that William James speaks of, the whole universe coagulating about the sufferer into a material of overwhelming horror, surrounding him without opening or end—and no other conception or sensation able to live for a moment in its presence.

"I quoted this to B, but told him his contention completely untrue. Must be—and it must be for us to make certain of it. For man of his quality and education apparently to believe it. . . . Less inexcusable for the barbarians of the East who have never been under same influences, same traditions. But if common grounds on which our civilisation built is destroyed, *nothing* left of value on the earth.

"At this B began to say something about Christianity, but told him Christianity only part of story. Many men in West reject religion or its dogmas. *This* is wider, draws from *all* beliefs—Jewish as much as Christian, Greek as much as either. Everything we've learned, breathed, inherited, irrespective of race, creed, kind. To reject it is the ultimate betrayal.

"Of course should not have got so hot about this were it said by anyone whose opinion I didn't care about. You laugh at the fool but get angry with the man you respect.

"After time he followed me out of tent and apologised —whereupon apology from me, and a greater harmony than before. But after it a discussion on contemporary vegetation in lake muds falls noticeably flat. These last weeks our talks and arguments together seem to have become of greater importance than the excavations."

I didn't sleep well, partly because of what I had read. There were not many more pages of notes now, and I was tempted once or twice to switch on the light and spend the rest of the night finishing them. At about a quarter to five I got up and shaved and put on a blue seaman's jersey and a pair of grey denim trousers and started off.

It was still very dark, and after I came out of the narrow alley and turned down the motor-road I saw that there were no stars out. A heavy cloud hanging over the island had snuffed out the sky. We had arranged to meet at the Piccola Marina to avoid disturbing people at the Villa Atrani, and it crossed my mind as I went down the hill that the assignment might be a drunken jest which none of the others would remember this morning.

The darkness before dawn is like no other part of the night, and the island was very still. When at last I got to the last hairpin I saw three figures moving across the little jetty and caught the flash of a torch. By now in the farthest reaches of the sky there was a stain of light, and imperceptibly the land was less dark.

As I crunched across the pebbles to join them, Jane said: "Ah, here he comes. Good morning, Philip. I'm sorry to say there's quite an argument in progress right now. Are you weather-wise, darling?"

"Scarcely ever," I said. Leonie was standing very still against the wall of rock. Da Cossa, who had said no word of greeting, was paying off some slack rope and staring out to sea. "Where's White?"

"We couldn't get him up," said Jane. "He said he wasn't feeling too good, but I think it was that party. It went on for quite a while after you left, darling. And now Nicolo refuses to go because of the weather."

Da Cossa turned. "There is a storm coming. I have repeated that three times. I know the signs too well."

138

"What sort of a storm?" I asked, my eyes on Leonie. "If it's a thunderstorm, it shouldn't hurt us."

"If it is a thunderstorm it may not *hurt* you—though it will certainly wet you. But the wind will get up. You think because the sea is so calm it is always calm. Nothing is less true."

Jane shrugged. "Well, I suppose you should know. But I surely do hate to give up after all the effort of an early rise. I shall be awful mad if we stay ashore and nothing happens. You're taking a great responsibility, Nicolo."

"Very well, I take it."

"What does Leonie think?" I asked, trying to draw her in.

She did not turn.

"Leonie thinks we should go," said Jane.

"I agree," I said.

"That's three to one, Nicolo," Jane said, patting da Cossa's arm.

"What Norton does is his own responsibility. He is of age and may please himself. But I too am the same. I have lived on this island all my life. I dived and swam here before you were born, Jane. I shall not go to the Grotto to-day, and I shall ask you not to go either."

The paleing in the east only showed up the pall of cloud. "Oh, well, perhaps we'd better call it off."

I said: "The boat's seaworthy, isn't it?"

"Of course."

"Da Cossa need not come."

"Jane must not go," said da Cossa. "It is not safe——"

"What about you?" Jane said to Leonie.

She spoke at last. "Oh, I don't mind. Give it up, if you like."

"Why should we like?" I said. "Da Cossa has put it fairly enough. We can go on our own responsibility."

139

"Not Jane," said da Cossa again.

"It's up to her," I said. "Anyway, perhaps Leonie will come with me."

Leonie looked at me then for the first time. "Do you think that would be a good idea?"

"I think it would be a good idea."

It wasn't easy to see, but I felt we stared at each other then with that antagonism which had got into us and which wasn't antagonism any more.

She said: "All right. I'll go with Philip."

It was quite chilly when we started. The outboard motor puttered away easily enough, and I sat in the stern with it. Leonie sat in the bows. She had got as far away from me as she could. It wasn't very far.

I'd thought at first, from her silence on the quay, that she had been prepared to carry on the vendetta from where we left off yesterday. Now I knew it wasn't so. My blood seemed to be beating rather thickly. Even the fact that we said nothing for the first ten minutes made no difference.

The run from the Marina Piccola is a good bit longer than from the Marina Grande. Seen from a tiny boat, the rocks are very grim, and I steered well out to begin. Then as the light grew I came in close beside that thousand-foot cliff we had been peering over a couple of days ago. The sea here was probably sixty or seventy fathoms deep. Thunder mumbled in the distance.

I said: "Is it much farther?"

"I don't think so. I've only been once before."

A flicker of forked lightning lit up the cliffs and the cloud. We both waited; the thunder came quickly; when it had gone the sea seemed quieter, more oily, slithering and sucking round the boat. I steered out to avoid a nearly submerged rock that raised its snout on our bow. Presently we rounded the second headland.

I said: "Leonie."

"Yes."

"Why did you agree to come out with me this morning?"

"Shouldn't I have?"

"I thought you might want to side-step a private meeting."

"Was I very rude last night?"

"I gave you cause."

"Some time I hope I'll be in a position to explain why."

"It wasn't only the most obvious reason, then?"

"What reason?"

"My searching your room."

"No. . . ."

The breeze was blowing her hair and she put up her hands to fasten it.

I said: "I'm glad you feel better to-day."

"Do I? It isn't all that straightforward yet."

I watched her. "You look like a caryatid supporting the world."

"A small and rather shabby part of it."

"If you told me about that I might be able to judge."

"I wish——"

"What?"

"You still puzzle me, Philip. I w-wish you'd tell me something more about yourself first."

She lowered her hands, but the breeze was having none of that. It blew the new tidiness after the old so that her hair was unexpectedly doubled in quantity and made a shining cloud about her face, fluffing and ruffling in the drawn light.

"Tell me at least one thing," she said.

"What's that?"

"Why do you feel so strongly about this—about your brother's death?"

"That doesn't seem unnatural to me."

"No, not unnatural. Not if it was just grief. But is it just grief? There seems to be something else as well."

"You're perceptive."

"I don't know. . . . There's the opening—beyond this next rock."

I peered at the low narrow hole we were coming up to. She said: "There's usually a boat outside to collect the fees, but we're ahead of them."

I felt a few spots of rain on my head. Then another scribble of lightning lit the sky, and the thunder grew heavier as it rolled downhill.

I said: "It may not be safe in the cave if the sea gets up."

Full day was coming now, but it was a coffee-coloured light dominated by the cloud.

She said: "Who wants to be safe."

She'd never been like this before. I shut off the little motor and unshipped the oars and paddled nearer. After a minute or so I said: "Duck your head—in we go."

The entrance is so small that you have to crouch in the boat and pull yourself in by a chain fixed to the roof. I did this, and the boat slipped quietly into the still water of the cavern.

I don't know if Sanbergh had been right in telling us that this was the best time to see the place, but he was certainly right in supposing that the effect would be greater before the exploiters were at hand. We drifted for some minutes in silence gradually towards the back of the cave. As we did so the water got more blue and more blue and the entrance dwindled to a thin funnel of grey light. When I dipped the oar in, it was as if the whole blade was lit with blue incandescence. When I stirred the water it was like tearing shot-silk.

After what seemed a long time I said: "Tiberius used this cave, didn't he?"

"Yes. There used to be a way up from inside the cave to his villa. He'd come down here and watch the swimmers and swim himself from a ledge somewhere over on the right. Then the cave was lost for eighteen hundred years."

"What became of the ledge?"

"It's still there. And some of the steps. But they don't go all the way."

I said: "When I was seven my father shot himself. He thought he was alone in the house, but I was in the garden and heard the shot and went up and found him. Grevil was seventeen at the time and Arnold twenty-one. Four years after that my mother died, and from then on Grevil did almost everything for me. I thought he was wonderful, aped him in all the ways I could, but unfortunately didn't have his brilliance. People used to say I was like him—not merely in looks but in impulses and tendencies. They said I was like my father, too. . . . So when they both die, apparently after the same fashion, that's both barrels at once, as you might say."

I dipped my oar in the water again and looked at it, glittering and luminous. She sat very still. I'd noticed before this quality in her, able to watch or listen or think in absolute silence.

She said: "Why did your father——"

"His doctor had told him he'd got a growth, might be malignant, he didn't know—they'd have to operate at once."

"Well, then, surely that's a good enough reason for anybody——"

"But it wasn't malignant—the autopsy proved that."

After a pause she said: "Yes, but all the same it's not an inexcusable thing——"

"No, of course not. I didn't say it was."

Now that I'd stopped paddling, we seemed to be drifting slowly towards the entrance.

I said: "I don't believe for a minute that Grevil did kill himself, but if he did, then on the evidence we've got at the moment that was inexcusable. Wasn't it. In fact if what you've told me so far is true, no motive that we know of existed at all."

"No motive that we know of."

"Anyway, that's my story."

She looked at me thoughtfully. "I don't think I can be as frank as you."

"You can be. It's whether you want to be."

She shook her head. "You have a loyalty. Perhaps I have too."

I waited but she didn't speak for a minute or so. There seemed to be some peculiar sound from outside, so I paddled right up to the entrance.

The daylight was bright on our eyes. At first it looked as if the sea outside was alive with fish. Then I saw that the bubbles were caused by rain—a tremendous downpour hissing on the face of the sea. There was another flicker of lightning and a muffled rumble of thunder. I turned the boat away again and moved off into the semi-dark.

The rain was like a thick wet curtain that cut off interference from outside.

I said: "We're here for some time."

"Yes. . . . Are you going to swim?"

"Well, I didn't bring anything. It didn't occur to me. Did you?"

"Yes. But——"

"Swim if you want. I'm in no hurry."

"If I tell you as much as I can, will you—as a favour —promise to cut this and leave Capri?"

"Will what you tell me explain what I want to know?"

"No. I don't know myself."

"Then the answer's what you must expect."

"You won't leave?"

"No, Leonie, you're wasting your breath in asking."

"Yes—oh yes, I suppose I am."

"I'm not at all sure I'd be willing to leave right away, even if you were able to tell me all about Grevil."

"Why not?"

I watched her trailing her fingers in the water. "Go on, swim. I'm sorry I can't join you."

"It's putting off the evil moment."

"Ten minutes. You can't get away this time."

She hesitated a second or two longer. "Perhaps it will help to clear my brain." She got out a white bathing-cap and pulled it on, tucking in bits of hair. She was already wearing her swim-suit underneath the jersey and slacks she had come in.

I said: "I'll pull in to the side."

The boat wobbled as she stood up, then rocked violently as she dived. For a few seconds the splash and the settling water hid everything—then as it cleared I saw her swimming under water near the boat.

I suppose I should have expected it but hadn't. Her whole body was lit by the pale blue incandescence. It was like some sort of a miracle in which fire and water met to make a new element. She swam easily, lazily, as if water came natural to her. Every movement of her long finely rounded arms and legs, every balanced thickening of her beautiful body was outlined by this incandescence. But it was etherealised, intellectualised, above and beyond ordinary sexual attraction. She was more like something out of the brain of Praxiteles.

She came to the surface and swam away. The ripples of shot-silk ran in lines towards the walls of the cavern. The water broke and glittered fiercely as she found some hand-hold on the rock.

"This is the ledge over here. I wonder where the steps are."

As she left the water all the jewels fell from her and she abruptly disappeared from view. I paddled slowly nearer. "Can you see them?"

"There's an opening of some sort, but I can't see how far it goes."

I waited but she said no more. I couldn't see anything of her at all. After a bit I saw an iron hook in the rock and hitched the bow-rope to it. Then I climbed on the ledge after her. It was much darker here because we were away from the reflection of the water. As I went in she turned suddenly and almost bumped into me.

She said: "Heavens! I didn't hear you. I thought you were Tiberius."

"No. He's older and fatter."

She went back to the edge of the rock and looked down. I stood beside her. Then she looked up at me, taking rather deep breaths.

I said: "There isn't anything I can say to you now that won't sound forced and phoney. And there isn't anything else that I want to say."

Her mouth curved in a quick smile. "I don't think it was ever phoney, Philip. Forced perhaps. But what you say now doesn't—come from the same stable at all." She added: "All the same, I don't want you to say it."

She took a step forward, put her hands up and dived cleanly into the water—and instantly was changed again into that inhuman, elemental thing she'd been before.

For some minutes she played about in the water, turning over, twisting, changing her strokes. I climbed down into the boat and paddled round. The sea was slapping up and down at the entrance to the cavern.

Presently she came to the side of the boat and began to pull herself in. I leaned to help her, grasping her elbow and hand, the boat tilting. She got in, and again the change took place, only this time it was the other way round. She sat in the back of the boat and I sat near her and looked at her. She pulled off her cap and shook out her hair. She looked a creamy colour in the half dark.

After a minute she said uncertainly: "Philip, let's go. The rain won't matter."

"No," I said, "the rain won't matter."

She never took her eyes off mine. "It's time we had ... the Thermos is in the bag."

I put my hands on her shoulders. It was like grasping a

146

warm fish. The droplets of cold water were still clinging to her skin. I bent over her and kissed her. She didn't make a fuss but she didn't play back. My hands slid under her arms and I began to kiss her face and neck. She tried to speak but did not. Then she suddenly kissed me back, but at the same time tried to free herself. She slipped in my hands as if still partly a fish.

"Philip, don't," she said. Her eyes were half shut.

I looked very closely at her face, so much closer than it had ever been before, watching the movement of brow and cheek and lip.

"In case of doubt," I said, "this is the other reason why I won't leave."

"If that was true——"

"It's true."

But after a few seconds she began to struggle again, and when I looked into her eyes I saw they were brimming with tears.

"Oh God," I said, "if Grevil didn't commit suicide because of you, I could." I let her go. "What is it, Leonie? Why are you like this? I can't keep pace with your moods or begin to guess what they mean. You say nothing, give nothing, take nothing. If I could have one minute's insight into what goes on inside. . . . If I had one single clue as to why none of the normal lines run straight. . . ."

She sat up, put a hand across her eyes. "I'm s-sorry. Blast. . . ."

"I'm sorry too." I moved back to my seat by the oars.

"Could you throw me my things, please."

I handed her her clothes and she began to struggle into her sweater.

"You can't sit in that wet suit," I said. "We may be here for ages yet."

"I'll be all right."

"Don't be a fool. I'll turn my back."

"Oh. All right."

I did so. After a bit she said: "I'm O.K. now."

In silence I paddled nearer the entrance. It was still raining heavily.

I said: "Drink?"

"Thank you."

I poured some coffee into one of the cups and she took it. I swallowed some myself. I needed it.

She said: "I'm sorry I'm so unsatisfactory."

"It depends which way you mean."

"You know which way I mean."

"Well, I don't want to be unfair. Æsthetically you're a pleasure to look at."

"Thank you very much."

There was a long silence. At last she said slowly: "What I've done, what I do now, may seem out of focus to you. It doesn't to me. Perhaps when I've explained as much as I can, perhaps then it'll seem slightly more reasonable. I've got to go back to when Tom and Richard died—or soon after. It'll be a bore for you, but it all dates from then."

"It won't be a bore at all."

"After they died I rather let go of the reins for a bit. There didn't seem any clear way for me to go or any reason for me to go anywhere. Then in this sort of drift state I met a man. It was at St. Jean de Luz. He had come in there for a few days. He was older than me, nice to be with, cultured, attentive, all the sort of things I seemed to need." She stopped, wrinkling her brows. "I think, right from the beginning, he appealed to something, a recklessness if you like. He didn't run to pattern. You could be with him and know him and yet still wonder about him, where he'd been, the exciting things he'd done. There was always something new that you didn't know, because you'd missed the earlier instalments. And I think he had—has the kind of imagination that can get inside someone else's mind and interest itself in what it finds there. It could be a great gift—it *is*; but a dangerous one too. . . . Well, at the time there didn't seem much reason to me in anything, but there was reason in *him*." She paused again, thinking it over. " We teamed up."

" I see."

" It didn't seem to matter then—and after a while I came to care a lot more about him. That sort of feeling isn't to rule, is it? You can't turn the page, say that's that, just when you want to or think you ought to. *That's* something that doesn't follow the normal lines."

The warmth of the coffee was welcome. I unwrapped the sandwiches and she took one.

" But after a time, after about three months with him, I couldn't any longer make things read quite right even to myself. And there were hitches over money; we ran through what I had that wasn't tied up; his attitude is queer, not exactly dishonest, but he acts sometimes as if he's above the ordinary rules. . . . We made efforts to patch things up. Then he went out to the Far East and I heard nothing of him except two letters in nearly twelve months. . . . One day I got a cable. It was sent from Jakarta—you know, it used to be called Batavia."

" Yes, I know."

" He asked me to meet him in Amsterdam. I had to go. . . . I—had to go. When you're attached to someone, you forget some of the things you didn't like, and those you don't forget you hope have changed. So it was a bitter disappointment to find that they hadn't changed."

" Was Grevil with him?"

" Yes. And he was travelling under another name."

" Buckingham?"

She looked at me. " Yes. They were very friendly, this man and your brother. I could tell Grevil was sincere, even though I'd only just met him, it was obviously an honest affection, very strong, good. But Buckingham—the false name to begin—I could tell, knowing him, that somehow he was going to cheat. I wasn't sure how but I know the signs. I wanted no part in it. If that was the price of coming to terms again—helping him in something shady that he wasn't even prepared to explain—then the price was too high." She stopped, rubbed her finger carefully along the edge of the boat. "You can guess the rest."

"You mean that your letter was meant for Buckingham? But how did it get into Grevil's pocket?"

"I gave it to him to give to Buckingham. I didn't want to see Buckingham again. With him it isn't just a question of uttering the words. . . . Or it might have been if I'd cared nothing at all—but when you're still divided within yourself and have to face a man who isn't and always has a terrific talent for getting his own way. . . ."

"He wanted you to go back to him?"

"Yes. He talked as if he'd made money—or was coming into it, wanted me to stay with him on the Continent, spoke of settling somewhere on the Mediterranean. But of course I didn't know how much notice to take of that. He's always a man who, as soon as he has some money, speaks as if he has an unlimited amount. . . . I'm sorry I'm not saying this very well."

"What I still don't understand is what made you give the note to Grevil."

She put her bare feet into her sandals and buckled them. Her feet were still damp and the straps seemed tight. I said: "You haven't eaten your sandwich."

She straightened up and bit at the bread. Some ends of her hair which had been wet were beginning to dry and curl.

"When I got to Holland I stayed at a hotel in the Nieuwe Doelenstraat. The next day they came. Dr. Turner stayed at a hotel called the Grotius. Buckingham would have put up at the hotel where I was, but it was full. We spent quite a bit of that first day together, and the second day we'd all arranged to meet at the Grotius. There was some sort of arrangement that Dr. Turner should take us—or take me—to the Indies Museum. But by then I felt it was no good to go on."

She hesitated. "Of course I could just have left and caught a plane without a word, but I didn't want ever afterwards to shout coward after my own shadow. So I decided to face—Buckingham. And then when I went round he was *out*. So I went to Grevil's hotel to see if he was already there, but he wasn't, and the receptionist said Grevil was engaged, so I waited. And while I waited either for Buckingham to come or Grevil to come down, my good intentions began to side-slip. If I stayed and Grevil came down first, the opportunity would be gone; I couldn't say what I wanted to in front of him. So I wrote a note. I was going to take it back to Buckingham's hotel, but just as I was writing it Grevil came downstairs with two men. I scribbled the last few lines while he was seeing them off and then gave him the letter and said would he give it to Buckingham when he came. He said he would and that was the last I ever saw of him."

I offered her another sandwich but she shook her head. I put the top on the Thermos, wrapped up the other sandwiches, put them back in the carrier.

"Did you seal the letter?"

"Yes."

"The envelope wasn't torn. I suppose the water soaked the gum off it and the flap came open. Did you address it?"

"No. There seemed no need—and the whole thing was done in a hurry."

"These two men who were seeing Grevil, what were they like?"

"I don't remember much. Dutchmen I should have thought, middle-aged, in grey overcoats."

"Did Grevil look worried when you met him?"

She folded back one sleeve of her jersey where the cuff had come down. "Yes. Yes."

"Did he say anything unusual?"

"I don't think so. He said he was waiting for—Buckingham."

"And then?"

"Well, that's all I can tell you, Philip."

There was a silence. I said: "I think it's stopped raining."

"Yes."

I began to speak and then waited.

She said: "Do you believe me?"

"Of course—so far as it goes."

"There's no 'of course' about it."

"Well, there is for me."

She glanced at me with a queer, rather worried look. "You're still determined to stay—to make things worse by——"

"By staying. Yes. I've told you. There are two reasons now."

"There shouldn't be."

"There are."

I rowed the boat back to the opening. It was risky, but we could get through if we picked our time.

"And you won't tell me any more?"

"As it is, I've said too much."

"Did you tell him you were going to tell me this much?"

She glanced up swiftly. "I believe we should go now, Philip."

The light coming through from outside was unbearably bright. I stared at her a minute longer and then gave it up.

"Ready?"

"Yes."

I shipped the oars and hurriedly clutched the chain. We lurched through into the morning. Warmth met us and a dazzling brilliance. From under the roots of the cloud the sun was shining across a rough grey-brown sea that was not recognisably Neapolitan.

For a bit I could see nothing, and anyway was too busy pulling the boat away from the cliff. Then I saw a boat; the one that came each day to collect the admission fees. The two Italians in it looked astonished to see us shoot out. But it didn't take them long to get the thing straightened out in their own minds. I started up he engine and puttered over to them.

"How much?"

"Two hundred lire, if you please, *signore*."

Two notes changed hands. I said: "The colour is very fine to-day."

One of the men glanced at Leonie and smiled at me sympathetically. "Oh, *signore*, please do not mention it: I feel as you feel."

Chapter Fourteen

I said: "We'd better make for the Marina Grande. The sea may be too heavy at the other side."

"All right."

As the cloud lifted, the sea on the horizon was already changing colour.

I said: "Leonie, why have you changed your mind from when you were in Holland?"

"How?"

"Well, there you were finished with this Buckingham apparently. Now you're trying to protect him from me."

"I'm not sure that that's the way round I think of it."

"He's on this island, isn't he?"

She bent to pick up her bathing-suit. I looked at her crouched figure, the ruffled shining hair, the long curve of the dark jersey.

"If telling you anything more, Philip, would bring your brother back to life. . . . But it won't. And you have your own life to live."

"I seem to have heard that before."

"Well, it's true."

"If I left this as it is now, I shouldn't be a very happy companion to myself."

"I don't know that. But——"

"Do you believe this Buckingham is a dangerous man?"

"In a *way*. . . . Very."

"According to what you tell me, you couldn't betray him if you wanted to—because you've no idea what happened. All you could tell me is his real identity—is that it?"

"Yes, but that would lead to much more."

"Perhaps in some ways I already know more about him than you. The name Buckingham isn't new. He's been in scrapes under the same name before. And unpleasant scrapes, the sort that leave a bad flavour in the mouth. . . . Leonie, it's your turn to believe me now. I'm not lying to you."

She looked at me. "No, Philip, I didn't suppose you were."

"You didn't know that, though?"

"Not in so many words. But I never supposed his past to be blameless."

"It's probable he's a murderer. You realise that?"

She put her swim-suit on the seat beside her, folded it, didn't speak.

I said: "Yet you still shield him."

"If that's what you call it."

"Well, what do you call it?"

She said: "Stop it, Philip, stop it! I've told you as much as I can. If you want to call in the police, then call them in. They won't learn any more from me. I *can't* say any more. I *can't*!"

Her lips were quivering.

"All right," I said. "Leave it at that. There's just one last thing I want to ask, but you needn't answer if you don't want. Do you still care about him?"

After a pause so long I thought she'd given up, she said: "Yes, I still care about him."

When I got back to the hotel there was a letter for me from Java which had been forwarded on. I expected it was from Pangkal, but I shoved it in my pocket unopened and went in to Martin's room to find him just finishing his breakfast. Between mouthfuls he was jotting down notes or something on the back fly-leaf of his Cervantes.

I was feeling pretty low.

When I had explained what had happened he shut the book and put his pencil away. His chair scraped on the bare floor as he pushed it sharply in and went to the window. He said sombrely: "God knows, I wonder if we're not wasting our time here. What truth can we get out of either of them if they don't want to talk?"

"We'll see about that."

"The threat of the police won't cut much ice. You know, it still seems to me that if there is anything to be made out of this mess it will be in Holland. I can't get away from it. Your brother's death took place on Jodenbree's doorstep. On his doorstep——"

"We may finish up there yet. We've got to tidy up this end first."

The morning was perfect after the storm. The curious effect of getting up very early once in a while is to add another complete period to the day. I let Martin go on to the beach because I had to call at the bank about my dollars, and even then I was down on the beach myself by eleven-thirty.

I went to our usual spot and saw da Cossa lying sun-bathing with Jane, but there was no sign of the others. I stopped some distance from the sun-bathers, but Jane heard the crunch of stones and raised her head and coo-eed. I waved back and made gestures to say I would join them later, having no intention of doing so. Da Cossa had looked up but made no welcoming sign.

I suddenly spotted Martin and Leonie sitting on some rocks across the bay. They had evidently just swum there, because you could see their skins glistening. I stripped to bathing-trunks but decided not to join them. Perhaps he might in some roundabout way get information out of her that I'd failed to get. I didn't put it beyond him.

I lay back for a bit, letting the sun soak in. I felt rotten inside, and tried to persuade myself that it was entirely because I was making so little progress in what I'd come about. Most things I did seemed to block their own exits.

Perhaps I was taking too much on myself. If there was good in the world it wasn't my sacred mission to preserve it; if there was evil I was not born to root it out. The universe would continue on its usual messy disunified course without caring twopence for the moralities, and I had best give up trying to make a unity of it. Rather irrelevantly it seemed to me then that I always either asked too much or gave too little. At selling jet engines or helping Arnold I would get by because I was fitting into a ready-made groove like millions of other people, not trying to organise a world of his own, as a true artist must.

Leonie had said twice that I had my own life to live. But what exactly *was* my own life? What were my own concerns? San Francisco and the Midlands seemed equally remote, and what went on there shallow and unreal. This thing had come to stand across my life—all of it, Grevil and Buckingham, and now Leonie—and now Leonie—so that everything else was overshadowed.

After a bit the sun seemed to relax things, and I half dozed, glad to forget the disappointments and the failures. I dreamt I was on a beach in England, and staring into a pool in which the depth and the colours constantly changed. After a time I thought it was Leonie's eyes and I could hear her voice saying: "If I could bring your brother to life again. But I can't, I can't. He's still in that Dutch canal." And now I could see Grevil's body floating in the depths of the pool. I stirred suddenly and looked up from the pool, and saw Grevil walking towards me across the sand, but instead of his feet making no sound there was the steady crunch as of breaking bones. I sat up, really awake this time, and saw a tall Italian woman who had passed close beside me, her feet rattling the pebbles.

The scene hadn't changed. The sun-bathers had not altered their positions. Leonie and Martin were still sitting on the rocks. I remembered the letter from Java and fished it out of my pocket. It was from Dr. Pangkal, in answer to the letter I had written him from Holland. Still a bit drowsy, I began to read it.

" Dear Sir,
    " I thank you for your letter reaching me recently. The death of your honourable brother will have brought grief upon all who knew him. So it has upon me, and I submit condolences to you and to your family. A noble man in whose name research will continue.

" You question me in some length referring to Mr. Jack Buckingham who helped him during my lamentable disease. I append hereunder such information as I can submit to you. I should say that I have already faced police inquiries emanating from Amsterdam, but these have lacked goodwill on both sides.

" Mr. Buckingham joined our party since four days in advance of my illness, and these days were all that I saw of him. Your honourable brother met him in the home of a Dutch planter in Surabaya, and they returned together to our camp, where my first meeting was with him. He came without gear, his explanation was that he had lost his ship in a tropical storm off the coast and is alone the survivor. His manners are full of goodwill and grace and he tells of matters archæological in enthusiasm and intelligent fashion. In this he is an amateur and has not any of the learning of Dr. Turner, but his knowledge is widespread in the field, from Toltecs to Tiryns and from Indonesia to Easter Island.

"But what they talk of that first night, and long into the night, for I hear it through to where I sleep, is Mr. Buckingham's claim of having found fossils in Urtini riverbed 30 miles south of Trinil site. He is not able to convince me, but Dr. Turner feels that this story shall be examined, more so because our now investigations are less good. So on the successive days we move camp. Here, as we are to set off, an attempt is made in the early morning by outlaws, regrettably of my race, to steal the provisions and two jeeps. When Dr. Turner arrives all becomes ugly, for no fight is shown by the bearers and it may well be that he is kidnapped for a ransom. But Mr. Buckingham here shows himself resource and ruthless and shoots dead the two ringleaders and the rest flee.

"The next day we arrive at river-bed and sufficient is seen to show that Mr. Buckingham is unmistaken. I think it is much later than the period we seek, but Dr. Turner disagrees. There are several disputed finds, and here I am ill, the fever strikes very severe and soon I am taken to hospital.

"You ask me about Mr. Buckingham. I have the impression that he is English; he spoke before us as if it was so—but he spoke several languages with an appearance of ease. In conversation with Dr. Turner he referred by name to places and peoples to which my scientific education does not give me the key. I am twenty-eight, Mr. Turner, and from fifteen to nineteen I spend all my time in the bush fighting the Japanese, and from nineteen to twenty-two it is the Dutch. This is a grave loss for any man.

"I know nothing of the many weeks your honourable brother and this man work together in my illness, but I will try to describe him to you in the best ability that I can.

"I am always in error surmising a European's age, and

158

this more when bearded, but he might be forty. Perhaps he is younger. He is tall in build, and spare, perhaps seventy-seven or eighty kilograms, and of above middle height for a European, perhaps 1.75 metres or a little more. His hair is nearly black and straight, his complexion to my thought noticeably pale, his face is long with strong bones, his eyes looking brown in the sun, black out of it, like olive stones, deeply put in, very handsome but seldom smiling. He wears a small black beard on chin only and cut to a V. His forearms are hairy and he has two moles on the left forearm about nine and eleven centimetres above wrist. His teeth are his own, but somewhat stained from tobacco smoke, both eye-teeth have been filled and the tooth behind the eye-tooth of the left side of the mouth is missing. There is unevenness of flesh and bone on his face so that if the light strikes sideways peculiar shadows are created. When he smiles the sadness goes from his face and warmth and sympathy are in it. But sometimes I think it like the devil smiling, flattering to deceive, do you say.

"Many people he impresses, and Dr. Turner is much taken of him, often to an exclusion—not intended I am sure—of myself. I query if your letter about him, and this Dutch detective coming, means that your honourable brother came to hurt because of him. He has a good singing voice and sings songs I do not know. Dr. Turner called them German Leader, I think. When he sings his hair falls over his eyes and he pushes it away with the two first fingers of his right hand.

"This, I regret, is all I can give you for description of his man. I trust you will excuse because since I am ill and that is bad for the memory.

"Sir, I send you my respectful greetings and deepest condolences on your honourable brother's death.

"Yours faithfully,
"Gani Pangkal.

" P.S.—I am not certain whether it was the left or right upper bicuspid that was missing."

I folded the letter and put it back in the air-mail envelope. The paper crackled in my fingers as I folded it again and stuffed it in the back pocket of my trousers and fastened the button. I folded the trousers and laid them beside me with the shirt and sweater. Jane had finished grilling her back and had now turned over to face the sun. Da Cossa was sitting up and tossing pebbles into the water. From this distance they made a tiny *plop-plop-plop*.

Someone's head was bobbing in the water quite near the shore. It was Leonie's. She had been swimming in while I was reading and had left Martin, who was following her, well behind. Presently she got to her feet and walked in, putting her arms up to take her cap off. She saw me, hesitated a second and then came across, shaking out her hair.

" I didn't see you come down," she said.

" About ten minutes ago."

" What's the matter?"

" The matter?" I said. " Nothing."

" You look pale."

" I've just been to sleep—had a dream. Perhaps that's it."

She smiled and sat down a little behind me, partly in the shade of a rock. She never took off the thin gold bracelet that she wore on her wrist. " What was it?"

" I dreamt that good was evil and evil was good, and that nobody could tell the difference."

" I don't believe you."

" No, you're right. A dream would never be as contrary as that. It takes real life to make the grade."

She stared at the black head slowly coming nearer. Then she bent and began to unlace her rope-soled shoes. Her shoulders were golden in the sunshine. There was a smear of tar on her ankle.

160

I said: "We're coming to dinner to-night, aren't we?"

"Oh?" she glanced up. "Oh yes, I believe so."

As Martin came in, she climbed to her feet again—I thought a bit defensively—stood very quietly against the cliff watching him.

Martin in bathing-trunks didn't quite confirm what Martin in clothes suggested. The impression made by the long delicate bones in his face, the shadowed eyes, the hint of ill-health in his colour, was blown off-stage altogether. His powerful, easy-muscled figure was as delicate as a newly-commissioned cruiser. There was over-tenseness somewhere, strain and a hint of nerves, but it didn't alter the complete picture.

He said: "Not to swim in the lead o' th' current were almost to sink. You're a trifle too fast for me in the water, Mrs. Winter." He sat down on the stones, scattering droplets. For a second his eyes flickered cautiously across us. "Strange I never was as much at home in the water as on it. At a pinch I can do half a mile, but that's about my limit. Not swimming, Philip?"

"Any minute now. Will the boat be all right in the main harbour, Leonie? I feel responsible for it."

"Oh yes. Charles is back. He's sending a man down to pick it up. . . . I must go and change."

She walked towards da Cossa and Jane. Martin's eyes followed her.

"So Charles is back. That's Sanbergh, isn't it?"

"That's Sanbergh," I said, watching him push his black hair away. It was all there that Dr. Pangkal in his jealousy had acutely observed, even to the moles on the forearm. The original hunch, scarcely more than a wisp of suspicion at first and twice since discarded, had been right after all.

Chapter Fifteen

Perhaps when you live with death at your elbow, as Mme Weber claimed she had been doing for the past fifteen years, it comes natural to need other company to relieve the *tête-à-tête*. So having the means to do it, she filled her house with guests and added as many outsiders as she could decently fit in. There were twelve at the dinner party, and Charles Sanbergh was there when we got there. I introduced Martin and watched their meeting with an interest quite different from what I might have had yesterday.

Sanbergh said to me: "I hope you enjoyed the Grotto this morning, Mr. Norton."

I looked at him, expecting sarcasm and enmity, but didn't find it.

"Thanks. It was impressive—and rain-proof. Your boat was safe?"

"Yes. Please don't hesitate to ask for it again if you need it any time."

"Thank you very much," I said, foxed now at this apparent change of front. It would be too ironical if for some reason he now changed his attitude towards me. "You must see Sanbergh's yacht," I said to Martin. "I imagine the sea is the first woman in both your lives."

Sanbergh smiled obligingly, his mouth curling up. "Happily our mistress has no locked doors and no other appointments, so jealousy is out of place."

"It doesn't at all follow," said Martin. "I'm jealous of any man with the money and the freedom to exploit her. I've always found the sea a harlot; she gives her best to the highest bidder."

Just before we went in to dinner I caught Martin's eye and he turned his thumb down. It was an agreed signal. I'd wondered what he would do about the agreed signal. All day since reading that letter there'd been a queer taste in my mouth, like copper, like blood. Every now and then I was caught by a rush of anger, burning and blackening. This afternoon I'd had another letter—from Inspector Tholen—but so far had been quite unable to make up my mind about it. For the moment decision was suspended; all I could do was wait and watch.

We dined and wined expensively. Towards the end, talk turned on petty theft which, according to Mme Weber, was practically unknown on the island; normal sins, she said with a raffish smile, were rare, Tiberius having left a legacy of abnormality which had never quite died out.

Da Cossa said: "I never understand what is meant by abnormality these days. Has not psychiatry shown all behaviour to be a series of simple variations on the same theme."

It was a good enough red-herring, but I didn't suppose anyone in that company would rise to it. However, both Sanbergh and White began to say something, and after a second White got the floor. He'd been quiet to-night, probably still suffering the dying kicks of yesterday. "Well, d'you know, I'm prejudiced against that view. I earn my living in the courts, and time and again I see psychiatry explaining away this crime or that so that there's nothing, no behaviour it hasn't got the answers for and the excuses for. And that's a thoroughly bad thing."

"Why is it a bad thing?"

"Because the criminal stands there and listens to the medical evidence explaining that, poor guy, the beastly crime he's just committed isn't really his fault at all, and you have to unload the blame on his father or his mother who did this or didn't do that when he was rising three. It doesn't always wash with our judges, but it's bad in any case because it sends a man up—when it does send him —with a feeling that he hasn't done anything wrong at all but that society has misunderstood him."

Martin put in quietly: "I've always believed that psycho-analysis was all my I."

Missing the joke, Sanbergh said bitterly: "But surely that is the chief aim of psychiatry, to take away the sense of guilt—and one of the reasons why it is so popular. Someone said once that if God didn't exist it would be necessary to invent him. In the twentieth century that would be truer of Freud."

"Well, and isn't that a good thing, Charles dear?" said Mme Weber. "Surely what our forebears suffered from more than anything was this sense of guilt. It ruined their lives. Devastatin'. I know it ruined my mother's. She lived under a constant cloud of sin. I shall never be sufficiently grateful to Sigmund for selling off all the hair-shirts at a cut price."

White was looking at Sanbergh. "I didn't know you were anti-Freudian, Charles. In the States I'm custom-arily a voice crying in the wilderness."

"So you are likely to be in most countries," said Sanbergh; "for it is such a comfortable philosophy, so much more comfortable than religion."

Jane Porringer said: "It's never sounded particularly comfortable to me."

"Well, it is, my dear, it is. Because aren't we told that what we do comes from urges in our subconscious, and that for these we are not responsible? They tell us that as soon as we are made aware of the causes of our conflicts, then we don't any longer answer to them. No effort on our part is needed. That's a great line to-day, isn't it. No effort." Sanbergh's eyes went round the table, met mine with a smoky gleam. "Indeed, they say we must *not* fight what is within us because that causes the repression we're trying to avoid. We sit back and the analyst unravels the string. By giving way to our impulses we do away with further conflict. By letting our children root in the dirt and wreck our homes and copulate at an early age, we lay the foundations for a settled generation in the future."

"For an unsettled generation," the Master of Kyle was heard to say, "and we've had two, three of those already."

"Personally I don't see what's wrong with an unsettled generation," said Martin, his eyes down, peeling a peach, "whether it's the outcome of Freud or common sense. That's a reversion to natural conditions again."

"More likely a reversion to anarchy," said Sanbergh.

"Well, if you call it that. Why not?"

"I think there are reasons why not," said Sanbergh, "but I think you're right in supposing it is coming. Because once we feel we're not at root responsible for our actions, or at least for yielding to the desires that prompt the actions, then it's an end to the meaning of good and evil as we've always understood them, and an end to moral law as an influential force."

"I think we should maybe invent a new mythology," said Mme Weber. "Eve ate the apple in Eden and discovered the knowledge of Good and Evil. But somebody now has eaten a grapefruit in Freud's garden, and that has anæsthetised us from the after-effects. Divertin'."

Martin said: "Mme Weber, you're one of the most enlightened women I've ever met."

"That's not enlightenment," said Sanbergh, "that's naughtiness."

"Really, Charles. . . ."

Martin put down his knife. "But seriously, isn't it time we all came awake to what's happening. Isn't it time we stopped picking endlessly over the ruins of our late civilisation and realised that a new one is already on its way up. People talk about a second Renaissance. Well, maybe you can call it that if you want a comfortable phrase. But what's happening with us is not the birth of new *art* forms, it's the birth of new *moral* forms—whether we like it or not. The old prohibitions mean nothing any longer. Not a damned thing."

I watched him. "The old prohibitions?" I said gently.

"Yes, Philip. A man who takes up a moral stand on this principle or that, merely because his grandfather or his great-grandfather believed it, is like someone reading the Riot Act in a Mississippi flood. There's no *magic* in a thing because other people have thought it. The only magic is in thinking for ourselves. In the last twenty years *all* the barriers have gone down in the physical world. Now it's the turn of the moral do-nots, the mental do-nots that get in a man's way at every other step. They're going, and it's time they went! We just have to start thinking afresh if we don't want to die in the mud like the megatherium and the dinosaur."

There was a sub-tone in Martin's voice that made it different from the rest of the talk, that undertone of passion that can creep in when a man gets on his pet subject. Or perhaps it was even more than that.

The Master of Kyle looked up, like an old dog whose bone has been touched. "It's not a question of what your father thought or of what your grandfather thought, Martin—it's what has been agreed among men for thirty centuries. There are some values that are absolute —or as near as can be in this world. If a man doesn't perceive them, he's a fool. If he perceives them and ignores them, he's a knave. There aren't two ways of thinking about it." He withdrew under his lids again.

Martin said: "It was agreed among men for centuries that the sun revolved round the earth—until Copernicus made them think different. If we——"

"Yes," I interrupted before he could go on, "this is a nice talking point for a Sunday half-hour. But it's all pretty vague and generalised, isn't it? I'd like to get down to particular cases for a change, if we could." I smiled at Mme Weber. "Martin Coxon, for instance, argues for a return to anarchy and the rest—but he does it chiefly for the sake of argument. Don't you, Martin?"

Coxon's sombre eyes met mine for a second. Then he bent over his peach.

"Don't you, Martin?" I said.

He looked up. "No. No, I think it's an inevitable trend."

"A general trend," I said.

"Well, yes. General certainly. World wide."

"Not world wide yet. There are many who set their faces against it. But I agree with you that the danger's there. Now what are we, who do set our faces against it, to do? We can't deal with general trends, but we can with particular cases—sometimes."

"What do you mean?" said Leonie quickly.

As she spoke Martin turned his head to look at her, and I saw the light falling across his face in the way Pangkal had described. I saw his face as if seeing it for the first time, the little bumps between the eyebrows, the full bottom lip drawn in in the middle.

I said: "Well, there are quite a few men who really disagree with the rules the rest of us accept. They're not psychopaths or abnormal in any recognisable way. They've no twisted childhood, no case history to explain it—there's no apparent reason for them to be different from their next-door neighbours. Yet they become criminals apparently from deliberate choice. What are we going to do about them?"

After a minute Hamilton White said: "I still think you ought to particularise a bit more."

I began to answer him and then stopped. Suddenly I saw the way before me open wide, and I saw where it was leading and wasn't yet ready for it. If there was going to be a reckoning between Martin and me, it couldn't begin here. And unless I was prepared for that, it would be crazy to say what I'd intended to say. I went on quickly, covering up: "Well, what of the murderer, the man who suddenly, and after an apparently normal life, kills somebody coldly and quite deliberately and often almost without motive. Where does he come into the picture?"

It seemed to me then a terribly tame ending, but no one apparently noticed it. Perhaps this was because Charlotte Weber took up the running.

"Dear boy, those are the people the psychiatrists are most use to. People who commit murder usually haven't, for some reason, been able to adapt themselves. As children they haven't found themselves able to cope, and the sense of inferiority has driven them to seek compensation in revolt. That's Adler's theory—or somebody's, my memory isn't what it was. But it's usually the beginning of all the trouble, and the outcome is split personalities and wish fulfilments and the rest."

Sanbergh made a comical face. "There we go, you see. A man murders because he is seeking compensation in revolt. It isn't his fault, it is his father and mother who are to blame. But if you asked the social reformer he will say, no, no, it is not the mother and father; it all happened because of the conditions in which the man lived. Then again the biologist will say it is nothing of the kind, he has simply inherited too many of the wrong genes from an ancestor. Anything to take the blame off the man who has done it."

"The biologist is nearest right," said Hamilton White. "If you go on endlessly dealing a pack of cards, sooner or later someone is going to get a straight flush and someone else a pair of deuces. It's the only explanation for the type of apparently senseless crime that Philip means. And such things do happen. They've come my way."

Martin took a bite of his peach. "The crime you call senseless is probably only senseless to you—because you see it as something abnormal and out of line. But crime is just as biologically normal to some people as walking down a street. Murder can be an expression of a man's personality. So perhaps can suicide—only in that case he's like the bee and allowed only one sting. You don't probe into the reasons why a child is born with a desire to play the piano or stigmatise him when he fulfils it. Nor do you if he wants to become a doctor—or a pathologist, who spends his time among the dead—or a butcher, who is always slaughtering animals—or an airman who may be asked to throw fire on a city. No, those professions are all right because they come inside the bogus rules that some old men in the past set up. But step outside them—not always to commit murder but to live your life as you believe it ought to be lived—and you become the prey not only of the police but of every pet psychiatrist and phoney reformer who's looking for another victim. It's they who should be locked away in asylums, and I believe they will be when humanity comes of age."

Da Cossa smiled. "That is a very interesting proposition. But it all boils down to the same thing, does it not, that a man's behaviour is determined by circumstances and events over which he has little or no control? There are mental deficients, moral deficients, physical deficients. All should be treated alike. You don't blame me, I trust, or wish to lock me up because I was born with a club-foot."

Sanbergh said : "A man can be locked up for what he *does* with his club-foot. So you can blame or praise a man for the use he makes of any disability."

Da Cossa said nastily : "I do not think I should like you to be my judge."

Sanbergh stared at him. "I have no desire to be one for anybody. I've lived my life and been no angel. But I still believe in sin, which is behaviour injurious to the individual. And I still believe in crime, which is behaviour injurious to society. Call them what new names you like, I don't believe a person's responsibility for what he does can be evaded."

She'd been in the garden with Martin. When she came

back her face was flushed and her stammer was more noticeable. Afterwards I saw her slip out of the room, and a few minutes later I followed her. There was no one in the hall, but as I got to the foot of the stairs she came down.

Three steps from the bottom she stopped.

I said: "I want to apologise for getting in your light so much in the last few days."

She half smiled, but looked past me towards the door. "I thought we'd gone into that this morning."

"This is the postscript."

"Well, have you decided to write off the—the search for——" She didn't finish.

"Yes," I said. "I have."

That brought her head up. "Really, Philip? If you...."

I didn't like the look of relief in her eyes. "Partly, anyway. I'm going back to Holland for a couple of days. I've had a letter from the Dutch inspector who was in charge of the case. Read it if you like."

I gave her the letter from Tholen which had been forwarded by Arnold. I could follow her eyes as she read it.

Dear Mr. Turner,

"We are now in the possession of fresh data in reference to your brother's death. This I cannot send to you fully because it is confidential and better that such information is not all commit to paper. If you find the convenience to come to Holland again, I shall give you this information by personal word and so help to clear up the perplexity of your mind.

"If it is not the convenience for you to come, pray let me know and I shall try to write you what I can.

"Yours very truly,
"J. J. Tholen."

She handed the letter back.

" I wonder what that means."

" It's what I'm going to find out."

" Yes. Yes, of course. Well I hope——" Again she didn't finish.

" That it means nothing at all?"

" No. I hope that everything will go well."

" Thanks. In the meantime I'll leave Martin Coxon here to look after you."

She kept here eyes down.

" That'll be fun."

" Yes, he's very good fun."

" Are you going to tell this inspector about me?"

" I haven't decided. But I don't think so."

" Surely you should."

" It depends what he has to say."

" I'm still puzzled why you're telling me this, Philip. Haven't I yet convinced you that I'm in the enemy's camp?"

" No."

She was silent, rubbing her finger along the side of the banister. I said: " One thing. I wish you'd promise me one thing while I'm away."

" What?"

" You may think this pretty cheap . . . but I have to risk it. I never knew your husband; but I think he must have been a nice fellow."

She didn't speak.

" And I imagine you had the sort of feeling for him that you haven't quite had for anyone since."

" Well?"

" Well . . . would it be a good thing to think of that?"

She came down two more steps until our heads were level. Her hand was still on the banister but I didn't touch it.

" It's queer you should say that."

" Why?"

" I've been thinking rather a lot about Tom to-day." She hesitated.

" Go on."

" It's too difficult to explain now."

" I'd like to know."

" We must go in——"

" No." I put a hand on her arm now.

It was like touching a restive young animal. I thought she was going to push me away, but suddenly her mood changed. " It's impossible to say in two words, Philip. . . . You see, when he died—when Tom and Richard died I was in hospital. I'd been taken away from home rather ill but not desperately ill. Tom and Richard were all right. *I* was the sick one. It wasn't until three weeks later that they told me. I couldn't *believe* it. When I went home I kept waiting. . . . I'd not even seen Tom ill for one day. It was just as if they'd both disappeared into air. . . ." Her nostrils flexed. " Of course the house and stuff were sold—I couldn't go on living there—and after a time I realised about Richard. A four-month-old baby—that's somebody you've hardly got to know. But what I'm telling you all this for is to say that I've never *quite* understood about Tom. I knew what had happened—went about my ordinary life. But at the back of my mind. . . ."

" You've always had a half feeling that somewhere he was still alive. . . ."

" Yes. Yes, that's exactly it."

After a minute I said : " When I mentioned your husband just now—perhaps you can guess why I did——"

" Yes, perhaps."

" Forget it. I still perfer to fight with some holds barred."

She put her hand on top of mine for a second and then moved past me.

I said : " All the same, I wish I could help you, Leonie."

" Perhaps you already have."

"As progress, I rate that the high-water mark so far."

"I'm sorry. . . ."

"Don't take it back now."

"I wasn't going to."

She walked towards the door of the living-room. I followed her.

She stopped and said: "What I wanted to say and haven't said so far is that to-day"—she looked at me thoughtfully—"to-day I've realised fully for the first time about Tom. It's . . ." Her eyes were large and brilliant and seemed to reflect more light than there was in the hall. "It's like realising, at the same time, that something vitally important to you is both better and worse than you thought."

When I walked home with Martin a half moon was nearly setting and looked as if its other half had been broken up and distributed as largesse over the water. It was difficult now acting it out, but vitally important that I should. I told him how utterly at sea I felt knowing now that Sanbergh was not Buckingham, that I felt I'd been chasing a complete will-o'-the-wisp and that all was to do again. The only ray of light anywhere was Tholen's letter, and this I showed him. He read it under a lamp, puckering his eyes.

When he finished he said: "I know—I told you. The rest of this damned jig-saw is still in Amsterdam. It stands to *reason*." I noticed a slight quickening in his voice. He was evidently pleased to get me out of the way, to set me still further on the wrong track. "You'll go of course."

"I'm not sure." I wanted to see what he would say.

"You'd be crazy not to. If you're unable or unwilling to press this girl, the purpose of staying here has gone."

"I don't think she knows any more, except Buckingham's real name—or what she supposes is his real name. It may very well not be."

"But you'll come back?"

"Yes."

We reached a place where the path opened out, and from this point you could see most of the Bay of Naples, moonshot and starlit. But his face was in shadow. "You want me to stay on here, Philip?"

"I shall be gone no time. Beautiful, isn't it?"

"Yes. . . . 'The Gods in bliss scrabble a baby jargon on the skies for us to analyse.' How does it go after that?"

I said: "I don't think chemical analysis provides all the answers any more than psycho-analysis."

"What guff we were talking to-night. It's all this bogus deification of the ego. Did you get any information in that letter from Java this morning? I saw one in your pigeon-hole before you got back."

I stared after a firefly that flickered across the path. "It was from Pangkal—that's the man who was Grevil's assistant and fell ill and Buckingham took his place. You can read it if you like."

I felt in my pocket and took out one or two letters. "Oh, it doesn't seem to be here. Anyway, it wasn't very helpful. Pangkal doesn't seem to have liked Buckingham."

We walked on.

"*Grevil* must have liked him," I said. "I still don't understand why."

"Buckingham is a very intelligent fellow. It's not unlikely that they got on well. He knows a lot."

"A lot of what? Cheap tricks and sharp practices and shoddy ways of making do."

Martin stopped to light a cigarette. The long lines of his pale wicked face seemed for a few seconds cut out, hung up in the darkness of his thoughts.

"You'd make a mistake to underrate Buckingham, Philip. If your brother was an exceptional man, so is he. There's nothing second-rate."

I said: "I wonder if there's something of the split personality about him, the schizophrenic."

He shook his head emphatically. "People like him are all of a piece. They're more not less consistent than the ordinary man. If you want press-button-A reflexes and Mr. Wet-Mrs. Fine personalities, go to the man who has toed the line all his life because the sham laws he's hedged about with have prevented him from behaving as he wants to behave—not to the natural renegade who's always done what he wanted."

"Sometimes you give me the impression you have a sneaking admiration for the fellow."

The light flickered out.

After waiting a minute I said: "Seriously, he seems to me no more than a prize bounder and small-time racketeer. If he had any exceptional quality he ought by the time he's forty to have been able to live off his past coups, not be a seamy down-and-out in Java."

"Taking risks is part of his temperament."

"I doubt it. These dunghill cocks usually run at the sight of danger."

He made an abrupt impatient movement of his cigarette. "Oh, *hell*, forget it. . . . You don't know him—and probably never will. I do—a little. I think maybe I understand why he does some of the things he does. I don't necessarily like him any better for them—or necessarily condemn. It's an attitude of mind. I think of Juvenal's ' *Fœdius hoc aliquid quandoque audebis.*' "

We walked on without saying any more. It gave me great satisfaction to feel I had touched him on the raw. It seemed to me just then that the hatred I felt for Martin Coxon now didn't stem from to-day and the definite knowing that had come to me to-day. Its roots were deep, in our first or second meeting, and had been growing hardly noticed because judgment had been held back, in abeyance. Now judgment was no longer held back, and suddenly I found the thing already grown to fit the new certainty.

And it seemed in that moment of distorted clarity that

the hatred was deeper, far deeper because its roots were in liking and trust. Just perhaps the same as Grevil's had been—except that Grevil had not had a chance of recognising the true man until it was too late.

I wondered if what I felt would show. It would be very risky to let it show. Martin Coxon had killed Grevil, or been present at the killing, in some manner and for some reason I had yet to discover. If he knew I knew, he and I would be on the verge of the same thing.

It was very necessary just now for me to walk carefully. Otherwise it might not only be Mme Weber who lived with an uncomfortable companion at her elbow.

Chapter Sixteen

I woke in the night and knew he was in my room. I'm a light sleeper, and he may have made some slight sound.

After a second or two I went on breathing at a slow regular rate, and after a second or two he began to move again.

I'd never done any fighting except a bit of boxing in the Navy, and I knew that against a man who would know every trick in the bag, such genteel experience would be as useful as an umbrella in a typhoon.

But I saw he had moved towards the wardrobe, and although I did not stir I guessed he was searching my pockets. So then I knew what he was after.

I waited. Next he went to the dressing-table and looked all over it. He got the two top drawers open without a sound, looked through them, shut them again, bent to a chair on which I'd thrown a few things in my usual untidy way.

I must have changed my breathing slightly without intending to; at once he was up and watching. It's very hard to sound as if you're asleep when under stress. Presently he began to move towards the bed.

I knew the shape of his hands and what they'd feel like. Trouble was I had to keep my eyes shut.

I'm not sure, but I think he bent over the bed. In—out; now wait; not too hurried; in—out; boat-race crew approaching Putney; in—out, don't let it catch. He began to move away again. As I opened my eyes he was going out through the open window.

I'd re-read Pangkal's letter just before going to sleep and pushed it under the pillow, otherwise he would have found it. And Grevil's notes—which might at least have told him I had access to information he knew nothing of—were under the bed.

As he went out some light from outside caught his face. It seemed to me that the look on it made it thinner and more tense than I had ever seen it before.

I said: "I'm so sorry to disturb your breakfast, but I came to apologise about the portrait. I certainly hope to get down to it when I come back."

"There's no hurry, dear boy," said Mme Weber, pulling down the sleeve of her Japanese kimono. "I don't suppose I shall change much before the end of the month; my hairdresser's away. Are you sure you want to go on with it?"

"Quite sure. I should be back to-morrow evening or Friday morning."

She salvaged a wriggling Bergdorf who was about to take a plunge off the silk counterpane, and stared into his ear. "I had a maystiff once that had a canker. Most distressin'. Philip, are you and Leonie . . . Is there some possibility . . ."

"No. . . . At least I'm afraid not."

"Be still, Bergdorf, I'll not hurt you. You must learn to trust Mother. A pity. Or I think it's a pity. She needs to marry again. It's time she did. This over-developed sense of loyalty."

"I'm not sure if it's quite the sort of loyalty you think."

"Down, dog. Keep your paws to yourself. She'd be happier if she was more fickle. I've told her so. A woman *needs* a man—keeps her metabolism right. And I think you'd do for her, Philip."

"Tell her that some time, will you."

"Being an artist you've finesse, could humour without spoilin'. And tenacity. Women who won't remarry—very difficult; especially when they're lookers. Deceivin'. Pity for a girl with *all* the guns not to use them."

I said: "She uses them."

"I remember when I met her first after Tom Winter had died, I said sorry, sorry, sorry, how she must feel—trying to be comfortin'—you know. And she said: 'Oh, that's all right; you're tough when you're young.'" Charlotte Weber dropped the wriggling puppy gently over the side of the bed. His paws made a plop on the floor. "As a generalisation, nothing ever truer. But about herself —couldn't be wronger. Wronger—is there a word? Leonie's toughness wouldn't fool a child. What's more, she's driftin'. Seems to me half the time she doesn't know her own mind, because what she's been thinking of and remembering doesn't make good knowing."

"Or doesn't bear knowing."

"Quite so, dear boy. It's like buyin' furniture. There are certain things in the mind one can live with and certain things one can't. When it's the 'can't', it usually means you've got to get 'out of yourself'—as the sayin' is—in order to live at all."

As I stood up to go she looked at me and smiled tolerantly. "And don't bother about the portrait in the least. I'll keep. I've kept so long."

I knew I shouldn't have much difficulty in persuading Martin to stay on the island until I got back. I knew I was taking a chance in proposing it, but it was a definite line now for the first time since the very beginning, and the chance had to be taken. As I waved to him as he leaned over the wall watching the steamer leave, I wondered what his own dark thoughts were and what they had been all through the process of this grim farce. With the boat moving out of the harbour I saw him turn and take a book out of his pocket and walk slowly off the quay towards the funicular. Good-bye, Martin, I thought, what shall I bring you back to-morrow?

It wasn't until I'd been on the boat for about half an hour that I saw that the Master of Kyle was among the passengers. When I joined him he stared at me resentfully from under his cap as if he half expected me to do him some injury. When I didn't, he unbent sufficiently to explain that his financial arrangements were with the Banca d'Italia, which did not have a branch on Capri, and I told him I had to fly to Amsterdam on a business matter.

He said: " I notice Martin isn't going with you."

"No, I shall be back soon. We were talking of you last night, sir. You were a close friend of his grandfather's?"

"His closest." Kyle lifted a hand from his stick to pull the cap more firmly over the ancient monument where his eyebrows had been. " Callard and I were friends and neighbours for five and twenty years. I doubt Martin has been telling you a long story of the fine times he had at Gaitweed when he was a lad. I have not seen the sight of him since Callard met his death. The present earl, his uncle, will have no truck with him."

"Why is that?"

Kyle hesitated, chewing something. " Ah, well, that's how he feels, and no doubt he's entitled to his opinion."

A tall yacht was sliding out of Sorrento harbour, its sails gilded with the sun. I said: " Is Martin the son of a younger son?"

"Very much so. His father was born on the wrong side

of the blanket. Callard had an affair with some actress, and Fred Coxon was the result. Fred died young, but Callard took a fancy to Martin and made much of him—too much of him."

I said: "I've known Martin only a very little time."

Kyle grunted but did not rise to the bait. Whatever he was chewing obviously didn't please him. We sailed on.

I tried again. "He's very amusing company."

"Who?"

"Martin."

"Oh, aye, he's all that, I grant you."

"What the cocktail-shakers would call good value."

"I've no doubt they would." Kyle stopped chewing. "And sometimes they have to pay for their good value, eh, just when they're least expecting to."

"I haven't known him long enough to know if that's true of him."

"Well, he's your friend, Mr. Norton."

Kyle wasn't the easiest of men to pump. I gave him three or four minutes. "Martin is very devoted to his mother."

"You surprise me. I have never met her."

"Did Lord Callard bring him up?"

"He paid for his education. Then Martin would come up for his holidays and they would go shooting and climbing together. Wild as a young eagle, he was, and as handsome. He was ever at cross with the rest of the family because they thought he was too much the favourite. And so he was. So he was." Kyle turned up the collar of his jacket and moved his back to the wind. "Martin used to act as if *he* was the heir. Callard would come to me and complain of the young man's extravagances, and I'd say, 'Pshaw, you encourage him—what else can ye expect?"

I waited. But he had begun to chew again. "And that all changed when Lord Callard died?"

"Aye, that all changed."

"Had Martin no claims on the rest of the family?"

"How should he have?"

A boy came across selling sweets and cigarettes, but the old man waved him irritably away. He muttered for a minute to himself. Presently I heard what he was saying. ". . . a stroke. One day Callard was a hale and hearty man of sixty-odd, the next he was helpless as a felled tree, snoring his life away." Kyle stared angrily across the water at Vesuvius, as if he would like to lay the blame somewhere. "Nasty shock for Martin Coxon. He expected to have been well taken care of, but Callard's will was fifteen years old. So Martin got a couple of thousand and went his way. He had always had the true aristocrat's attitude to money, had Martin—that it existed only to buy him what he needed, and that it must always exist in a sufficient quantity for him to have the best. . . . It would be different when he had to start cutting his coat. . . ."

I said: "But all that makes me sympathise; I still don't see why you dislike him, sir."

"I didna say I disliked him," Kyle snapped. "That's putting words in my mouth."

"Words into your mouth perhaps but not thoughts into your head."

Kyle stared at me suspicious. "I'm not at all sure, my friend, that you like him so much yourself."

"Well . . . supposing I don't?"

Kyle grunted. "Well, then, ye don't, eh? And why do you not?"

"My reasons are vague. I think that yours are not."

"I would not be so sure. But I dislike him, for one thing because of his damned charm, Mr. Norton, that's what. I may say I never had the least difficulty in resisting it myself, but I saw others go down before it like—like icicles in the sun. His grandfather for one, a hard-bitten old campaigner you would think, but the boy had him on a string. Then there was his cousin, Mary Falconer, and his aunt, Lady Maud Falconer, and at least two girls and . . . Well there were plenty."

"Did he ever marry?"

"Yes, in the thirties. But she divorced him. I've forgotten her name; it was in the papers because of some marriage settlement. I do not believe he has cared a finger's snap for any one of the people who have loved him; he has taken their friendship and sacrifices for granted. And you can tell him that from me if you've the mind to carry tales." Old Kyle tapped me on the arm. "Oh, charm, yes, no doubt. But ye judge a tree by its fruit, and his has been bitter. He has taken what others have had to give him—all his life, young man—and very few there have been who have been the better off for knowing him—many have been worse off, let me tell you that, badly worse off. There has always been a *darkness* to him, a pessimism, even in his youth—ye heard him the other night—always he was a destroyer, a puller-down of good things."

I nodded but did not speak. Kyle stopped there and I didn't pursue the subject. In a very small way the old man had given me a glimpse of Martin Coxon's beginnings. I thought I might myself possibly be able to fill in the end.

I had cabled Tholen, and when I got to Schiphol he had sent a car to meet me. I saw him about eight that evening, and I was surprised to find Van Renkum there as well.

Tholen said: "It is good for you to come. I have not wished to feel that anything has been left undone. Perhaps now we can clear your mind of this distress. Mr. Van Renkum is here for our Foreign Department, and I shall ask him to explain. His English language is so good, and much that he has to say is concerning his office, too. So that is the best way."

Van Renkum said: "Will you take water with it, Mr. Turner? Some English prefer that, I know, but I have forgotten. . . ."

"Thanks. Either way." I was not interested in the glass he was filling.

"Perhaps we should apologise about your last visit, Mr. Turner. Then we were not in a position . . . how shall I put it?—the net was still out. To draw it then would have been to lose some of the fish. But now it is different—the sweep is over."

"I'm glad to know it. Thank you."

He took a second glass to Tholen. "I think I must plunge in and tell you what is the worst from your point of view. We now have evidence to bear out what Hermina Maas told us."

I stared at him. "You mean about my brother?"

"Yes."

I looked at Tholen. He had put down his drink and was nipping the end of a cigar. "You mean about him having—jumped into the canal?"

He looked up. "Yes, Mr. Turner. I know you did not believe that, but I am sorry to tell you that there is the truth."

After a minute I said: "What sort of evidence?"

Van Renkum said: "We had always hoped that someone else might have seen what happened on the bridge that night. You remember we said we were still searching. But the difficulty was in tracing them. People who visit De Walletjes are not usually forthcoming. We offered a reward. In the end we found a man, one connected with the Harbour Board. He had been in the house opposite, had seen what the Maas woman had seen." Van Renkum took a typewritten sheet from Tholen's desk. "The evidence is here for you to read if you would like it. The English translation is on the back. Also, the man speaks a little English, and if you wish it we can arrange for you to meet him in the morning. We want you to be quite certain in your own mind."

I took the paper and stared at the Dutch version. I

didn't bother to turn it over. There was a scrawled signature at the bottom that I couldn't read. The black lettering of the type had little red edges where the ribbon had been out of true. Van Renkum said: "Briefly what it says there is that he saw your brother talking to someone on the bridge. They separated, and your brother stood for a minute or two watching the other man out of sight. Then he stepped on the parapet and jumped into the canal. The witness is quite certain that there was no one else on the bridge at the time."

With no knowledge of the language I could still make something of it. "On the night of the 30th March . . . when I let up the blind . . . no cry for help. . . ."

Van Renkum said again: "The translation is on the back, Mr. Turner."

I handed the paper to him. I got up and took out a cigarette. Someone gave me a light.

"Do you say you offered a reward?"

Tholen cleared himself of smoke by waving his open palm. "I should like it that you would see this witness, Aahrens, to-morrow, to judge for yourself. He is a man of honest repute and incurs some risk to his home life by giving this testimony. He would not be tempted by a few guilders."

Van Renkum said: "There is much more to explain yet, Mr. Turner. If you will sit down. . . ."

I said: "So Grevil . . ."

In the street outside you could hear the bicycle bells. They must have been getting impatient at some traffic jam because they were all ringing together.

Van Renkum said: "We no longer think he took his own life because of a broken love affair. That was in fact never an explanation we altogether believed."

"Then *why* did he do it? Why?"

"We must ask your patience to go back. Take a drink and sit down and we will tell you the rest."

I sat down. I felt sick. "Well?"

"Before the war the import of opium into the Dutch East Indies was a Government monopoly and strictly controlled. During the war all imports from Persia naturally stopped, but the Japanese brought in a good deal and encouraged its use in Java as a matter of policy. A drug-taking population is a quiescent one, you understand. So after the war the new Indonesian Government found itself in possession of some twenty-five tons of opium. The sale of this it controlled and restricted at first in a thoroughly responsible way; but during the trouble with our Government the Indonesians were very short of money to buy arms, and so they decided to sell some of this opium in the international market. You may remember the scandal that arose."

"No."

"Well, in the confusion of that time a quantity of the opium was pilfered by lesser members of the Government and much to-day is still unaccounted for. In March of this year our agents in Java reported that a substantial amount was about to be smuggled into Holland and a close watch was kept to intercept it. Later we were informed that it was being flown into Amsterdam on a particular K.L.M. flight, so when the plane landed at Schiphol it was impounded and all its passengers and crew and their luggage searched—all that is except some cases of archæological specimens which were the possession of Dr. Grevil Turner, whose reputation was above reproach."

"And right to be so," said Tholen.

"In any event, four of the five cases went direct to the Rijksmuseum where they were at once examined. The fifth, remaining in the possession of Dr. Turner, presented a greater difficulty." Van Renkum frowned at his cuff and fingered the embossed silver cuff-link. "Before taking any further step we cabled again to Batavia and again were assured that, according to information there, the opium had left. So Inspector Tholen and another plain-clothes officer called at Dr. Turner's hotel and explained the position to him and requested permission to open the fifth case. Dr. Turner refused."

I looked at Tholen. "He refused?"

"Yes. He was—angry at the suspicion. He says it is an insult that he shall be so accused. I explain that it is not to accuse him that we come but to clear up our own minds. I tried to explain, you understand, to say that it is our duty to stop this traffic. He will not agree that this is the way to do it. Then I must insist. I have authority by Netherlands law to search his possession. To this he submits with not-good grace and we open the case. In it there is many kilograms weight of opium."

I took a drink now. There was no water in it. I didn't want water.

Tholen said: "Sometimes the police work has great difficulties. It is necessary to sum up, to form opinion at short notice. This is the first time I meet Dr. Turner. To look at he is like his reputation. Who would think? But often one has been forced before to say, who would think? Facts, evidence, that is all to go on. And here the evidence is as black as can be. When we discover the opium Dr. Turner looks very ill, very angry. He states there is no knowledge to him as to the opium or of how it is come in the case. He declares he is angry too at the loss of some things which should have been there. He speaks of some mistake, but cannot explain at all how the mistake is made. I request a statement. This he says he will not give until he has seen the British Ambassador. I agree and phone Van Renkum and also phone to have the opium removed. Then I make the grave mistake of leaving him."

Van Renkum had finished with his cuff-link. "If we had treated Dr. Turner like an ordinary criminal he would still be alive—but we felt we could not do that. With his distinguished record and his connections in the Netherlands. . . . It would be better to give him time to reflect.

A confession might come, and with it information, invaluable information. Or he might make some move on his own which would be almost as useful. We posted a man to watch Dr. Turner's movements, and sent two men round to interview the companion who had accompanied Dr. Turner from Java. Unfortunately the man was not in his hotel. He never returned and his travelling-bag was left unclaimed. Still more unfortunately, during the evening Dr. Turner evaded the detective who had been left to watch him, and by the follow morning it was too late."

"In other words," I said, "he put the seal on his guilt by killing himself."

Van Renkum looked pained. "If we had thought that, we should have had less excuse to withhold the facts from Dr. Turner's widow or, indeed, from you. We chose to withhold judgment."

The Bols was going down inside me, fiery and full of sham good cheer.

Van Renkum said: "It would not have been to our credit to lay a very unpleasant crime at the door of this distinguished scientist unless we were convinced it must be so laid. In the end the information that our man has brought back from Jakarta, and what we have found here since suggests something rather different."

"It was Buckingham's doing?"

"Yes. We've discovered the source of his supply in Java and his contacts here. Last week we made a clean sweep of them here, including their head, whom we were most anxious to bring in, a man I believe you met called Jodenbree. Although we shall probably———"

"Jodenbree," I said. "You've got him. . . ."

"Yes. He's coming up for trial next month, and we shall make sure of a conviction. It may be that Dr. Turner knew all about it and helped Buckingham—some points suggest it; his refusal to let us open the case, his visit to

De Walletjes where Jodenbree lived. But on the whole we think it much more likely that he was duped until the very end."

I rubbed my cigarette out. Tholen's cigar had a long tube of white ash unbroken at its end.

I said: "Then why do you suppose that he—committed suicide?"

"Not because he was guilty but because he had no possible way of proving himself innocent. Faced with what seemed to him an intolerable situation, notoriety, imprisonment, disgrace, he chose what seemed to him then the only escape."

There was a long silence. I pushed my chair back but didn't get up. A tram clattered noisily in the street.

I said: "Although by taking his own life he very much increased the possibility of being thought guilty, although he did that, you're still prepared to give him the benefit of the doubt and consider him innocent?"

"Yes, now we know what we do know."

"Then I wonder why he didn't reason that way at the time?"

Van Renkum said: "It's easy to be wise after the event. It's easy to say, 'I wouldn't have taken that course.' But with the thing full upon you. . . . He may well not have realised how much we should be able to discover. And also, if I may say so, it is not a verdict of not guilty that could have been brought in; but not proven. In such a case the mud will always stick no matter what you say in your own defence, no matter even what is proved afterwards."

Too late Tholen moved his cigar towards the ash-tray. A shower of white ash drifted down towards the carpet like stage snow. He had been watching me, like a doctor with a troublesome patient.

"I know how it is over this," he said. "I know how you are disappointed. But it has been my duty to tell you."

"Did Grevil ever phone the British Ambassador?"

"No."

"And Buckingham? Have you been able to include him in this net?"

"No," said Van Renkum. "It's the one gap. We've given what information we can to the British police in case they can trace him."

Tholen said: "And you, Mr. Turner? Have you made some progress on your own?"

I met his eyes. They were sharp just then. I said: "On the evidence you now have—if you should find him in another country—would you be able to proceed with an extradition order?"

"Yes. If we were able to establish identity. But I think it is perhaps quite difficult to establish that."

Chapter Seventeen

I found there was no service for Naples the next day. The best offered was a 3.15 p.m. plane for Rome, so I decided to take that. That way I could see Aahrens in the morning. Anyway, I had suddenly lost the will to hurry back to Italy.

That one night in Amsterdam I sat up late drinking coffee at one of the street-side cafés. There was some sort of a fête or anniversary on, because the streets were decorated and more people than usual were about. Watching the homely agreeable respectable faces pressing by, it came to me to wonder if this busy, attractive but slightly provincial city was the same one in which a district known as the Little Walls existed. It seemed improbable. It seemed improbable that many of these people would know of its existence. It seemed improbable that Grevil should have done.

I wasn't yet properly taking it all in. It was like being stabbed with a weapon that partly froze the area of damage. The injury was something you couldn't pin down to the locality of a limb or an organ—it was outside them all and within them all.

Two or three times I tried to face up to what it all meant to me, but it was too soon. I seemed altogether to have lost my sense of judgment. When the cafés began to shut down some time after midnight, I got up and began to walk and must have wandered round the city for two hours or more. When I finally turned in at the hotel my legs were tired and my mouth was dry and bitter from too many cigarettes. I lay down on the bed and waited for the morning.

About six I was up again and looking for a bathroom—curious the lack of them in hotels in this clean city—and when I had washed and shaved I lit up again and finished off the last of Grevil's notes. As I might have expected, they ended on a reference to Buckingham.

"Came back from two-day shoot better for the mountain air. Glad J. B. persuaded me to go. Bivouacked for night above forest; the quietness at sundown most noticeable after the customary chorus of insects; even the wou-wou silent for long periods. Returning found and caught fine specimen of the *chalcosoma atlas* beetle. J. B. full of his usual odd quirks of knowledge. Pressed me to spend few extra days making expedition Boro-Budur—should much have liked to but feel have been here long enough. If I come back next year shall invite Jack to come with me.

"He is returning home with me and have promised to get him job with expedition to Euphrates in autumn under Massey. This beneath his obvious talents but a beginning, and certainly better than the thing he would normally drift into. Shall miss him when we separate. There's an acid refreshment in his company, a challenge, a stimulus. Consider him the perfect companion for such undertakings as this. The attractions of opposites, no doubt, and rather an obsession."

That was the end. That was all. But perhaps it meant a lot, those several long entries about Martin Coxon in a book intended solely for notes on the excavations. Grevil, the single-minded, whose concentration on his work was a stock joke among his friends.

I saw Aahrens at eleven. It didn't help much except that it made the testimony more real for me and more conclusive. On the way to the Leidseplein I bought some magazines to read on the flight; but I might as well have saved the money, because in the air it was just the same as on the ground. I kept saying to myself: Martin Coxon didn't kill Grevil, no one did; he killed himself. He killed himself. I had to keep on telling myself, so that presently perhaps I should know it to be true. Everything else beside that was unimportant.

Crossing the Alps by plane always reminds me of Operation Moon a little ahead of time. I stared at Mont Blanc rearing its austere head among a score of lesser peaks, and the ring of white summits was a pearl necklace about the throat of Italy. (Or perhaps it was a hangman's rope.) Then there was the opal-blue Mediterranean and Elba, and tree-covered mountains, and snow on Corsica, gaunt in the distance.

I had kept Grevil's references to Buckingham separate from the rest, so I was able to go through them now. I thought perhaps with this new knowledge. . . . But the only one which on second reading seemed to have a greater significance was where he said, referring to some discussion on spiritual degradation: "If it were true I think one would be capable of that desperation absolute and complete that William James speaks of, the whole universe coagulating about the sufferer into a material of overwhelming horror, surrounding him without opening or end—and no other conception or sensation able to live for a moment in its presence."

He'd written that just after he'd been ill with a bad bout of fever. Impossible to say how far he had thrown off the after-effects; nobody would ever be able to say what sort of physical or mental health he had been in when he flew home.

Nobody except perhaps Martin Coxon.

Much, much, was still obscure. Perhaps it always would be. That Grevil had taken his own life was the thing that stuck.

I slept better in Rome. It was probably because I was fagged out, and just for the time there seemed nothing more to think about, nothing that was worth thinking about—nothing that wasn't shoddy and rotten and futile and worthless—nothing that did not feed a black and bitter rage.

Next day I took the train for Naples and caught the afternoon boat. There wasn't anyone I knew on the boat this time, and I was glad. I didn't want to talk to anybody. When I saw the craggy outline of the island coming closer, I felt I didn't even want to return. Perhaps in a way I was coming back to something in myself that I hadn't yet faced up to. It would be dangerous to meet Martin in this mood.

Martin was out. They said he'd been away all day. I sat on the balcony and drank some wine and tried to read the magazines. In the narrow lane outside the hotel a fat woman in a cheap print frock was trying to get on a donkey. The donkey-man, with a brown face and a halo of gold curls, was trying to help her and trying not to laugh. She was dead serious about it, and so was the little man in the cloth cap and spectacles who was holding the donkey's nose. The fat was creased round her bare elbows, her neck and face were red and peeling. She looked awful. I wondered if they were English or American. I wondered where Martin was and how much I should tell him. I wondered why in the first place he had linked himself with Buckingham in the eyes of the English police. Probably it wasn't that way. Perhaps they had known of his being in the blockade-running off the coast of Palestine at the same time as Buckingham and had asked him for information, and Martin had given it to divert suspicion from himself.

The woman got on the donkey at last and they began to lurch up the lane. I heard her voice.

"*Nimm Acht, Karl! Ich habe heine. Lust zu rennen.*"

I decided to go to the Villa Atrani.

The sun had set before I got there, and a few stars, keeping their distance, were showing in the remote sky.

Only Charlotte Weber and Charles Sanbergh were in, and I felt I'd interrupted a private half-hour. Mme Weber said: "Dear boy, you've kept your promise. People say, 'darling, I'll be *back*', and the next time you see them it's the following decade. . . . How was England?"

"Amsterdam. All right. Have you seen Martin Coxon?"

"Not since this morning," said Sanbergh.

Mme Weber screwed another cigarette into her long cigarette-holder. After she'd lit it she waved the match in zigzag lines until it reluctantly went out. She said: "Leonie's gone away."

"Away? Where?"

"To Rome. She heard some friends were there, and took it into her head to rush off yesterday afternoon. I warned her. That monument to Victor Emmanuel is such a bore in the hot weather. Overpowerin'. Gimbel, don't make those disgusting chewing noises. Charles, do something about Gimbel."

Sanbergh stirred the dog with his foot. "Your friend Coxon was up here yesterday evening. We had dinner together on my yacht. An interesting character, your friend Coxon."

"Yes?" I said.

"I think he went fishing to-day. I saw him at the quay this morning hiring a boat. Excuse me, I must telephone." He got up and went out of the room. Again this evening he was friendly enough. It would all have been very puzzling if I'd had the interest to care.

Mme Weber said: "Draw up your chair and talk to me. I'm a poor substitute, but Leonie will be back."

"What makes you think so?"

"A feeling I have. Psychic. Philip, what is the mystery going on around you? Provokin' not to know."

"Did she say she'd be back?"

"*Kick* Gimbel for me, will you. He's being exploratory. Yes, she said I was to say to you that she had to go and that she thought you'd understand. I don't know why I *permit* him in the drawing-room."

"She thought I'd understand."

"Don't you? Very difficult. There are some things one can't do by remote control. Sorry."

"It isn't your fault."

"I don't know. I was reading Proust at the time, and he's demandin'. One has to *pursue* him, like a coy bachelor. Philip, I wish I could help you."

"I know. Thank you."

"Tell me about the great world outside. Not that I don't shudder to know. Your Martin Coxon is quite a spark, isn't he. Those sombre dark eyes. Engulfin'."

"Did she leave her address in Rome?"

"Should think he's been quite a Pied Piper for the women. We women love a hint of mystery, you know. Adolescent. No, she didn't, Philip, she said she'd write. Is that Jane and Nicolo back already?"

It turned out not to be Jane and Nicolo but Mlle Henriot, so I refused an invitation to stay to dinner and left. This was something else I had to think out now. I felt I needed a new brain to deal with Leonie's going (was it flight?)—a new detachment to set it in its perspective. The trouble was that all the uncertain feelings of a man properly in love for the first time in his life kept trying to crash in at this point. It shouldn't have made any difference to the older and more recognisable loyalties—and didn't in sum—but it set them out of focus, made me less certain of my judgment, when, if ever, I needed now to be objective and keep my hands cool.

In the hall Sanbergh was talking into the telephone, but as I went past he hung up and said: "You are going early. Have you had a drink?"

"Thanks, no. I expect Coxon will be waiting for me by now."

His eyes slid over me in that expert way they had. "It is a pity Leonie has gone."

"Yes." I didn't want to discuss it with him.

"She didn't hint at it before you left?"

I stopped at the door. "I don't think I quite understand you, Sanbergh. Three or four days ago you made it rather plain that you didn't want me around. Well, I stayed around. I was sorry about it, but I could live without your approval. Now . . . the hate campaign seems to have been called off. I'm not quick enough on the change."

He shut the little cubby-hole where the telephone was kept and came over to the door, stood with a hand on it looking out at the evening. "I'm glad you mentioned it; I had intended to. On Tuesday Leonie told me a little about why you had come here. I don't understand the whole of it, but I understand enough to acknowledge my misjudgment."

"I still don't know what the misjudgment was."

His mouth curved, Pan-like but formidable. "I am Charlotte Weber's oldest friend. Twenty years ago when she was even more beautiful than she is to-day, I was her friend in another way. Often she has helped me. Sometimes I have been able to repay." He shrugged. "But she's a gullible creature. That's how she married so often. Such a mistake. And she's very much liable to be imposed upon, especially by the sham æsthete, the artistic dilettante. No doubt she has a heart big enough for all, but that isn't the point. To see her taken in by every smooth little cheat. . . . There are many come to

195

Capri . . . and because she is rich and easy . . . There's one such in her house now—to my shame an Italian like myself——"

"Da Cossa?"

He nodded. "He has battened himself on her for twelve months. On so many things she listens to me, but if I try to pick her friends she says I'm jealous and we quarrel."

I said: "And you thought I was another?"

"Does it surprise you? The approach could hardly have been more well-worn: the scraped acquaintance, the pretence of being able to paint, the unsubtle flattery. . . . Then when I sent to the hotel and found you were not even using your own name here, I thought it might be a matter for the police."

"I'm sorry. I do paint, you know."

"Oh yes, I understand that—now."

He came out of the door, and we stood a minute on the steps listening to the quiet sighing of the night.

I said: "When I first met you I thought da Cossa was a special friend of yours."

"Was that why you showed a dislike of me?"

"No. . . . I don't think I can explain my mistake as easily as you have yours."

"If it was no more excusable, it is no less pardonable."

A liner was coming into the Bay of Naples. It glittered like a telescopic view of the Milky Way.

I said: "You might ask da Cossa some time to do you another pastel like the one of the Faraglioni Rocks."

"Why?"

"Because he never painted it. He's bogus even in that."

Sanbergh was a step lower than I was, and he turned and faced me. "Are you sure? Why are you sure?"

"I've seen him at work. How would you know if a man could sail a yacht?"

He walked with me thoughtfully to the gate.

He said: "You are—interested in Leonie Winter?"

I didn't somehow mind the direct question now. "Yes."

He opened the gate. "She hasn't gone to Rome."

"Where is she, then?"

"At a place called Poltano. It's a village in the hills above Amalfi."

"Why has she gone there?"

"I thought perhaps you might know about it. I wasn't sure."

"Did she tell you?"

"No. She left on the afternoon boat yesterday, and by chance the captain of the boat mentioned to me that she had got off at Sorrento. You do not get off at Sorrento for Rome. After that it was easy. You see, I know almost everyone."

It occurred to me that if Sanbergh was likely to be an uncomfortable enemy, he might also be a very useful friend.

"Does Mme Weber know?"

"She must. Leonie is staying in one of her villas."

"One of her villas?"

"She owns property there. You may remember we went up on business connected with it the day you came with us to Amalfi. There are a number of small houses and flats."

I didn't speak.

He said after a minute: "I don't think you should feel that this is anything Mme Weber has done against you. I can only imagine that Leonie found some need to leave the island for a few days and asked Charlotte to help her. She must have sworn Charlotte to secrecy if Charlotte has kept it even from me."

I said: "Do you know the name of the place she's staying? How would I find it?"

I think he smiled in the dark. "It is number fifteen Piazza San Stefano. It is easy, for there is nothing at

Poltano except the Piazzo and the Cathedral. If you find Poltano there's nothing more to find.''

Coxon still wasn't back, so I had dinner and then sat and waited for him. All I'd learned in these last few days fairly milled in my head. I kept trying to think why Leonie had gone and what I should do about it. It fitted into a pattern but not a pattern I liked. Then I got undressed and lay in bed and smoked and drank Soave and listened for footsteps in the next room.

For a change I *tried* to think about Grevil, but now for some reason his image escaped me. I tried to think what he looked like, and wished I had a photo to bring the blurred lines up. After a bit my mind went back to 1942 again and the meeting I had with him just before I went into the Navy. He had just thrown up his scientific job and was trying to get posted into the Commandos—a target he never made. I remember he seemed pretty elated at the time, like someone who has just got a load off his back—but also exasperated because some of his friends, knowing nothing of the scientific stuff he'd been working on, looked on his decision to go and fight as a patriotic act. He was young, twenty-eight, and so they thought he'd nobly decided that he wouldn't accept the safety of the back-room boy any longer. I remember him saying to me: "Well, yes, of course, I'm patriotic. I'm loyal to king and country and the rest. In any case, who could help but be, with the enemy what they are? But if anything this is an act of unpatriotism—to the group —because it's an act of loyalty to the individual—myself —and what I believe in. God knows it's not a ‘gesture’, it's not brave, it's not in the very least self-sacrificing, and any attempt to label it as such is drum-thumping crazy. Nor is it noble or a ‘gesture’ for the opposite reason. I'm neither a better nor a worse man because of it. I am what I was before. If a person doesn't know his own mind and his own conscience, he doesn't know anything at all."

I wondered if Grevil had so surely known his own mind in those last minutes of his life in Amsterdam.

Something Count Louis Joachim had said at our meeting kept recurring, but I couldn't get it right. Then suddenly I remembered. "Always he was one to set himself the almost impossible task. How would he, I wonder, tolerate failure from whatever source it came? The ordinary person does not risk as much to begin or feel as much to finish. Whereas the man of high ideas sometimes has not the spiritual ambiguity to compromise. He cannot or he will not. They must conquer or die who have no retreat."

Had Louis Joachim understood Grevil better than any of us, after all?

While I was wondering, I heard the man who—whatever the full explanation—was directly responsible for Grevil's death come into the room next to mine.

Seeing him standing in my own doorway a couple of minutes later you could forget for a minute or two he was not at heart a sailor; the blue jersey, the quick-footed easy standing, the subdued air of being used to command; you could forget it until you saw the tight-skinned pallor of a face that never seemed to catch the sun, the long elegant cheek-bones that would have pleased a twelfth-dynasty Egyptian, the handsome wild eyes. He'd been drinking, and for once it showed in his eyes.

"Well?" he said.

"You've been out late," I said. "Had a good day?"

"Fairish. I didn't really expect you till to-morrow. What's the news, good or bad?"

I stared into his eyes. It was a good effort on his part, and I could tell the interest was pretended only because it was overdone. "I don't know which you'd call it."

Perhaps something in my own voice wasn't as easy as usual. He went to the french window and began to light a cigar.

"They've found somebody else who saw Grevil jump into the canal. It's genuine enough : I met the witness. That was the chief item. Then there was some story about dope smuggling." I went on to tell him the details. I thought, the longer I can speak the truth to him the longer I'll be able to keep up the pretence.

He said when I'd finished : "So—he did do it after all. . . ."

"Yes. My—our hunch was wrong."

He threw his match away, stood with his hands in his pockets for a minute or so. His shoulders were broad in the doorway. I watched him and waited.

He said : "What do you feel about it?"

"Blind angry."

"Who with?"

"Chiefly myself. I've been clinging to something as to an absolute article of faith. Well, that's gone up the chimney. It seems to me that if Grevil wasn't murdered, there isn't much worth-while left to discover."

"So what are you going to do?"

"Drop the whole thing. It's *finished*, Martin. Done with. Over."

He turned. "Some feelings go sour on you, go rotten if you plug them too long."

"Help me finish this bottle."

He shook his head tautly. "Are you going to give up the search for Buckingham?"

"What chance is there of finding him? Next to none."

"You've been up to the Villa Atrani?"

"Yes. They say Leonie has left for Rome."

"She went yesterday. I didn't know about it until she had gone. I couldn't have stopped her but I might have followed her." He looked at the end of his cigar, his mouth pulled down, apparently bitter. "I doubt if we shall see her again."

"You think she's gone to join Buckingham?"

". . . Yes."

I drank some more wine. He stood irresolutely in the middle of the room.

"I'm *sorry* about Grevil," he said abruptly. "Damned sorry. You know that. Because I know how much it meant to you."

Perhaps it was what he had drunk, but again it seemed he was overplaying his hand. The sham sympathy was like poison to me."

I said: "What have you been doing to-day? Catch any decent fish?"

"I gave most of the catch to the boatman and saved just a few of the best for the *signora* downstairs. We shall get it for breakfast, don't worry."

"Have you been out all day?"

"Since about eleven. There seemed nothing else to do, since I was wasting your money and time. About Grevil——"

"I was thinking of taking a boat to-morrow. What did you do for food all that time?"

He hesitated a second. "Oh, we landed at Amalfi. I had a meal there and then walked about a bit. It's pleasant enough. Have you been?"

"Yes," I said, my skin prickling. Because at that moment looking at him and seeing something in his face, I knew with absolute certaintly that he had spent the day with Leonie. I knew it just as if he had told me, and I knew that Leonie had gone back to him.

After he'd left, I went back and sat on the bed. Some ash from his cigar made a white pyramid in the ash-tray. The smell of the smoke still hung in the room. I went and tipped the ash out into the garden. I came back and lit a cigarette. My hands weren't quite steady. I knew now what I was going to do.

I slid out of the room and went down the passage, and so to the foyer of the hotel. There was a telephone box in the corner. I called the Villa Atrani. I wasn't too late. Sanbergh was still there.

I said: "I'm very sorry to trouble you at this time, but do you remember offering to lend me your outboard motor-boat if I ever wanted it?"

"Of course. When would you like it?"

"To-morrow perhaps—to-morrow morning. I'd like to have a day's fishing. That's if you're not using it yourself."

"It exists for the convenience of my friends. Ernesto will be on the yacht. If you should be there before me in the morning tell him you have my permission."

"Thank you very much. . . . I hope to catch at least one fish."

"That's not very ambitious."

"It could be."

There was a pause. "Well, that's your business, isn't it?"

"Thank you for being so incurious."

"I'm not incurious . . . only discreet. Oh, I mentioned the picture to da Cossa when he came in to-night."

"Yes?"

"I think I have a stick and shall use it carefully. It will give me great pleasure."

"Good luck."

"Good luck to you," he said.

I went back to my room and dressed again in a sweater and a pair of denim slacks and old tennis shoes. Then I sat and waited until his light clicked out. After that I gave him half an hour.

It wasn't necessary to go out by the stairs again. The other morning when going to the Grotto I'd simply shinned over the balcony and made a way out through the forecourt. I did the same to-night.

It was nearly two when I got down to the Piccola Marina, and the moon had set, but there was enough light to see the yacht riding at anchor in the bay. I'd been prepared for a swim but it was not necessary. The little boat was moored alongside the stone quay and was apparently open for anyone to steal. As Mme Weber said, that wasn't the sort of crime they went in for on Capri.

There was no light on the yacht, and it took only ten minutes to check things up and do what I wanted to do.

Then I went home to bed. I didn't sleep well, but at least I dozed fitfully through the rest of the night and don't remember having a single nightmare. Perhaps the nightmares were reserving themselves for the coming day.

Chapter Eighteen

We had breakfast together on his balcony. He seemed in a strange mood, over-taut but quiet, his eyes shadowed.

When we had nearly finished I said: " Sanbergh has offered me his motor-boat for to-day. I think I shall see if I can get ashore on the outer Faraglioni."

" It's only another rock, isn't it?"

" Well, there's this tale about the blue lizards."

" Any proprietary brand of Scotch would give a better yield."

I said: "Well, we've nothing else to do until we decide to go home, and I don't propose to do that for a day or two in case Leonie does return. Coming?"

He ate in silence for a minute, staring rather blankly at the blue line of the sea. It was a perfect day but hazy. " I don't think so, Philip."

"What's the matter?"

"Matter? Nothing."

"You seem quiet."

"I'm all right."

"You feel you've wasted your time?"

"No, why should I?"

I said: "I don't feel excessively sunny myself."

"I know that, Philip. I know how you feel."

Do you? I thought.

In the end I persuaded him to come, and we went down to the beach about eleven, taking sandwiches in case we wanted to stay out. Sanbergh wasn't down, but he'd been there and Ernesto knew all about the boat. I started up the engine and we puttered slowly away from the towering cliffs. From the beach Jane waved an exhausted hand.

It was unusually hot for the time of year, and the fog still hung about in a peculiar way, like steam that had lost the kettle. It would be without movement for a bit, and then unexpectedly a patch of it would drift across to another part of the sea or coast. I remember there was a speed-boat out carving a great white wound in the sea, and the man driving it seemed to take a special delight in roaring his way into a cloud of fog and suddenly shooting out at the other side. I thought it might be hard luck for anyone in a rowing-boat who happened to get in his way in the fog. A good distance out there were a few fishing-boats, and beyond that two coasting vessels leaving the Bay.

Martin sat in the bows in a blue T-shirt and a pair of linen trousers. He'd suggested taking charge of the motor, but I said that was my job. He didn't have much to say, but began at once unravelling a fishing-line he found in the bottom of the boat, frowning occasionally when the smoke from his cigarette drifted into his eyes.

After a time he raised his eyes and said: "You're taking a wide course for those rocks."

" I'm not making for them yet. We've all day."

He said : " You're the skipper."

The engine was sputtering a bit, and I turned and tinkered with it. I didn't want anything to go wrong with that.

" It was queer Leonie going off suddenly," I said.

" Was it? I think we should have expected it."

" You said last night you thought she'd gone to join Buckingham."

" I thought it likely."

" Yet she left Holland apparently to get away from him."

" Did she tell you that?"

" The letter that she left behind proves it."

He drew at an end of the twine, pulling a loop out. " Perhaps women don't ever get men like Buckingham quite out of their system."

" I've often wondered about that," I said.

" About what?"

" Why so many women make fools of themselves over cheats and rogues."

" Because what you call evil is always more attractive than good."

We purred farther out into the bay. I didn't look back, but could just see the rocks out of the corner of my eye. It was going to be a point of nice judgment.

I said : " I've been thinking some more about Grevil."

" God, I thought we'd talked ourselves out. What more is there to say?"

" I couldn't see, if he was innocent, why he should stand in the way of the police when they came to his hotel. It argued foreknowledge. But now I don't think that. I think when the police came, all sorts of bits of evidence probably came up from the back of his mind —perhaps something odd in Buckingham's behaviour in the matter of the crates, whisperings in Java or between officials at the airport—all the bits came together and he suddenly realised what was in the packing-case along with his own specimens. So on the impulse of the moment he tried to cover up for Buckingham, not condoning what he'd done but trying to save him from arrest because of their friendship, and not at first thinking of himself at all."

"You've got a good imagination."

"It's not all imagination. Did you know Grevil kept a diary?"

He scratched his arm, stared at the place, and took all the time in the world. "No."

"It wasn't a proper diary—just notes on his work, but he got so preoccupied with this man . . . It helps to piece things together. I'm sure Grevil saw Buckingham as a quite exceptional person who'd somehow got on the wrong track. When he found out how he'd been let down he decided he didn't care, he'd still go on protecting the fellow out of friendship, and out of a deep sense of loyalty and trust."

"You seem to know all about it."

"Not all. I don't know what happened after the police had left Grevil. I suspect that Buckingham must have got wind of their visit somehow—he probably watched the hotel until they left and then phoned from a local call-box to see what had happened. He would probably find Grevil feeling pretty furious, and he would arrange to meet him at the bridge in De Walletjes that evening. After their meeting there, realising how deeply he was involved himself and how much he'd been cheated and played for a sucker by Buckingham, Grevil found he couldn't face the situation and committed suicide."

Martin flung down the fishing-line. "*Why?*" he said savagely.

"What d'you mean?"

"I mean, *why?* Is there anything you've told me to provide *one valid motive* for jumping in a canal?"

I stared at him. He'd taken out another cigarette and was lighting it from the last one, which was barely half done.

I said: "It's a motive of a sort. The man who flies high has farthest to fall. Suicide at best is an act of unreason."

He threw the half-used cigarette away, watched it drift towards me. "That's right, tell me your brother was a religious fanatic without a spark of humour or a sense of proportion. A Saint Theresa in khaki shorts and sun-blinkers. A Saint John of the Cross persecuted by nobody but himself. Pity we didn't realise that before. It would have saved a lot of trouble."

I said: "I don't see what you have to whine about. It saved you a hell of a lot of trouble when he jumped in the canal."

He slowly bent the new cigarette until it snapped. The muscles of his arm rippled as he threw the white paper and the crumpled tobacco after the first. There wasn't much obvious change in his face except that the bones seemed to become sharper, his temples more hallowed.

He said: "When did you know?"

"Pangkal's letter on Tuesday."

"Before that——"

"Oh, something. A hunch. No more."

"When?"

"At the beginning. That tin of cigars you had on the table in England. El Toro."

"Why?"

"They're made by Claasen of Hapert. They're the brand Grevil always smoked when he could get them. Did he give you them?"

"Yes."

"You can't get them in England anywhere."

He glanced at the land, at me, at the glittering empty sea. He was sizing everything up. "You were surprised when I agreed to come to Holland, then?"

"I thought if you were mixed up in it in some way you

207

might be afraid of what I should discover. But now, from that angle, I see you'd nothing to fear."

He stared at me grimly. "Nothing at all."

"Then why did you come?"

"Does it matter?"

"It was to trace Leonie, wasn't it."

He shrugged. "She'd disappeared without a word—or apparently without a word. I didn't know what had become of her. When I got to England I went to see her mother, but she wouldn't tell me where she was."

"You left Amsterdam a day too soon. That was careless."

"When I knew there was a man coming from Java, I knew it was time to leave. And then—after the brush with Jodenbree—I was afraid of him informing."

We sat there not speaking in the hot sun. The speed-boat had got tired of its game and had disappeared towards Naples. We watched each other with careful hatred.

I said: "That farce you played at De Walletjes put me off. I thought then that my hunch was wrong."

"What farce?"

"What you call your brush with Jodenbree."

"Ask him if he felt it was a farce!"

"Then why did you do what you did?"

"You wouldn't understand if I told you."

"Suppose you try."

"Some other time."

"There won't be another time."

I had changed course so that we were making a slow arc back towards the island. A smear of fog lay right in our path. He turned his head because the island was in my view now and out of his. He said with a sudden taut movement: "If you've got some plan, Philip, drop it now."

I said: "When I invited you to Capri, that put me off too. I thought if you were Buckingham and I could confront Leonie with you, the shock would be certain to make her give it away. But it didn't. I don't know how it didn't."

"I wired her I was coming, as soon as I got the address from you—at Naples airport."

There was a pause.

I said: "Now that we're out in the open, now there's nothing more to hide, what happened at your last meeting with Grevil?"

He hesitated, looking me over. I thought he was going to refuse; but perhaps he reasoned that the longer he could keep me talking. . . .

"We had a set-to on the bridge. He accused me of getting him into the mess and told me I must get him out of it. I said how could I? I'd hoped all along to get away with the whole dreary business of the dope-running without him knowing—would have done with any luck at all. I tried all ways to come at that case in his bedroom, but he didn't give me one single chance. I think I could have got the stuff and delivered it to Jodenbree before the police moved. The afternoon they did move I'd at last persuaded Leonie to get Grevil out without me. That was to have been the arrangement, but it went awry. . . . Well, it *went* awry. I told Grevil that. I told him he'd no reason to be surprised that I was making use of him. I'd never pretended to him for an instant about my own character or my own philosophy of life. If he cared to build up some elaborate make-believe system of his own to explain it and then tried to fit it on to me for his own pleasure, it wasn't my responsibility if the thing fell off at the first test. If he was let down, he had only himself to blame!"

The fog patch was much nearer. "And what did he say to that?"

"What you might expect. That it was a choice I had to make—something of that sort—a challenge to meet on my own. I told him I'd have none of it and left him there."

"Then he could be sure."

"Sure of what?"

"That you wouldn't perhaps change your mind and go to the police."

"Oh yes. I left him in no doubt. The moral issues were his, not mine. I told him he was free to do what he pleased about them. Let him go to the police if it pleased him, and maybe they'd believe him after all. Or if he didn't want to do that, he was always talking about principles and the virtues of self-sacrifice and giving up the best for others. Well, here was a chance to show there was something in it. The challenge existed for him as well as for me. If there was anything in this stuff about ' greater love hath no man ', then this was the opportunity to prove it!"

I stared at Martin. "If Grevil got what he asked for you won't kick, I suppose, if you get the same?"

He knew he was in for trouble. He'd been in too many tight corners before, and as the wisps of fog closed round us he knew it was coming now.

"No," I said, as his eyes travelled over me. "I've got no gun, no knife. You can't hang for Grevil. After all, it wasn't your fault, was it? Well, this won't be my fault either."

He sat and watched me with that hint of delicacy in his face strangely heightened. It was as if the closeness of danger refined his senses.

As the sun went in I said: "Rats swim. You swim, you bastard, as Grevil never had the heart to."

I reached down and pulled the bung out and threw it away over the sea. As he came at me I lurched to the edge of the boat, kicked at his clutching fingers and jumped into the water.

When I came up we were well into the fog. The boat was still afloat but settling quickly. He was aboard and trying to wrench the outboard motor off to lighten the weight. It wouldn't budge. I'd seen to that last night. I clutched at the bows and half hauled myself in. My weight rocked the boat as I scrambled aboard, and he turned to ward me off, but the boat was foundering under us. I dived off again as he lost his balance and fell forward. When I came up he too was in the water. The fog was only thin and you could see a corner of the island through it; it was blowing over us. The boat went down quickly. It should have done, because there were heavy stones under the stern-sheets. It would be a long swim home.

I swam towards him, dived, opened my eyes, saw him just above. I grabbed one of his legs, began to drag down. It was hard to avoid his other kicking leg. I held on till no breath any longer, then let go and surfaced. Eyes smarting, I gulped at the air. He came up a few seconds later. He saw me but didn't attack. Instead he headed off for the island. I swam after him.

We were out of the fog before I caught up. I dived again. But this time he was fighting. He curled round in the water with exaggeratedly laboured movements, reached his hands to my throat. Before he could grip I slid away, managed to get above him. With my foot I kicked him on the back of the head as I swam up.

He was late surfacing this time, and coughing. He swam quite near to me and our eyes met. He didn't say a word, but again turned away, began to make for the shore. For a bit I kept my distance. Once or twice he looked back, knowing I was behind. The island was still a long way.

I dived and got a hand round each of his ankles. He kicked with a slow-motion frenzy, but I held on in bitter obstinacy. We went down. Again he doubled up; this time he got his hands under my chin. He was pressing my head back. Mustn't let go. This was how Grevil had died. Water in the mouth, in the lungs, in the head, voluntarily giving up his life. Water in the brain. Clean water here, but foul and lethal to the human heart.

Martin Coxon was going with me. Going together. Wasn't as intended. A life for a life. Good Old Testament ethics. Not two lives for one, that neither ethical nor common sense.

I loosed his ankles and at once he gave up his grip of my neck. His face for a few seconds was close mine as I swam up. Far gone. Soon he would be floating lifeless.

I surfaced, but it came late. Water and air breathed together, I coughed and retched, knew just enough to keep afloat, to keep buoyancy. For a few seconds I was almost out. The sun had gone in again, the noise of the water was shouting, the fog inside me a part of exhaustion and break up.

His hands got me. I'd thought I'd done for him, but he had the last reserves of strength. I tried to fight, but he was too strong. In this last attack he seemed to speak with several voices. Then something was hooked under my arms and I was hauled out of the water. The sun came from behind the shadow of a sail as I was lifted on deck. . . .

A fishing-boat and a new-landed fish. I gasped and lay flat in the sun. A man was bending over me talking Italian, but the chief centre of interest had shifted. Two others were leaning over the stern chattering like a sub-machine gun to someone in the sea. Then the one man moved away, and I lay there and listened with intense bitterness to Martin Coxon being rescued.

His shadow blackened the deck, and he was slumped down near me. Companion in distress. They'd done a good job, these Italian fishermen. Seeing me stirring they began to shoot questions at me. It took a long time, but then I realised they were asking if there'd been any others in our boat. When I shook my head they seemed satisfied to let me recover in my own time while they worked on Coxon.

He was really out and a bad colour. I thought for a bit that the job was done and that this interference was too late. But one of them understood artificial respiration, and in about five minutes he began to come round. Then one of them ducked into the tiny cabin and came out with two cups and a *fiasco* of Chianti. Martin couldn't drink it at first, but I had some and it made me feel better. Better in health, that was.

One of the Italians, a fat little man who looked like the boss, squatted on his haunches beside me and asked a question in labial Italian. When I shook my head he thought it over and pointed to himself and made a circle to include his ship. "Salerno."

I nodded that I understood. Then he pointed at me. "Capri?"

I hesitated. Coxon was recovering. We couldn't go back from here. We had to go on.

The little man tried again. "Sorrento?"

"No," I said on the impulse. "Amalfi."

He showed his gold eye-tooth in a beaming grin —perhaps because I'd understood, perhaps because that was on his way home. He called to the helmsman, and it sounded as if they were cheerfully speculating on whose boat it was we'd lost with our clumsy seamanship.

The strength was coming back quickly. My shirt and trousers were drying in the scorching sun. Underneath Coxon was a dark stain of damp like blood, and his sandals were steaming on his feet. They had brought him into a sitting position, but I couldn't yet see his face. I was interested to see his face. Then I heard his voice for the first time. He evidently knew some Italian.

It's queer when you've got to know a person pretty well and then suddenly tried to kill him—and have narrowly failed and now must meet him again; there's no precedent in your affairs to go by, no euphemisms to hide behind. The swords have been out. Nor in this case had violence and passion cleared the air. None of the enmity had been split; the feud between us wasn't of that kind. Even if the past had been forgivable, there would have been the

future. Even if there had not been Grevil between u.
there would still have been Leonie. That was how I fel:
I knew he felt the same.

I thought he felt the same. But when I saw his face
wasn't sure any longer.

Chapter Nineteen

He said: "I want—to talk to you."

I shifted round so that I could see him better. Hi:
lips were putty-coloured.

He said: "When you want to kill someone—it's alway
a mistake to fight by the rules."

I said: "Never worry. I'll try again."

He wiped his mouth with the back of his forearm
There were two Italians squatting beside me, but the
didn't seem to understand any English.

He said: "Try again. . . . Maybe. But you can't ye
—so I'll tell you something, as you've got this mania t
know."

"I think I know enough."

"Not quite." He swallowed and lay back for
minute not speaking. Then he shifted and tried to si
up. One of the Italians moved to help him. Marti
nodded and vee-ed back his lank hair. "I wanted to sa
this before you sank the boat, I wanted to put straigh
one or two ideas you'd got in your head about Grevil an
me. You think I made use of him. Well, so I did. Yo
think I let him down. Well, so I did. That's all i
keeping. But if you think I thought nothing about him
then you're not even using the right language. I felt mor
for him, you *fool*, than I've ever felt for an other perso
in my life, or am likely to do again—certainly for any othe
man. And I'm not a homo—perhaps even you will coun
me out on that."

He shut his eyes. The little skipper went past and beamed at us. He was as proud as if he'd made a record catch. Perhaps he looked at it that way.

I said to Martin: "What are you trying to say?"

"Simply this. That we met, Grevil and I, and stewed together in that damned hot-house for two months, the only white men in miles. At first I'd got to; it was the only chance I saw of getting the opium home. But after a bit I *wanted* to. We were spending our days looking for another example of *pithecanthropus erectus*. We began that way. But we ended putting in more time on the archæology of our own final causes. And not merely in Aristotle's sense. It was—do you understand what I'm trying to say?"

I said: "I might if I was prepared to believe it."

He stayed silent, and I wasn't sure if he'd even heard.

"He was the ablest man I've ever met. He was different and his brain was different. He was clever as hell. We talked—yes, we talked—night after night, any subject on earth. We sharpened our brains on each other—raised argument to a new pitch that I didn't know existed before. Perhaps he didn't either. You know the sort of kick you can get in higher mathematics, mounting one peak on another. You know the stimulus of reaching for something bigger than you can ever grasp. . . ."

The sail flapped over our heads as some straying breeze took it, and the timbers of the boat creaked. We were nearer the mainland.

"That's something I've—missed ever since. . . . Of course we quarrelled too. His way of looking at things was the dead opposite of mine. But you can respect a fighter. And after a time that sort of thing can bring you together. The harder a man hits, the better you know his quality and understand him. There's an *intimacy* in battle. Even when you quarrel with the things he stands for you can acknowledge the way he stands for them. He was unselfish and—and uncorrupt. . . ."

I said: "You thought so much of him that you let him down, cheated him, left him to make his own way out of the mess you'd landed him in. Is that it?"

He fumbled in his pocket, took out a sodden packet of cigarettes, stared at it with a sharp contraction of the eyebrows. "I don't claim any virtues, but I claim consistency. Strange, isn't it, in your nice little pigeon-holed Jekyll and Hyde? Because I *was* consistent, I let him down. So what? I've *told* you, I never deceived him for a second about what I thought or believed. . . . That opium was worth a fortune. I'd sunk every penny; and nearly my throat cut as well. Are you suggesting I should have tipped it in the nearest river?"

"Yes."

"And with it the opinions about everything that I've had all my life, eh? Should I have gone to him and said, 'My dear Grevil, I have been redeemed by the soul of a good man!'"

Although he'd been speaking quietly he threw the packet of cigarettes out over the sea with a furious gesture of recovering strength. His fingers were trembling.

I said: "So now you're telling me that to score a theoretical point over him—"

"Theoretical point be damned! Why deny sincerity to my opinions because they happen to differ from yours. . . ."

"Well, then, because you wouldn't give way to yourself, you let this man you'd come to think more of than anyone else you've ever met—that's right isn't it?—you let this man carry the can for your own nasty little crime and left him to commit suicide in a back-street canal."

"I left him in a back street! That was all. We'd had a set-to, as I told you. I was flaming angry because the whole scheme had come crashing, and I felt if he'd done *one single* thing to help, we should have put it through. *And* I was bloody angry because he seemed to expect a self-sacrifice that I wasn't even prepared to consider. Why should I! I left him there and made my way back to England—by motor-boat as it happened. It wasn't till two days later that I knew he was dead. I didn't believe for a *second* that he had committed suicide. I felt sure Jodenbree was at the bottom of it—Jodenbree or one of his lot. I didn't believe any intelligent man could be such a *fool.* . . ."

The Italians had drifted away from us. They probably thought we were quarrelling over the sunken boat. One was standing staring at the mainland.

Martin said again in a voice hardly above his breath: "I didn't believe any man could be such a fool. Even up to yesterday. . . ."

"You mean you thought you could shift the blame."

"I thought I could make sense out of it. Does it seem sense to you, even now? Why d'you suppose I took the risk of going back with you to Holland in the first place? Why d'you suppose I laid myself open to being found out by you? Because of Leonie? She was a side-issue. I'd have found her in time. Why d'you suppose I encouraged you to go on when you looked as if you might give up? Because we *both* wanted to prove the same thing—because we both believed or wanted to believe the same thing. Isn't that so?" He sat up, propping himself against the crate behind, whispered: "It was a challenge, he said. God Almighty, what an *attitude* to take up! His suicide doesn't *prove* or *justify* anything—not a thing. It only *wastes* something, throws it away for a gesture, throws it away. That's what I can't get over. He threw his life away."

He was so bitter that for a minute or two I was convinced. Nobody could be so bitter who didn't care. It seemed to me for that moment that the antagonism was gone from between us. We'd had a common aim—now we shared a common defeat.

After a time I said: "Maybe I can see some sort of twisted sense in it."

217

"For God's sake, don't tell me you think it was a good thing to do."

"No. . . . But I'm trying hard to put myself in his place. Perhaps he found or thought he found there was some truth in what you said, that the finger was on him as well as on you. Perhaps it was a personal choice. I don't know. That's the way you put it to him, wasn't it? Greater love hath no man . . .

"Hell, I was *angry*, we were quarrelling; people don't always measure up their words!"

"No, but you did say it; and perhaps he suddenly thought, that's right on my doorstep, what am I going to do about it, because however much he's let me down this man is my friend? We've been arguing for weeks on just these issues. What am I going to *do*?"

"Did he think he was saving me by what he did? Why on earth——"

"I couldn't understand Grevil, with the beliefs that he held, taking his own life. Now I'm coming to see that it was just those beliefs—and you—which put him on the spot. To a Christian, suicide is the worst failure, isn't it? But where does suicide end and self-sacrifice begin? They can be almost contradictory. What about that fellow, Oates wasn't it, who crawled out of the tent on Scott's last expedition? What would you call the thing he did?"

There was a long silence. Martin Coxon said: "Yes, sometimes you're so much like Grevil. . . . It might be him talking—and his damned habit of making a moral issue of everything. Perhaps you'll tell me what it's all supposed to mean to me. If it was supposed to be a sacrifice on my behalf, what was it supposed to save me from? Arrest and imprisonment? I could have got clear of that without his help. Being wanted by the police? I already was wanted—under that name. No, instead of that he's burdened me, or tried to burden me with

—with this. . . . It was an *insufferable* thing to do. Why should I carry that with me all my life!"

"You haven't got to," I said. "You can sneer it off. It all depends on whether his estimate of you was the right one."

Unnoticed we'd been coming inshore, and I recognised the towering cliffs behind Amalfi. As we ran in under them the skipper came across to us and said something to Martin. Martin turned sharply to me.

"Why did you tell them we came from Amalfi?"

"Because I didn't want to go back—yet."

"Why?"

"Nothing's finished between us, is it? I'm sorry to disillusion you."

He stared at me, his face fine-drawn as a fencer's. Then he was helped to his feet. I got up on my own. It was siesta time, and there was nobody about on the quay except two men sleeping in the shade of a wall. There was hardly anybody to be seen anywhere, but a bus palpitated, just about to start, on the sea front.

I shook hands with the skipper, thanking him in a few halting words for the favour of his rescue. He beamed and patted my shoulder. Coxon said nothing at all.

As we came right in and it was almost time to land, he turned to me and said: "These men come from Salerno. Why have you chosen Amalfi?"

I said: "Isn't this where Leonie is?"

Chapter Twenty

Weak and unsteady, we stood together on the quay like rescued comrades, and watched the fishing-boat luff up into that faint air which did duty for a breeze and make off under her own diesel for the southern headland of the bay. I never knew the skipper's name, and if I read the name of his boat I have forgotten it. We stood together alone, Martin Coxon and I, still damp in the heat of the afternoon sun.

He said: "This thing has gone far enough between us."

"It's gone too far. That's why it can't stop here."

He started at me. "What d'you propose to do—fight it out with bare nails on the quay?"

"No . . . I'm going up to find Leonie."

"*Look*," he said. "Leave her out of this. Leave Leonie out of it. She had nothing whatever to do with Grevil."

"No, but she's had something to do with me."

"You fancy she had, but it meant *nothing*. She's come back to me. I warn you to keep out."

I ran a hand through my hair, trying to flatten it, took out my handkerchief and squeezed it but it was already dry. As I turned away he said: "Where are you going?"

"I've told you."

"And what good will it do you if you find her?"

I said: "You're free to catch that bus if you want to, Martin. I can't stop you. You're free to go. But you've something to gain by following me, because as long as I'm alive you'll be a wanted man."

I walked off along to the end of the quay and past the bus and turned into the centre of the town, past the cathedral and up the narrow street where Leonie had bought the scarf. I found I could only just keep steady on my feet. I didn't turn to see if he was following.

The shop where she'd bought the scarf was shut, along with all the others, but two of the older children were playing with a kitten on the doorstep and they recognised me. I knew just enough Italian to say: "*Dove Poltano*", and then "*lento, lento*" as their replies flooded over me.

One of them knew a word or two of English, and in the end I understood. If I wanted to follow the motor-road I must go back along the sea front for a kilometre to the next village and turn sharp inland past a church with a clock tower; but if I did not mind the climb, then

I should continue up this street and follow the dried-up bed of the stream until I reached the second of two ruined mills, when I should see the main road above me to my right and could climb to it over the rough ground between.

I thanked them, and as I turned to go on Martin was standing at the end of the street watching me.

The street climbed sharply uphill and soon became a track, first flanked by orange groves and vines and then almost overgrown with rank weed, with a few broken-down cottages, and hens picking among the rubble. Then I saw the bed of the stream, pebbly and overgrown, winding ahead of the valley.

I stopped once but saw nothing more of him. The sun hammered down like a July day, and soon I was sweating as I climbed. It grew to be desolate, lonely country, and when I got to the first ruined mill there was no other house in sight. The sides of the valley had narrowed sharply, and it was now almost a ravine. Just then I didn't think much, because my mind was fixed on what I had to do and on the effort of doing it. By the time the second mill came in sight I was feeling very tired. I stopped once and waited in the hope of catching sight of Coxon, but he didn't come, so I went on.

I made a circuit of the second mill and looked about. Not a bird stirred in the bushes. Here and there, among the more familiar things, plants of cactus stood up like the listening ears of strange animals. The stream-bed wound on and up, but I'd been told. . . . And then I saw the road.

It was two or three hundred feet above me. The hillside climbed sharply and the green scrub was broken by sharp bluffs of rock. Evidently the boys scrambled up this way, for nearly all Italian children can climb like monkeys, but it wasn't exactly going to be an easy job.

I got about half-way, tacking a good bit to avoid the loose boulders and the denser thickets, and then I stopped to look down the valley. There was still no sign at all of

Martin. It looked as if he'd not taken up the challenge. Perhaps I'd been a fool to suppose that he would. And yet . . .

I turned to look up, and saw him watching me from the road above.

At first I thought he had found some even shorter cut than mine, but then I realised he had probably taken the Salerno bus as far as the foot of the hill and walked up the main road. So he had got ahead of me. Evidently he wanted to reach Leonie first.

As I went on I saw there was another reason. He had three or four big stones on the parapet wall beside him. They may have weighed about twenty pounds each. He called out: "Can you hear me?"

I didn't answer but went on climbing.

He said: "Go back, Philip. I've warned you. You're not coming up this way."

As I went on, it came to me at that odd moment to wish I still didn't feel something about Martin Coxon. It would have been ten times better if I could have gone about this cool and detached. But I couldn't. An old deep-rooted liking makes the disliking more bitter and more intense. If I hadn't muffed the struggle in the sea he would have been finished before the fishing-boat came up. If I could have felt no hatred now my hands wouldn't be fumbling over stone and rock.

As I got nearer I could see the sweat on his face. He said: "This is as far as you'll come, Philip."

We stared at each other. I still had about twenty feet to climb to the parapet. As I took another couple of steps he flung the first rock. I flattened myself in the undergrowth, and it flew wide over my head and crashed away down the hillside.

Lying there I looked to right and left. It might be possible to edge along and make the road a hundred yards down, but I supposed there was nothing to stop him following me. I took two more steps and another rock crashed past.

"The next one will finish you," he said.

I was of the same opinion and lay quiet for a few seconds. Where I was now I was partly sheltered, though with a bit of luck he might get my legs, which wasn't a nice thought.

I began to edge over on the new tack. He could probably see me, but I was still in semi-shelter. I made about ten yards of side progress this way and then raised my head, rather expecting him to have moved also. But I found I couldn't see more than a few feet of the parapet from here, and he wasn't to be seen in this limited area.

I went on, expecting a stone any time, and at last came to clear country where there was no shelter at all. He'd disappeared from the parapet and was nowhere to be seen. Neither were his remaining stones. I tried to consider it for a minute or two, not to get over-impetuous or in a sweat. There was still nearly twenty feet to go from here. If I waited to get my breath back and rushed it. . . . He might be waiting over the top ready to knock in my head, but it was a risk I was prepared to take.

I got my breath back, and then I gathered my strength and jumped up.

I got to the parapet unscathed and clawed my way shakily over it, ready for the worst.

The road was empty. I looked up at the overhanging cliff above the road and ahead to the next hairpin bend. It was unlike him to give up a position like that without making good use of it, but that apparently was just what he had done. All he had done was delay me five minutes. If there was a catch somewhere, I couldn't see it.

I made the next hairpin, but the road was climbing steeply and I couldn't get a clear view. It wasn't until I'd climbed for another five minutes that I briefly caught sight of him on ahead. He was walking quickly and had established a good lead. I tried to break into a trot but gave it up after a minute or two.

We were right out of the valley now, and the road had probably risen seven or eight hundred feet. In the distance the sea glimmered hazily, and all round were the mountains in knotted clusters like the muscles of an old giant. Beside the road the foliage was grey with dust, and here and there a crumbled wall stood to mark the site of a dead cottage. I wondered why people had gone, whether industry had moved or whether some pestilence had struck them a century ago.

When I saw him for the second time he had gained on me; he must have been almost trotting, and it showed his condition after being nearly drowned. I put on a spurt and tried to think of Grevil, because thinking of him seemed to feed the right fires; hatred curiously did not seem to come from that, but determination did and a greater detachment.

And so thinking, I came round a corner and found an inhabited house, and then another, and suddenly was in Poltano.

By now, a thousand feet below us, Amalfi might be moving into the afternoon shadow, but in the square of San Stefano the sun hammered down with all its midday heat. It was dusty and deserted except for a few pigeons pecking among the loose stones. A half-dozen plane trees drooped in the centre of the square and not a leaf moved on them. Two sides of the square were occupied by small houses, a third by the inevitable café and a few shops, and the fourth by the cathedral, a queer flat-faced church in black and white marble with a Campanile beside it and olive trees climbing steeply behind. In front of the cathedral a car was parked and three or four bicycles, the only sign that life had not left here as it had left the mills and the cottages below.

I looked at my watch and wondered because it was past siesta time. But the only things stirring were the swallows. They broke both the stillness and the silence. All round the cathedral dome and the Campanile they flew, darting and swerving and endlessly twittering, in no order or sequence, crossing and recrossing each other's flight scrawling swift meaningless lines over the slate sky. Martin Coxon had gone. He had been perhaps three minutes ahead of me, and had evidently made good use of the time. Number 15, Piazza San Stefano, Sanbergh had said. I walked round the square and saw 10—it would be on the other corner. It wasn't a detached villa as I'd expected but the corner house of the row, a narrow two-storied place with a balcony with some hibicus in pots. I went to the door and knocked sharply

There was no answer Only the hot sun and the dust and the silence. I knocked again and then tried the door. It opened. There were steps up and a door on this level. I chose the steps and was half-way when the door opened and an old woman in black looked out with a suspicious angry face.

"Signora Winter?" I said.

I got the expected gabble of Italian, but I did pick out the word *Duomo* and could easily understand the pointed trembling hand. "The man?" I said. "Signore Coxon. Where is the man?"

"Si, si, si, si." She nodded her head and pointed impatiently. If Coxon had in fact been here, this was the second disturbance she'd suffered in five minutes. The pointing hand began to wave up and down from the wrist indicating that she expected me to go.

I turned and walked across the square to the church. The noise of the swallows made the silence more intense, as the humming of bees will. A couple of pigeons edged cautiously away from my footsteps. I pushed open the door of the church and went in.

Chapter Twenty-one

I shall never forget going out of the dusty empty silent sunbaked square into the hum and light of a church full of people. It was like finding a dynamo in a desert. All the way from Amalfi I had only seen three people apart from Martin. There were half a dozen men standing by the door, and they turned to stare at me before looking back towards the altar. A funeral service was on.

Of course the church wasn't full, but it had that first look—there were probably fifty or sixty people in the centre aisle; until a minute ago I should not have thought there were sixty people in five miles. The coffin lay under a silk catafalque; there were more candles than people, and the yellow light threw a discreet sheen over the jewelled cross and the madonnas and the emblazened saints. The dull black of the family mourners pointed the contrast between earth and heaven.

It took me only a minute to pick out Leonie. Her fair head was alien among the dark ones. She was on the edge of the crowd, against a twisted rococo pillar; and Martin was beside her. They were both looking towards the door, and they had both seen me.

I began to edge my way towards them. It wasn't easy because the priest in his rich white robe was just then waving a censer over the coffin, and the people were kneeling and crossing themselves.

When she saw me coming towards them Leonie said something sharply to Martin, and he began to edge out of the crowd in the opposite direction. I think he pressed her hand before he went. After he'd slid out of the crowd, he moved away up the side aisle towards one of the unlighted lady chapels.

Although the Italian Church is tolerant of people moving around when a service is on, I got one or two black looks from the people I had to negotiate. She was edging her way out to meet me. She had moved to cut me off, in case I went straight after him.

We were still among people when I said: "I'm sorry. This is the wrong funeral. I arranged a much quieter one."

She stared into my eyes. "Martin told me. Thank God it didn't come off."

"Is that the way you feel about it?"

"It's the *only* way to feel. Philip, the Old Testament eye-for-an-eye can only do worse harm here. Please listen."

"While he gets away?"

"There's no way out that end. But even if there was. . . ."

Although we'd spoken in whispers the people about us were staring and frowning.

She said urgently: "Please listen, Philip. I want you to let him go freely. Revenge on Martin can do no good now. Nobody will ever know all the truth about Grevil's death, but it was not by Martin's wish nor choice that he died. Oh, I know what he did was about the lowest thing there could be—but they were two men living on different *levels*—of conduct, I mean. Your brother's attitude—his suicide—put what Martin did out of proportion, magnified it, made it something bigger than the contemptible trick that it was. . . ."

She broke off because the people had turned on us. I thought they were going to surround us with protests and waving hands, but then I saw that the service was over and the coffin was being carried to the door. We stood in silence to watch it until it had disappeared through the crimson curtains; then the people began to shuffle after it, pressing to get out. For a minute or so we were separated. My feeling for her, which had got smothered in the last hours, had flared up at sight of her again; but her trying to defend Martin, her quite obvious sympathy with him, her siding with him against me, turned it back on itself, made poison of it, so that her being that way got the reaction she most wanted to avoid, reanimating a purpose in me that had been half thrown off.

The crowd dwindled, like sand in the neck of an hourglass, fifty grains, twenty grains, and then the last was gone. The church was empty except for the priest snuffing the candles and myself—and Leonie standing out white in the darkening church—and somewhere Martin.

I moved up the side aisle. She came across to bar my way.

I said: "Keep out of this, Leonie."

"Stop it, Philip. You're—you're crazy."

"Yes," I said, "it's a family failing. I'm going to make the most of it."

As I pushed past her she wrenched at my arm. "You fool, that's just what it's *not*! There's never been a better-balanced person than you, Philip, nor a nicer one. Don't *let* this drive you to extremes. It isn't worth it—nothing is worth that."

The priest had put out the last candle. Evidently our voices had raised no particular alarm or interest in him, because he switched off the light above the altar and went out without even glancing at us.

The church was suddenly dark. It had become no longer a place for worship. Now it was empty, I noticed that the whole floor of the place sloped uphill towards the east. An extraordinary pulpit stood near the door, a thing with crouched lions supporting twisted columns and a stone chariot-like platform, tricked out with hideous gargoyles. More Assyrian in inspiration than Christian. So perhaps my impulses. Both came from the older things.

I heard Martin then. His footstep clattered against a stone step. It sounded as if he were at the extreme end of the church behind the high altar.

I pulled my arm free from Leonie's fingers. Probably if I'd looked at her then it would all have been different.

I went up the hill of the central nave.

At best it must have been a dark church, because there were hardly any windows high up for the sun to come through. But I think the place had just now come into the shadow of the steep slopes behind.

I said in a fairly loud voice: "Martin!"

He didn't answer. Near the main altar I went more slowly, sensing danger but not sure where it lay. So far as I knew he had no weapon—though weapons of a sort could be had in plenty in this church. The clip of a sandal on the stone floor told me that Leonie was following.

I saw him as I went round behind the altar. He was standing at the top of some steps which looked as if they might lead to a crypt. There were similar steps at the other side. In the half light I couldn't see his face properly, only the shadows that lay across it, and the dark sockets of his eyes. He had nothing in his hands.

He said: "Well, Philip. . . ."

"Well, Martin."

"Leonie thought she could turn you back. She over-estimated her influence."

I said: "Will you come outside or have we to finish it here?"

"I'm not going to fight you."

"I think you will."

"I've told you."

"It's too late for talking."

It seemed then to me that it was vitally important that I should give neither of them any more time. If I did I should be out-manœuvred, with the two of them against me. I went slowly up to Coxon.

As I got to him he stepped away from the threshold of the steps, suddenly came at me with both fists. It didn't surprise me but I took more on the face and head than I needed, watching for the foul or the villainous kick.

They didn't come. But he did, following up, I could see, to put me out in the first rush because his strength was half spent. Reeling, I went back against an effigy of St. Peter, and a chair slid screaming across the stone floor. There, against the railings, I shook myself and stood up to him and gave blow for blow, no gloves on this but bone against bone, like old fighters whom exhaustion has robbed of the last finesse.

Then I drove him away before me and we lurched against a table with candles on it; the candles leaned all askew and a bunch of them rolled chattering to the floor. He slid away as the table overset, and turned and stumbled down the steps to the crypt. Leonie cried out something to me as I went after him.

Not a crypt, but the tomb where the sacred relics of the patron saint were kept. A single blue point of light burned above the sarcophagus. Before I could reach him he had come to the ledge before the tomb—there were more candles, but on it also a tall wrought-iron candle-snuffer. He picked it up and turned. I stopped and we looked at each other.

There was blood on his face. The paleness was vividly stained. He looked like a wax saint come to miraculous liquefaction.

I walked towards him. He lifted the iron-snuffer. hesitated, took another step. With a sudden contemptuous gesture he flung the snuffer away; it clattered down upon the marble floor. He turned and walked away towards the other steps which led back into the church again.

I caught him, and we fell very heavily together. A sudden jerk up of the knee told me he could have fought that way if he'd wanted to. But now it was too late. I got him by the throat, and his own fingers weren't strong enough to break the grip. Then he looked at me and smiled slightly, and deliberately struggled no more.

I held on, but I had known instantly that I couldn't tighten my grip any more. At the last the mind has to direct the muscle, and the mind would not. It was not he who was cheating me by this last refusal to struggle —it was myself.

I let go suddenly, feeling my hands unclean, part guilty of an evil act. I stayed there for some seconds or minutes, I don't know which, because there was no breath left in me either and my heart was thumping in my ears.

"No," I said. "Your business . . . is to go on living."

I got up and began to shiver. I leaned against the wall of the crypt and shivered and shook, at first letting go in the complete reaction, and then struggling to stop it, struggling to get control. He lay on the steps where I'd left him. He wasn't moving yet.

The crypt began to go round, and I reeled up the steps, clutching at a slipping world. I got to the top and something in that small ascent was like climbing away from the Pit. Someone was saying something to me.

"No," I said to her, "I haven't killed him."

She covered her face in her hands. "Oh, thank God!"

"Yes," I said foolishly. "That's about it."

"You're hurt, Philip. . . . Let me——"

"No, I'm all right. . . ." I did for a second feel better. Only I wished the church wasn't tilting so much. In the increasing slant I saw her now clearly for the first time. I seemed to have been killing what I loved as well as what I hated.

"Dear Philip, I tried so hard——"

"Go down to him," I said. "I think he—needs some help. And—you're the person to give it him, aren't you?"

She looked at me slowly. "Yes. . . . I'm the person to give it him. He's my husband, you know."

Chapter Twenty-two

I don't remember much about the journey down, excep
for one bit of it. I suppose I must have left her then an
gone straight out of the church. I think she said somethin
else before I went, but I never knew what it was.

I do remember the shock, like another blow, to come ou
into the sun. The heat was going, but it seemed wrong tha
there was any light at all. And the swallows still darte
and wheeled and twittered, busy with a sky-writing n
one could read. There was something running down m
face and I thought it was sweat. I'd walked righ
through the empty dusty square and out of the villag
before something dripped on my hand and I saw it wa
blood.

I took out my handkerchief then and tried to close u
the gash that his knuckles had made. The people mus
still have been at the funeral, because I don't thin
I met anyone all the time I was doing this. I didn'
stop walking. It's the first and only time in my life I'v
known what it is to be punch-drunk. My legs carried on
all the time just about to fold up but never quite doin
that. Of course I wasn't only punch-drunk from Martin'
fists.

The thing I do remember was after I had been walkin
for a good bit I came to a piece of the road where a hairpi
bend skirted the edge of a precipice. The fall was probabl
a hundred feet, and at the bottom were a lot of loose whit
boulders like big skulls that had been bleached in the sun
I stopped there at last and leaned over the parapet an
thought very clearly about everything.

I thought, this is the lowest you'll ever be in your lif
—you've lost everything, Grevil and Leonie and all th
things you've come most to care about; you've failed i

everything you've set out to do, every single thing, and you've finished up by failing yourself. This is rock bottom. I looked over the precipice and thought, *this* is the time to take your own life—it no longer has the slightest attraction for you; indeed, far worse than that, it's a poison in the mouth that makes you want to escape. Well, here's the way. It's all laid on.

And I looked down again and thought, I really would at this second like to finish it off—but to do that there's not only got to be the thought, there has to be the impulse —and there just isn't any impulse, none at all. I could stand here for twenty-four hours and not even put my knee on the parapet. So perhaps that explodes *that*. I wasn't even going to be a failure in the grand style.

I remember smiling wryly to myself and thinking, perhaps there's more of Arnold in you and less of Grevil than you supposed. Perhaps this is why you never got to be a successful painter. Perhaps this is the advantage of being ordinary and commonplace and having both feet on the ground.

I went on then.

I suppose it took me best part of an hour to get down to the road to Amalfi, and then luck was with me, because a bus came along marked Sorrento and I put up my hand, and because I looked such a mess the driver stopped in astonishment and picked me up. The conductor helped me in through the mass of strap-hangers and someone gave me his seat, and I shook my head at the questions and just said "*accidente*" two or three times. Somebody wanted to pay my fare, but I found a crumpled thousand lire note in my pocket and booked all the way to Sorrento. From there I might be able to hire a boat.

I don't know how many miles it is to Sorrento, but it is by way of one of the most fantastic roads in Europe. It's as if the genius of all Italian road builders came to flower in it. It seems never to be more than six feet from a thousand-foot precipice and many of the hairpin bends are so acute that the bus has to stop and reverse to the edge of the cliff to get round. Now and then it swoops down into a bright-coloured fishing village, but soon it soars up again to the old heights.

Soon after I got into the bus I began to feel sick, and the swinging of the bus and the twisting panorama of sea and sky made the nausea worse. I didn't think of it then, but I'd eaten nothing that day except a roll and coffee for breakfast. Several times I thought I should have to stop the bus and get out, but somehow I stuck in my seat. After about ten minutes the conductor got some first-aid kit from a box at the front and insisted on pressing sticking-plaster on my cheek and dabbing something that stung on a bruise on my forehead and on my lip.

I knew now I'd been wrong to try again after the first attempt to kill Martin. That expenditure of spirit had been enough. The impulse to go on to the bitter end, provoked finally in the church, had sprung from the need to finish for ever with him and what he had done and the things he stood for. But it had been doomed and damned from the start.

I tried my best not to think of Leonie and the whole bitter mess-up of her marriage, but it didn't work. I saw the story she'd told me with different eyes now. It made sense of so much more of their behaviour, nonsense of mine. Marriage of course wasn't sacrosanct, but it was obvious that she still loved him in spite of his faults . . .

I don't remember what time it was when we got to Sorrento, but the sun hadn't quite set, because the cliffs looked as yellow as butter in the late sunlight. The bus stops near the quay, and I walked unsteadily along the long stone pier, feeling pretty weak and light-headed but mercifully free from the immediate need to be sick. There were a few small boats about and a group of men gossiping by the seats, but what at once took my attention was a yacht in the harbour with three men on it still in bathing costumes, and two of them were running up a sail. I'd seen this yacht in the harbour at the Marina Grande, so I walked as quickly as I could round to where I was within hailing distance and shouted to them.

They were Americans, all fairly young, and when I told them I'd had an accident and was stranded on the mainland they said, sure, we're off there ourselves in ten minutes, Ken'll come over for you in the dinghy.

I told them the best excuse I could think up, and one of them had a couple of bars of chocolate to spare, and somehow the intervening space of water was covered and by the time darkness had fallen I was standing in the funicular which mounts at about the speed of a water gauge from the port to the town of Capri.

In the dark I stared down at the harbour, which glimmered like a little Naples as we rose above it. The season was nearly in bud, and canned music floated up from a couple of quay-side taverns. Two old women with bundles murmured together close beside me, and in the next box-compartment a group of French tourists argued over the fish they had caught.

I thought of what Leonie had said about Martin and Grevil when I first met her in the church. I had brushed it aside with anger then, but now the argument cropped up again. Martin and Grevil had been two men living on different levels of conduct—wasn't that what she'd said? Was it true that Grevil's violent reaction to the way Martin had let him down had magnified it out of its true proportion—as it were, converted petty theft into grand larceny? Practised on a lesser man than Grevil, the mean betrayal of friendship—which, anyway, would never have occurred if things had gone right—would have had smaller consequences. Had his death, the whole rotten affair, been the bitter tragedy of a clash of two codes, of two different standards of life and behaviour? From the time of the discovery by the police, Martin Coxon had been struggling in waters too deep for him.

But for their friendship none of the rest would have followed. So it cut both ways, didn't it? If Grevil had been a lesser man, it couldn't have happened. If Martin had been a lesser man, it couldn't have happened. This was every bit as true.

To-day had made me understand far more about Martin than I had ever expected to. He was like an animal that had shaken out the barb of Grevil's death but carried the venom along with him. That was all borne out by what had happened to-day—the stones hurled too far away to hit me, the iron candle-snuffer thrown contemptuously on the floor. And he had fought fair with me all through, that was the queer thing. He had fought fair.

The central square seemed full of people as I pushed through it. Their voices murmured in the illuminated dark. There'd been some sort of a boat-load of new arrivals. I was held up at the entrance to the alley leading to the hotel, and people seemed to cross and re-cross so that there was no way through them. They were like an influx of new thoughts, trespassing on and confusing the old. Three men carrying loads of bricks, bowed down under their load waited patiently to get through. Some-one stared curiously at my face. Then we were in, plunging into the three-storey ravine that led to the hotel.

When I asked for my key there were a lot of exclamations and efforts of help, but I went straight up and stared at myself in a mirror, and I *was* a mess. I had some tea and cakes in my room, and when the boy brought them up he asked if Commander Coxon would be in for dinner. I said no. I wondered how often Martin left kit behind in hotel bedrooms. I didn't seem to care any longer. At least that much had gone out of me during the day.

I lay in a warm bath for about half an hour trying to let everything be soaked away, and after a bit it seemed to me that something did let go, something that had been at a stretch inside me ever since getting the first cable in San Francisco.

The telephone rang.

I waited a bit, hoping it would stop, but the thing went on and on. I stepped out of the bath, grabbed a towel and went into the bedroom.

"Hallo."

"Hallo." I waited again. It had been a man's voice, but now the line seemed dead. Probably someone had got the lines crossed at the switchboard. Then the voice came more clearly. "Philip Turner?"

"Yes?"

"Philip, this is Charles Sanbergh. I'm glad to know you're back."

"Er—yes. I'm back, I——"

"You remember Charlotte invited you to dinner?"

"Did she? No, I don't remember."

"Well, there's plenty of time. It's not until eight thirty. You can come, of course?"

The story I had ready didn't seem to work when it came to the point. "I'm sorry, no. But I shall have to have a word with you some time, Charles. It's about your boat——"

"Good. Then we can expect you in half an hour?"

I said: "I have to tell you that I lost your boat to-day. I think—I'm pretty certain I can arrange to pay for it in dollars—but it will put you out a great deal, I'm sure. I'm very sorry indeed."

There was a pause. "That's a pity. I'm sorry too. As you say, perhaps we can come to some arrangement."

Something in his voice. "You knew?"

"I don't think this is a thing to discuss over the telephone."

"No. . . . I'll come round in the morning."

"I shall be away in the morning."

I looked at the floor. Something, the tea or the warmth

or the rest, had put the ground back where it ought to be. I was still deadly tired, but I didn't want to miss the morning boat. "Perhaps later this evening I could slip round for a minute or two."

"Charlotte would specially like you to come to dinner. We have Langdon Williams here, and it is rather a special occasion. I think you promised to come."

Williams was the artist Charlotte had mentioned at our first meeting. If there was one thing I felt less like than light conversation about nothing, it was light conversation about art. "I'm afraid I'm rather a sight. I hurt my face."

"I'm sorry. But I think you should come. We counted on you to make even numbers."

The receiver crackled once or twice. "Oh . . . all right. Thank you very much."

When I put the phone down I went to the mirror again, cursing myself for being so weak-minded. The very last thing to-night. Yet what else could I do? I still owed Sanbergh a boat.

The sticking-plaster came off without more bloodshed, and luckily it wasn't iodine the bus conductor had used. But I still looked like a beaten middle-weight.

I began to dress.

And then at that point I realised I'd lost Leonie for good.

I think perhaps it was the telephone call that had done it. The phone ringing must have wakened some expectation that wasn't quite dead. I realised for the first time that it had to be dead. I realised for the first time how much had been going on inside me on the quiet. Somewhere hope had been plodding away.

I put on a clean shirt, and going for it saw Grevil's diary at the bottom of the case. I picked it up and turned it over in my hands. The pasteboard binding was cracked and coming to pieces, as if the extreme heat of the tropics had destroyed it. I felt at that moment as if I were saying good-bye to Grevil over again—and this time in some irrevocable way.

I tied my tie and combed my hair and put on a jacket and walked out of the hotel and thought: there were things I should have *said* to her, a different way I should have been; I was out of proportion; if I'd said to her . . . I should never have left her here pursuing that will-o'-the-wisp to Amsterdam. . . . I wonder why her passport was still under the name of Winter; probably she'd not bothered to get it changed and then getting his cable . . . why did I ever send for him . . . what did it matter whether he was Buckingham or Coxon. . . . I was crazy. . . . But it was done now and finished with. . . . In any case she was his, his all along. She had made that very clear. *She* had been the will-o'-the-wisp. I'd got to put it behind me . . . but if I'd said to her that night in the hall before I left for Amsterdam . . . I'd said the right things then. I should have gone on, gone on. But had she ever given me any reason to think. . . . Well, I had so thought; it hadn't been what she'd said but . . .

The walk down from Poltano was flower-strewn compared to the one I now made to the Villa Atrani.

By the time Macy and Gimbel were barking a greeting to me I wasn't feeling too good again on my feet and the outlook got even darker when I saw that all the usual gaggle were here: Castiglioni the big Neapolitan ship-owner; Mlle Henriot, and the awful woman who'd been at the other party in the toy hat. I remembered Langdon Williams as a shy man with hardly anything to say at the best of times, and he looked defensive in this company.

We had cocktails and talked. Sanbergh wasn't yet to be seen. Charlotte was sympathetic about my face, but I didn't get an inquisition from her, which made me think she too had an idea there'd been trouble. After a bit the woman with the hat, though she hadn't the hat on now, bore down and began to talk to me about the Kinsey report on the sexual behaviour of the Human Female. I'd thought she had her eye on me the other evening. I wasn't quite sure from the way she spoke now whether she thought I was a medical man, a psychiatrist, or just another male waiting to be shot to pieces to prove Kinsey wrong. I thought I ought to tell her about the blind, sub-human, infantile behaviour of the man she was talking to. I thought I ought to tell her that.

Charles Sanbergh was still not there when we went in to dinner.

You get to a stage sometimes, and I had got to it now, when you are hungry but can't eat, ache with tiredness but can't rest, and probably at such a time it's as good to be in company as out. Only it doesn't feel it. You wish you'd never come, and long to be able to do all the things you can't do but wouldn't enjoy if you could. I caught Charlotte Weber's eye on me several times. Jane Porringer was sitting next to me, and I don't think she found it easy going.

Then after we'd nearly got through the first course Mme Weber looked towards the door and said: " Ah, there you are, Charles. We had to start because everyone was famishin'." Then she beamed at me as if to say, you see, it was worth-while coming after all.

All the men had got up because Sanbergh had brought a lady with him. After a sudden hesitation she slipped into the empty seat opposite me and beside da Cossa. It was Leonie.

Chapter Twenty-three

She hadn't known I was there. I could tell that because of the sudden hesitation. She went a bit green and nearly turned away. I don't know when you're punch drunk

240

whether you can't feel the next shock; if so I wasn't, because I felt this all right. I should have been ploughed at any medical for D.A.H.

Then after a minute, after she said something to Charlotte and began to eat, I remember thinking rather stupidly that it was impossible that she should be here—or else all the stress and violence of this afternoon was a delusion or a trick of the sun.

I must have stared hard because when Berto came to take my plate I got in his way and knocked the fork off. Mme Weber was saying that Leonie was back only for the evening, and da Cossa, shifting his aim for a bit, began to ask, how was Rome? She dodged his questions as well as she could until Charlotte, looking irritated for once in her life, headed him off.

For the first time I glanced at Charles Sanbergh. He was dressed as usual like *Harper's* idea of what the well-found man should wear on a Riviera holiday, and he could just as easily have been either to a murder or to a Mass for all you could tell from his face.

I looked back at Leonie. Relieved of da Cossa's curiosity, she was sitting quite still in her high-collared turquoise silk frock, not even pretending to eat now. She had a look like an El Greco angel—fine drawn and slightly haggard.

A hand was touching my arm. I stared at Jane. "What? I'm sorry."

"Hamilton was asking if you would stay on the island much longer."

"I have to go to-morrow."

Da Cossa said with satisfaction: "The—er—portrait has not come on so well, eh?"

I didn't speak.

"I told you not to worry about it, dear boy," said Mme Weber. "The weather has been against it. Summery. One wants to bask. And this time last year one positively needed an *igloo*."

"Philip will return," said Sanbergh.

Langdon Williams said: "I'm glad you've not given up altogether, Turner."

"Of course," said Mme Weber, "what I've really always wanted him to do is a portrait of Leonie."

There was silence except for the clinking of a bottle as the Italian boy moved by the sideboard. The woman with the hat was saying to Signor Castiglioni: ". . . and apparently twelve and a half women out of every hundred don't get any fun out of married life at *all*. That's what it *says*, sweetheart. I often wonder how these statisticians work in the halves. . . ."

I said suddenly, sharply to Leonie: "Where is Martin?"

She hadn't looked at me before at all, but now her eyes came swiftly up.

I said: "Didn't he come with you?"

"Did you expect him to?"

"Well, yes."

I don't know what it was in those few words, but they must have had something because they stopped everybody talking as if we'd threatened them with a gun.

"Leonie phoned me," Charles said pacifically. "I borrowed Signor Castiglioni's speed-boat and fetched her."

"You—fetched her from Poltano?"

"Yes. She wanted to collect her things."

"Oh. . . ."

After a definite pause somebody decided to begin talking again and the meal went on.

"Why didn't you bring Martin back as well?" I said to Charles about three minutes later.

"He has a cracked rib. He will have to be strapped up for a few days."

Jane said to me: "Is that your friend Martin Coxon? Has he had an accident? I hadn't heard."

"It's nothing," said Sanbergh, still giving nothing away, still smoothing over.

". . . of course I've had no medical training," said the woman with the hat to Signor Castiglioni, "but when you take a cross-section of the public like that, the *only* ones who will *consent* to talk are the extroverts, and sweetheart, we know what extroverts are. . . ."

Another course got itself put in front of me. Leonie looked at me again, and this time didn't look away. We stared at each other. My pulses were fairly thumping.

I said: "I wish you'd told me earlier."

"What?"

"That he was your——"

"What good would it have done?"

"I wouldn't have had the hope."

She flushed.

I said: "You don't know how bitterly I've regretted ever having brought him back into your life."

"It was for the best."

"Well, it was inevitable I suppose—sooner or later—if you feel like that. Are you rejoining him to-night?"

"Yes. . . ."

"I see. . . ."

Jane touched my arm. "Mr. Williams was asking you about the States."

"I'm sorry. I didn't hear."

He smiled and repeated his question. I said: "I didn't do any painting over there at all."

There was silence for a second or two. Then Signor Castiglioni's voice broke in: "But, madame, this inquiry you speak of, this inqury into the private life of ladies . . . it is the American ladies, you said? And many confess they are cold? Then I would say they are very different from the Italian lady." He chuckled. "The Italian lady is—what is the English slang you use? —*sauce piquante*——"

"Mustard," supplied Sanbergh.

"Ah yes, Charles, thank you. Mustard."

I said to Leonie: "You've surely made some plans. What do you intend to do?"

"It rather depends on you."

243

"On me? Why?"

"Well, you told him, didn't you, that so long as yo
were alive . . . ?"

"Oh, God, let him do what he pleases. I'm sick o
revenge."

"I'm—so very glad to know that."

I said: "This afternoon I was too far gone to listen t
reason. You were right to try to stop me, but I just didn'
hear what you said. . . . The thing had got out of hand.
can do nothing more now. . . ."

She said in a queer voice: "Oh, Philip, I wish yo
could see . . ."

She stopped.

"Go on."

"No."

"Darlings," said Charlotte Weber, "don't you thin!
the conversation is getting a little starko? Not that on
minds but . . . Dear Mr. Williams, tell me about you
Paris show. I've only read a solitary account. . . ."

The boy waiter had bent to take the unfinished plat
from in front of Leonie. Her eyes glinted in the light a
she looked up at him when he asked her some questio
about it. When he'd gone she put up her fingers to brus!
back the wisp of fringe that always fell across he
forehead. For a second I was reminded of Martin's action
though the two were quite dissimilar. She looked at m
again. Up to then I thought I'd been the only one feelin
that polite talk wouldn't do. But I could see her strugglin
to say something and at the same time to say no more
It was on her lips and in her eyes.

"Go *on*," I said.

"I can't."

"Yes, yes, you can. Go *on*, Leonie."

"I know you *blame* me," she said, "for my loyalty t
him. . . ."

"No, no, not just that. . . ."

"When he first came here—the first chance—that wa

in the garden during the cocktail party—he told me everything about Holland. Don't think I was charmed. I wasn't. But what astonished me was that he was genuine —not sham. In Amsterdam I left him for good, I thought, just because he was sham. . . . But here he has been different. I've never seen him like it. When Grevil committed suicide he didn't only destroy himself, you know. . . . And if you marry someone you don't just marry their virtues, you take it all."

The Italian boy was holding out some dish for me. I shook my head.

She said: "I'm not defending him. Usually he doesn't care a rap about other people, but I think that he even welcomed being with you because of the odd resemblance you had to Grevil—he was seeking something in you that he'd lost."

"Darling," said Jane, "did you say you were somebody's wife? Are you married again? Or is this the separation?"

Leonie drew in a breath to speak, glanced at Charlotte. "Forgive me," she said, her voice cracking. "I think I . . ."

She screeched her chair back, moved swiftly to the door and went out.

There was another silence. Then the woman with the hat said: "I adore quarrels in other people's houses. One has the vicarious excitement with no anxiety about one's crockery."

"Philip, I don't think——" Charlotte began as I got up.

"I'm *sorry*. . . ." I went to the door, nearly upsetting Berto who was in my way.

But when I went out the hall was empty. That minute or so had been too much. She had probably gone up to her bedroom. Then I fancied I heard a sound in the big living-room and went sharply in. But the room was empty. As I came out I nearly cannoned into Sanbergh.

He said: "Hold hard. Let us take this a little more slowly. Measured in hours, life is quite long."

I was persuaded back reluctantly into the living-room. He switched on some more lights and offered me a cigarette.

I took the thing unsteadily, stared at it, my hand shaking. "Don't spoil your dinner, Charles. I'm sorry, but I felt I—had to come out."

He smiled. "Why not go back and finish your own meal while I try to persuade her to do the same."

I shook my head. "Thanks, but I've really—had enough."

"In more ways than one perhaps." He lit his own cigarette, holding it carefully in manicured fingers. "I have a message for you—from your friend Coxon."

"A message? For me? You saw him?"

"Yes. In the flat. We had—quite a long talk. He said I was to give it to you."

I stared at the bit of crumpled paper he had handed me. Something was scrawled on it in pencil. "*Quare vitia sua nemo confitetur? Quia etiam nunc in illis est. Maxima est enim factae injuriae poena, fecisse.*"

"My Latin's not good enough. . . ."

Sanbergh took the paper back. "It says. . . . Well, it says: 'Why does no one confess his sins? Because he is still in them. For the greatest penalty for having done an injury is the fact of having done it.'"

The paper was handed back to me. I folded it once or twice. I said wryly: "It's a bad mistake to underestimate the enemy, isn't it?"

". . . You haven't lit your cigarette."

I went to the mantelpiece, leaned heavily on it. "I don't think I quite understand you again, Charles. I don't know how much you and Charlotte know about this, how far you have tried to—to help or to hinder. . . ."

"Not to hinder, certainly."

"So it was a private arrangement of Leonie's that

Martin should join her in Poltano? Neither you nor Charlotte knew anything of that?"

"There was no arrangement of any sort. Leonie told me that to-night."

"But there must have been some arrangement between them! Martin spent all yesterday with her!"

"Not by her choice. Apparently da Cossa told Coxon where she was. He read the address on a letter Charlotte was forwarding and told Martin."

I stared at Sanbergh, trying to digest this thing. "But I naturally thought it meant she had gone back to him! She *has* gone back to him, hasn't she? Why otherwise did she go up there?"

"I gather it was her way of trying to get a perspective on things."

"A perspective?"

He screwed out his cigarette, watched the last spiral of smoke. "Does that surprise you?"

After a minute I said: "I got it all wrong—and her. . . . But in the end it has been the same thing."

"That was a matter she refused to discuss with me."

A surprised glance in his eyes made me turn and I heard a movement on the verandah. I ran to the open doors and saw her at the end of the verandah, moving to go down into the garden.

I overtook her at about the fourth step.

"Leonie. . . ."

She stopped short with her back against the balustrade. We were still in the light cast from the windows, but out of earshot.

I said: "You heard?"

She said: "Philip, I never expected to meet you to-night! It wasn't *fair* of Charles to bring you here!"

"That may be. I'm sorry. But I think I've got to talk to you now."

"Haven't we done enough to each other to-day?"

"Hurt, yes. But must that be the way it ends?"

247

She didn't answer. She looked angry, queer, frightened

I said: "D'you understand the mistake I made? thought you'd gone to Poltano simply to rejoin Martin I thought you'd left without a word as soon as my back was turned. . . ."

"And I thought . . . But it doesn't matter. It makes no difference, does it."

I said: "It does to me."

After a second or so she said: "I had to make up my own mind, and quickly, without other people's thoughts getting in the way . . . and I *had* to make sure."

I said: "And now?"

"Well . . . now I've made sure."

"It's a different choice from Amsterdam."

"Yes. It had to be."

I said : "Before you go on I want to tell you this. I love you and want you as I've not wanted anyone before. For me there's not ever been anything like this. . . . But that doesn't mean I want you to make the wrong choice. If you feel about him as you seem to, then don't be put off by anything I say, because nothing else makes sense as much as that."

Somebody passed in front of the light from the windows. It was Sanbergh moving in the room above.

I said: "But don't go back to Martin because you're sorry for him and think you can help him. And don't go back to him because you're married to him and think you must hold up your end of the bargain. It isn't enough, Leonie. That isn't enough. That way in the end you'd only do hurt to yourself. . . ."

There was a pause. I watched her breathing, which was being about as difficult as my own.

I said: "Do you love him?"

She passed her tongue over her lips. "I've made my choice."

"Leonie," I said. "Don't keep running away. Look at me."

She looked at me then. "Philip, I'm not running away. But I can't let him down. In many ways, I know, he's bad—but there's good in him too. Grevil knew that. And just now Martin is—adrift, without direction—the way *I* was when I first met him. Even women play fair sometimes. Even I don't—desert a sinking ship . . ."

"Do you love him?" I said.

She opened her eyes wide at me. "No!" she said in anger. "Not properly, not absolutely, not in the way you mean."

"Leonie——"

"But that doesn't mean that I'm—that I'm heart whole or free of him. I care what becomes of him! That's one of the—penalties and privileges of knowing him. Most people feel it. Much more so for me—being his wife. If I left him now there would be ghosts always that couldn't be laid! My only chance is to go back to him now —and let it work itself out. . . ."

There was a creak on the verandah and Charles Sanbergh came slowly down the steps. "Forgive me. It is ill-mannered for an outsider to interfere, but I am interested in what you have decided."

I said: "I'm going back with Leonie to-night, to see Martin."

"Philip——"

"Oh, there won't be any more fighting. That's over, spent. . . ."

"Don't be a fool," said Sanbergh.

I looked at him.

"If I were in your position," he said, "I should take Leonie on the first plane back to England—and then to America—if she would come." He raised an eyebrow. "I should take her perhaps even if she would not come."

Leonie said: "No, Charles, it's *impossible*. I've been explaining to Philip——"

"If you both go back to Poltano, Martin will win the battle of loyalty, as it is in his nature to do. Oh, I don't

249

blame him for fighting; who wouldn't? I don't blame him for acting according to his nature, which is egocentric and one-purposed. Your brother, my dear Philip, from what I gather, cracked that egoism wide open. It may be that as a result Martin Coxon is at a turning point in his life. But if he does find some new way of being, he can only find it on his own and in his own way. To go with him now, Leonie, to comfort and companion him, will very probably undo anything that Grevil Turner may have accomplished. Go with Philip, where you belong."

She was trembling. "I've *promised*," she said. "I promised to return to-night. Nothing will change that!"

"I heard you," said Sanbergh. "I'll go in your place —tell him what's happened. I have a broad back. Take her to England, Philip."

"*No!*" she said.

"Yes!" I said passionately. "Charles is right, Leonie. Even if you don't care so much for me personally, come back with me as far as your home. Start afresh—on your own. That's what you decided in Amsterdam, and that is right."

"It was right for then. It—it may be right some time in the future. But . . ."

"Leonie, it's right for now. Will you come?"

She didn't answer.

I said: "Do you care anything for me at all?"

She said: "Don't you see how impossible it is that you should have someone—close to you who had any feelings for Martin at all?"

I checked what I was going to say, hardly able to believe we had come so far, knowing even so that the whole thing still hung in the balance.

Of course, even supposing for a second that the balance might be tipped my way, she had put her finger on the vital spot. There couldn't be any sudden and complete break between her and Martin; the legal tie might be the least of it, but it was the material anchor which couldn't be slipped in a night. That much was obvious. But after that? What after that? Ghosts that couldn't be laid. . . .

I said: "Can you give me one thing. . . ."

She looked at me then.

I said: "Not loyalty, not friendship, not sympathy . . . but some part of your love."

She said suddenly in a low voice: "It's so much the largest part of my love."

Sanbergh made an expressive gesture. "What time shall I get you the boat?"

"But I *can't* go with Philip!" she protested. "*Neithe*i of you seem to understand! If I let Martin down now, ' let myself down as well; and that's not the way to—sta1 again. If I'm ever lucky enough to come to you, Phili1 then it must be with a clear slate."

There was a long silence.

Sanbergh said: "Let me put it this way. If you go back :o Martin Coxon now, for the reasons you have, you'll be doing the same sort of thing as Grevil Turner, and doing it *because of the same man*. People, I suspect, have been sacrificing themselves for Martin in a greater or lesser degree all his life. Grevil Turner did it in excess—or *in excelsis*—I don't know which. But, whichever it was, now is the time to stop."

After a while then I could tell there was beginning a slow give-way within her. It was a condition of muscle, not a movement. In a few sentences Charles had said things that she knew from her greater knowledge of Martin to be unanswerable.

"Leonie," I said, "after what you've just told me there isn't any argument that can stand."

"I shouldn't have said it, but you——"

"Don't take it back now."

She said: "There's nothing I want to take back."

I looked at Sanbergh. "One day I hope I shall be able to repay you and Charlotte—somehow—for the help you have given us to-night."

Leonie said: "Charles . . ." and stopped. It was still a protest, but it was becoming a defeated one.

Sanbergh turned to go. "You know, Philip, fidelity of heart isn't much in vogue these days—and it can be a little dangerous. For both of you I think it has been dangerous. Perhaps if you practise it towards each other, you will find it brings a more excellent return."

He left us then and went back into the house, to rejoin the company, and with a smile or a nod or an understood glance to satisfy Charlotte.

Winston Graham

'One of the best half-dozen novelists in this country.' *Books and Bookmen*. 'Winston Graham excels in making his characters come vividly alive.' *Daily Mirror*. 'A born novelist.' *Sunday Times*

His immensely popular suspense novels include:

Take My Life
The Sleeping Partner
Fortune is a Woman
Angell, Pearl and Little God

Winston Graham has also written The Poldark Saga, his famous story of eighteenth-century Cornwall:

Ross Poldark
Demelza
Jeremy Poldark
Warleggan
The Black Moon

And three historical novels:

The Grove of Eagles
The Forgotten Story
Cordelia

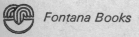 *Fontana Books*

Howard Spring

In 1938 his most famous book, *My Son, My Son*, was published; it was a world-wide success. Since then all his books, without exception, have been best-sellers and have earned Howard Spring a high reputation as an author of universal appeal.

'Howard Spring is a novelist of solid and considerable talent, whose ability to tell a story, sense of character, craftmanship and industry should put hollower and more pretentious novelists to shame.' *Spectator*

'He is not afraid of stark drama, and he writes with real feeling.' *Sunday Times*

Shabby Tiger

I Met a Lady

A Sunset Touch

Winds of the Day

These Lovers Fled Away

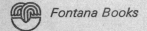 *Fontana Books*

Taylor Caldwell

One of today's best-selling authors, Taylor Caldwell has created a host of unforgettable characters in her novels of love, hate, drama and intrigue, set against rich period backgrounds.

'Taylor Caldwell is a born storyteller.' *Chicago Tribune*

Testimony of Two Men

Let Love Come Last

The Eagles Gather

Captains and the Kings

The Sound of Thunder

Tender Victory

This Side of Innocence

Melissa

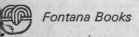 *Fontana Books*

Fontana Books

Fontana is a leading paperback publisher of fiction and non-fiction, with authors ranging from Alistair MacLean, Agatha Christie and Desmond Bagley to Solzhenitsyn and Pasternak, from Gerald Durrell and Joy Adamson to the famous Modern Masters series.

In addition to a wide-ranging collection of internationally popular writers of fiction, Fontana also has an outstanding reputation for history, natural history, military history, psychology, psychiatry, politics, economics, religion and the social sciences.

All Fontana books are available at your bookshop or newsagent; or can be ordered direct. Just fill in the form and list the titles you want.